THE RETREAT

Jill E. Friedman

iUniverse LLC
Bloomington

THE RETREAT

iUniverse books may be ordered through booksellers or by contacting:

iUniverse
1663 Liberty Drive
Bloomington, IN 47403
www.iuniverse.com
1-800-Authors (1-800-288-4677)

ISBN: 978-1-4917-1222-1 (sc)
ISBN: 978-1-4917-1224-5 (hc)
ISBN: 978-1-4917-1223-8 (e)

Library of Congress Control Number: 2013918985

Printed in the United States of America.

iUniverse rev. date: 11/18/2013

For my mother, Madelon Ficks, who faces all
life's issues with courage and grace

"How wonderful it is that nobody need wait a single moment before starting to improve the world."
Anne Frank

Prologue

Another Dimension

"Rose, come with me," said Julia.

In a split second they were in a media room with three other entities.

"I've never been in the Life Review Room before," said Rose.

"There was no need. But now you, Maddy, Vivian and Barbara are going to accompany me on an outing," said Julia.

"Finally," said Rose. "I've been polishing all my skills—I'm ready."

"Not quite, "said Julia, "you need to know the lives of our seven women. There may be an eighth, but we can deal with that later. So, review and study the paths they have taken so far.

And with that Julia was gone, leaving the others to observe their subjects.

PART I

CHAPTER 1

Hans and Kahn Cook

Lynn Kahn and N.C. Allen had started their careers in show business on the same children's show, 'The Bunnies.' Lynn played one of the silly bunnies who helped children sound out words phonetically. N.C. worked as an intern, for a year, and now was finally being paid to run errands for the assistant director. The show was only on for five months but the two women continued their friendship.

They worked well together so, when N.C. was hired to produce a cooking show, she suggested Lynn to be the co-host and "Hans and Kahn Cook," was born. The idea was to put a spin on the regular cooking shows by adding a TV personality, as sous-chef, interspersing topics of the day along with the food preparation; a kind of Kelly and Michael with food.

Lynn was fun and energetic in contrast to Hans's rather acerbic temperament. She wore five inch heels to compensate for her petite stature and counted calories, inwardly annoyed when the camera tended to exaggerate her curvaceous figure. Appearance is important in show business and, with her big brown eyes and curly dark hair, Lynn did not disappoint. She was referred to as someone who 'could think on her feet.' Her wit had provided the comic relief for the

German Chef, who had three popular restaurants in the Los Angeles area.

N.C. was similar in height to Lynn, about five foot four inches, but very slim with sandy hair and blue eyes. Her role as producer morphed into so much more as the weeks went by and trouble brewed. She became a referee, the one to placate egos, and the glue holding the show together. Her sincere, nurturing personality normally enabled her to extract the best from the cast and crew; but N.C. was faced with an impossible challenge.

"Hans and Kahn Cook," initially did well and, seemingly, had all the elements of success. They had a sleek kitchen set with stainless steel appliances, black and white floor tiles and colorful pots and dishes. There were delicious recipes and the provocative banter between co-hosts moved the show along at a fresh and lively pace. Unfortunately, jealousy reared its ugly head when the balance of fan mail flattered Lynn and made the menu appear to be of secondary interest. Hans was not above acrid displays of temperament and, eventually, congeniality gave way to sarcasm both on and off the camera. The chef's penchant for fomenting problems seemed endless. He made it clear that sharing the spotlight was not his style.

Lynn was a good sport about it all, and N.C. did her best to pacify the man, but every laugh that Lynn would garner only fueled Hans' anger. They were filming three segments one day when the verbal barbs became physical. They were standing behind the prep counter in close proximity.

"You're on my foot," said Lynn with a jaw full of clenched teeth, smiling at the camera. Hans gave an extra push before extricating his heel off Lynn's toe. A tear formed in the corner of her eye but she smiled.

"Oh Hans, how do you ever find shoes big enough for those feet of yours, they caught me again," she said still smiling.

Hans was seasoning a whole fish, head and all, and Lynn chose to put a few more inches between she and he, but still peering at the fish head.

"Gee, look at those big eyes. He could have been your twin, Hans," said, Lynn now looking toward the camera with a wink.

Hans threw the salt shaker at Lynn and the director yelled, "cut." Lynn pulled her shoe off to rub her injured toe.

"Stay off my feet Hans, or I swear I'll skewer your nuts," she said in a tone only he could hear. The crew knew she had put up with a lot but in L.A. it was best not to get a bitchy reputation.

They managed to finish the segment, but Hans could not contain himself for very long. The third meal was a pasta dish and Hans had a ladle of hot sauce in his hand. Lynn had just asked, for the benefit of the viewers, why he added a little sugar to the tomato sauce. Hans made a sharp turn toward her, accidently on purpose, and the liquid became airborne—landing on Lynn's skirt.

"Damn," she said pulling the soaking skirt away from her upper thigh. The thick lined material prevented a burn, but it still hurt. "You son of a bitch," she said, this time loud and clear. Of course, Lynn needed a wardrobe change and the set needed a touch up. Time is money and everyone involved was fed up with these annoying antics.

N.C. was saved the task of firing her friend when the powers that be recognized that, if Hans could not relate professionally to the affable co-host, there would be no replacing her. The show was cancelled. Of course Hans went on a tirade blaming Lynn for the plummeting ratings, and everyone involved was thankful there were no meat cleavers readily at hand. The Network had assured N.C. that they were pleased with her work and would be open to considering any future projects she might pitch, but two months later N.C. and Lynn were still picking up unemployment checks. They had consoled themselves in that they had developed an even deeper friendship and appreciated that at least something positive resulted from a negative experience.

The shows termination was an opportunity to abandon what had become an increasingly tense routine, and they wanted to explore other creative facets of life. Lynn did lots of craft projects, painting furniture and fashioning decorative objects in clay, but these were things she had done before. She utilized every inch of storage space and there were no longer any chairs or tables that needed attention. Cabinets bowed with an exhausting load of napkin holders, candle holders, vases and various knick knacks for holiday display. Lynn, who had once coveted her own creations, became more and more generous in her gift giving.

N.C. spent her free time riding her beloved horses, arranging flowers and visiting antique shops. It may have been an existence envied by others, but N.C. was a worker bee and needed to be challenged in some new area of creativity. She found herself being attracted to paintings on her excursions to antique shops. She pondered over their color choices and the balance of their composition. She hadn't been to a museum for a while and decided to organize an outing.

CHAPTER 2

The Getty

N.C. called Lynn and two other friends and, through a series of phone calls and planning the last minute logistics, the ladies had decided to meet at Sharon's house in Sherman Oaks. They could then carpool to the Getty Museum in Los Angeles.

So Sharon welcomed Lynn and N.C. to what N.C. had always described as "the most perfect little cottage." Sharon was a tall, thin and a rather regal looking woman, with big brown eyes and caramel skin she attributed to her mixed race background. She was a stylish set designer for a popular soap opera. The Los Angeles TV community was a small world, in many ways, and these ladies had crossed paths many times over the years. Gia, the last to arrive, was a little blond powerhouse at work, as a casting director, who turned into a shyer, thoughtful listener in social situations.

"Hey, glad you could make it," said Lynn, as Gia entered Sharon's spotless kitchen. The dark pine hardwood floor lay in contrast to the white cabinets. At the far end was a circular eating area with a round, white-veined black granite table top sitting on a thick, round, white iron base. The black surrounding chairs, though sleek and modern, were very comfortable. Sharon's collection of colorful fruit prints were framed in black and hung on the white walls. There were stainless steel appliances and granite countertops holding bold colored canisters. A green ivy plant, in a white pot on the floor, had thrived and totally framed the bow window beyond the table.

"Hey, it's only five minutes you slave driver," said Gia. "How quickly we forget. Who waited twenty minutes for you last week when your car was being fixed?"

Sharon handed Gia a mug of coffee and a spoon. The lazy Susan on the table held the cream and sugar and a small bouquet of peach roses interspersed with baby's breath.

"Mea culpa, that did slip my mind. I owe you another fifteen minutes," chuckled Lynn.

"I'm so glad you suggested this N.C." said Sharon, "I always get inspired at the Getty."

"Come on," said N.C., "you get inspired at the shoe store, the grocery store, the gas station—anywhere."

"You might be right," said Sharon smiling, "but there's different types of inspiration and every once and I while I need a 'museum fix'."

They finished their coffee and piled into Lynn's van.

Work gears up to a frenzy whenever the gloomy cloud of a strike hangs over the city of L.A. Nobody makes money without product and there is no product when there is a strike. The work load is bumped up in anticipation and, if the strike is avoided, as in this case, there is more wiggle room for free time. Thus, we have two women in-between jobs and two women in high-demand jobs all able to steal away for a relaxing day at the Getty.

The twenty minute drive, which would have been ten if not for L.A. traffic, provided the initial opportunity to catch up on industry buzz. A lot of who was working where, who was let go, what jobs may be opening up and, of course, a dash of who was sleeping with whom. They were not typically catty women, by any means, just interested in the latest power and politics of liaisons that might make a difference for future employment plans. And, according to Sharon, it was just practical to know the reputations of the men who crossed her path.

"Did you guys hear that cute little brunette, on the New World Soap, is dating the producer, Michael Dunn? There should really be a Hollywood Ingénue Handbook for young girls that come to L.A.," said Sharon.

"You know he's still married, I think to wife number three," said Lynn.

"I went out with him, oh, I think it was ten years ago. He took me to Mr. Chow's and luckily I ran into a friend of mine in the Ladies Room. She told me his m.o. was to have one wife, and at least one girlfriend at all times. Just like my ex—tall, dark and unfaithful."

The chit chat continued in the car, parking lot and the tram up to the Museum where the view overlooking Los Angeles was magnificent, even on an overcast day. The creamy buildings held so many treasures. They needed to decide in which direction to go. It would be impossible to see everything in a few hours. They split up and the plan was to meet, at twelve thirty, in the restaurant on the lower level.

Lynn and N.C. wandered through the prodigious halls of master artworks. At one point Lynn was laughing and called over to N.C., "you've got to see this." It was a small 9x11 oil by the Dutch painter Hendrik de Valk dated 1700 and titled "Amorous Old Man with Young Girl."

"Well, he had a sense of humor," was N.C.'s response to the vision of an old woman on one side of a screen peeking around to see a young girl being seduced by a much older man. The faces had a cartoonish quality and seemed to insinuate that the old woman was responsible for the meeting.

"See, dirty old men have always been around," said a smiling Lynn, to which N.C. replied, "Let's not forget the dirty old Madam."

Two hours slipped away quickly and it was time to join the others for lunch. They had once made a pledge, at a particularly festive birthday party, that they would never again bore each other with tales of woe about weight, body image or counting calories. So each ordered the meal they felt they deserved and they all agreed on a bottle of wine. Then they shared their morning experiences.

Sharon was the most enthusiastic, "You guys have got to go see the Turkish bed, and I don't understand why somebody hasn't adapted a modern version. I can't wait to take a model to David." David was a master carpenter who could literally recreate just about any project Sharon could invent.

"I sort of remember seeing it once, and thinking it was beautiful, but I also remember thinking it would be a bitch to change the sheets," mused Gia, smiling.

"Always the practical one, cutting to the chase," said N.C., "remind me to talk to you the next time I need a bubble burst" as she smiled and took a bite of her salad.

"Just sayin,'" Gia smiled back as she sipped her wine.

"Obviously, you didn't read the caption," Sharon retorted using an affected accent. "The beauty of the thing is that it pulls away from the wall, and the sides, so it should be easy to change," she explained.

Gia laughed, drawing out the 'excuse' in "Excuse me, my lady."

Lynn, whose attention had been on her tuna salad said, "I don't know what the hell you're talking about, I'll have to go see this for myself."

Sharon grabbed a pen from her purse and a napkin from the table and drew a quick sketch. "You see mine would not be in the French gilt style, I never really liked gold on furniture. See here, the back could be either a standing piece or actually upholstered on the wall. Then, see how high the sides are," looking around to see if her audience was still paying attention, "the whole bed pulls away from the wall so you can have front and back exposed for cleaning and changing the sheets." There were a couple of puzzled faces so Sharon just said, "Oh just go see it for yourself."

"So are we ever going to see you market this for the public or is this going to be one of those things you have in your guest room and forget about?" pushed Lynn.

"Yeah, whatever happened to the children's heavy cotton washable saddle bags for the car or stroller," asked Gia. "I thought that was a great idea."

"Well how about the bedside desk you had David make up. Did any of you ever see that?" N.C. said as she surveyed the group. They replied in the negative and N.C. proceeded to describe how, after visiting a friend in the hospital, Sharon designed a model of a bedside table in the shape of a U on its side that has a tucked away leg. You can use it sitting up in bed or you can pull down the hidden leg and lower the other leg and you have a regular desk surface or side table. David used several different exotic woods, it's just beautiful. You have to see it when we get back," she insisted.

"She talks like I'm not here," said Sharon.

"Well Ms. Crazy inventor," said Gia, "when is the general public going to benefit from your genius? Or maybe you'll open your home to 'The Friends and Family Turkish Bed Tour.'"

"I just don't get it Sharon. You have the perfect venue for displaying any of your ideas," Lynn said. "If people saw your bed on the Soap, and we are talking hundreds of thousands, all you would have to do is put up a web site. And I'm sure there are manufactures out there who would love any one of your concepts. I bet you could get on Shark Tank."

So the encouraging talk went on a while longer but none of her friends really thought Sharon would follow through, and they couldn't understand why. The conversation eventually drifted away from Sharon as N.C. asked Gia about the Manuel Alvarez Bravo exhibit. Gia's deep eyes grew wide as her face lit up with excitement. She was passionate about photography but usually only discussed it when someone else initiated the conversation.

"Oh he is just incredible," she poured out, "way ahead of his time. They call his imagery optical parables, they're just so powerful. The funny thing is" she said wistfully, "it's like the image goes right to the heart of things, without words. The vision is an experience you feel in a very primal way." The others could see that Gia was deeply moved by the exhibition.

They continued picking over their salads and sandwiches; mineral water was now the beverage of choice, their wine glasses having long since been drained. Munching and talking in between bites they concluded this outing had been a wonderful idea and a creative inspiration. Lynn and N.C. announced that they were going to find a painting class and make art a top priority. So, with new resolution, they continued their afternoon visiting each other's discoveries and comparing opinions in the car on the way home.

CHAPTER 3

Lynn and N.C.
Painting Plan

The feelings their museum visit had inspired lingered and, on Friday, Lynn and N.C. had a long phone conversation about how they would acquire their art education. They both wanted to learn to paint with oils. Lynn's husband, Chuck, was always helpful and supportive so, by Saturday, he was in his garage workshop making easels for Lynn's latest endeavor.

Art had always been appreciated in the Kahn household and Lynn's sixteen year old daughter, Amanda, was no exception. Lynn had always nurtured Amanda's talent and now, many art classes later, she delighted in how accomplished Amanda was at such a tender age. She proudly hung Amanda's work and, when visitors saw the displayed paintings and inquired about the artist, she beamed and referred to Amanda as 'my little prodigy.' So Lynn approached her daughter with a proposition she thought Amanda could not refuse. Lynn and N.C. would pay Amanda twenty dollars an hour for three hours of painting instruction on Saturday morning. Lynn knew Amanda would be excited about the prospect of earning sixty dollars for three hours of work. Amanda's artistic eye had carried over to her fashion sense and this new income would allow for additional wardrobe purchases.

Amanda, at sixteen, looked younger than her chronological age with her big brown eyes, heart shape lips and soft brown curls. It seemed ironic, to Lynn, that in so many ways Amanda's cherub face hid wisdom worthy of a mature woman.

Amanda was nothing like her mother had been as a teenager. 'Girls just want to have fun,' would have been an appropriate anthem for Lynn's youth. Her joy for life was ravenous and only matched by enthusiasm for new experiences. She did have a serious side and used her intelligence and wit to protest injustice and fundraise for charities, as she did in her adult life. But, truth be told, it was great fun and Lynn's charm and gaiety were the real tools that attracted others to whatever cause she might promote. The simple truth was that Lynn's success was the result of people feeling like anything was possible when they were in her company.

Amanda was a far more serious thinker. She was a diligent student and gave focused attention to whatever her current project happened to be. Her sense of humor was not the lively robust type, as her mom, but based more on sophisticated intelligent observations of life that would both amaze and amuse the listener. Lynn would joke with friends that she was pleasantly surprised that she had given birth to her polar opposite. "There doesn't seem to be any resemblance once you get past our eyes and hair," she would confess. Of course she adored Amanda and was happy that at least they shared a love of art and music.

But the onset of the teenage years had put a strain on their relationship. How foolish to think she could avoid the mother/daughter struggle, and yet she thought just that. They had been so close and she tried so desperately not to repeat the same pitfalls she and her own mother had encountered. But there was no fighting the hormonal surge that seems to polarize parents and children while the latter struggle for independence; Amanda was no exception. She was distancing herself from Lynn, for the most part, and any questions by Lynn were answered with grunts and half sentences.

Occasionally, Lynn would catch glimpses of the little girl of not so long ago. Amanda would venture into the TV room and snuggle up with Lynn and Chuck to eat popcorn and watch an old movie. Of course the battle for recognition, as a young adult, would begin again the next day but, for a brief time, Lynn had her baby back. Now, having a project that required a role reversal, Lynn thought they might develop a more adult understanding of each other. But, after their first session, Lynn's own maturity would come into question and her ability to allow Amanda to take the lead meant acknowledging how close her baby was to being an adult.

Saturday morning rolled around quickly. N.C. arrived at nine thirty A.M., rather than the scheduled ten, to beg a cup of Chuck's notoriously good brew that she never seemed able to duplicate at home. She was familiar enough at the Kahn's to let herself in the back door, usually left unlocked after the dog's first morning outing to the back yard.

She yelled a greeting, "Hi, I'm here, stealing coffee," while simultaneously grabbing a cup and heading for the pot. Happy to hear an, "Ok, relax, we're still getting ready," response from Lynn, N.C. grabbed the cream and sugar and enjoyed a few minutes of solitude to savor her coffee and admire the surroundings. The Kahn's modest Craftsmen Cottage home was a vision of simple elegance with a good measure of art and cozy. N.C. could gaze about the kitchen and see the results of Amanda's drawings and paintings bordering the entire room, above the cabinets. Chuck had left the space, for just that purpose, when reconfiguring the room. N.C. loved this kitchen that, unlike her own, reeked of family existence. The creamy cabinets looked down on a thick, round butcher block table. In the center, holding the napkins from straying off a square ceramic plate, was a primitive looking heavy, black goddess figure Lynn made in a 'mommy and me' class when Amanda was five.

The surrounding chairs were a family project using six colors, with each chair displaying a dominant color. The other remaining shades, plus black and white checks, were cleverly distributed on the arms, legs and backs. The baker's rack, filled with colorful pottery, was a wonderful contrast to the sleek stainless steel appliances and shiny black countertops where Lynn displayed the cookie jars she had collected over the years. N.C.'s respite was concluding as she could hear the bustling activity of bodies in motion about the house. She grabbed a second cup and wandered through the wooden frame door into the large L shaped living/dining room. The two shabby chic white couches flanked the fireplace directly across from the door and the dining room was situated to the left, with French doors leading to the garden.

Lynn and Amanda were finishing up covering the dining room table with drop cloths and strategically spreading other cloths on the floor around the table. The dining room chairs had been a family project that Lynn had told N.C. about. The oval backs and seats were covered in a rich butter cream fabric while the bordering wood of the backs and legs were painted in a leopard design under a beige wash. N.C. was more than a little skeptical of the project when told about it over the phone, but seeing the results, she was amazed and thought they were beautiful. So after 'hellos and hugs' it was N.C. who insisted on protecting them further with additional layers of cloth.

Lynn had purchased the supplies, as per instruction, and Amanda had arranged the table for efficient usage. She was obviously taking her role seriously and wanted a punctual, no nonsense commencement. She had painstakingly arranged a bowl of fruit and dramatically draped a velvet scarf across a small Chinese pedestal table that usually held up their old Buddha. This had been placed in the center of the dining room table and was the focus of several lamps and a spot light. Amanda pointed to the prepared canvases leaning against the wall and advised the ladies to grab one, and a piece of charcoal and start sketching, using a very light touch. "You look at these objects not as fruit, a table or fabric, but as lines, planes, circles and different values of dark and light," instructed Amanda with a tone of authority. She turned on the radio to a classical music station and they began.

Amanda was a tough task master and required Lynn and N.C. to follow her lead in a methodical, step by step program. Lynn was having a difficult time suppressing her own mother/daughter rebellion. There was no deviation from the program or even the subject matter. Lynn, being a fan of impressionism, wanted to do a French street scene and had spent the previous evening searching through art books for inspiration. But Amanda would not allow it explaining that, if she and N.C were serious about painting, there was a sequence of application techniques they needed to understand first. She didn't even allow the use of color on the first painting, insisting that they would master blending much better if they started out in black and white.

Perhaps they were both less than comfortable in their new roles as student and teacher for, while N.C. tried to follow Amanda's instructions, Lynn was making bad jokes about how these "forms" were tomorrow's breakfast. Amanda gave Lynn her 'look that could kill' and Lynn eventually settled down. It wasn't long then before she and N.C. were both in the zone of concentration where the grapes, bananas, apples and pears were competing for canvas space and the noise of the outside world ceased.

When the forms and shapes were finished, to Amanda's satisfaction, it was time to 'fix' the charcoal with a spray. Aqua net hair spray was cheaper than charcoal fixative, and just as effective, so the three of them marched outside with canvases in hand to do their spraying in the open air. Now they were to apply paint in various shades ranging from black to white with as much shade variation as possible. Lynn whined again about using color but Amanda was adamant and, as soon as she walked into the kitchen for a glass of water, Lynn turned to N.C. telling her "I've raised a tyrant, my mother put a curse on me when she said, 'just wait until you have your own.'"

It seemed like only a few minutes later that Amanda announced her time was up. Sure enough they checked their watches and it was one p.m. They were incredulous that the time had flown by so quickly and rather pleased with what they had done thus far. Amanda advised them that they were welcome to continue but she would prefer they stop now and continue next week under her tutelage. Her reasoning was that they were doing well and she didn't want them to run into any problems and become frustrated. With that bit of advice, and a few kudos on last inspection, Amanda ran off to meet with her friends and maybe spend some of her earnings.

Enthusiasm fueled their energy and Lynn had little difficulty convincing N.C. to postpone her errands, another hour, and continue painting. A half hour later, just as predicted, they seemed to have blurred their tone gradations and, without Amanda's quick catching eye, their paintings lost their crisp clarity and appeared to have a muddy sadness about them. Unsure about how to correct the murky mess, they took a step back, looked at their canvases, looked at each other and burst out laughing.

"This is a fine mess," N.C. declared, "teacher is going to punish us severely. I'm never listening to you again, or at least not this week."

"I think we'd better hide these in the garage, maybe we can have a 'do over.' I feel like a naughty little girl," admitted Lynn.

"Well you are!" laughed N.C. as she helped Lynn clean up and return the room to its original condition. "You know I'm really impressed with Amanda, she knows her stuff. I think she would be a wonderful teacher; is that what she wants to do?"

"Well she hasn't really been confiding in me lately but I heard her telling someone, on the phone, that she wants to be an artist," said Lynn, "but you know how that goes. I think she'll need a day job—or starve. It's a tough world out there for an artist to make a living, but hell, nothing is easy and at least she'll love what she's doing."

CHAPTER 4

Gia

Gia was facing a very long day. Her company was casting a cereal commercial using eight principals, mostly kids. They had seen dozens of kids and potential parents who were crowded in hallways waiting for their opportunity. Of course she had been around long enough to know they probably wouldn't wrap until 7p.m.

Gia was getting not so much bored, as a bit frustrated, with her life. She was confident that she was a good casting director and had a keen eye for matching the talent to the job. She was well compensated for her work and her accountant encouraged her to start looking for a house, or at least some rental units. If she didn't do something soon the IRS was going to take much more than its fair share of taxes. But she didn't feel motivated and was just coming to the realization that she didn't want to rattle around a house without a partner. She had been on her own too long now and feared she was facing years alone.

Most of the men she met were actors and Gia stayed away from dating actors, fearing that their intentions might be less than sincere. This was a lesson she had learned the hard way when first in "the business." She had succumbed to the invitation of who she described to friends as "Mr. Drop Dead Gorgeous". They dated for a month until an accidental revelation. One Saturday morning, while wandering around Melrose Ave. in West Hollywood, Gia saw Mr. Gorgeous and a handsome man having brunch at a sidewalk café; but he was supposed to be in San Francisco for the weekend. She was just a couple of feet from their table when Mr. Gorgeous caught her eye as Mr. Handsome was whispering in his ear while gently stroking his upper thigh. She had taken Mr. Gorgeous by surprise and the awkward fumbling introductions, excuses and half hearted apologies left Gia with a cold ache in her stomach.

"Gotta go," was all she could think to say as she rushed off, in the wrong direction. It took another ten minutes for Gia to round the block and find her car. She was so crushed and shaken by his deception that she vowed to herself never to date an actor again, or mention her work at parties risking some 'wanabe actor' following her around all night.

Gia called her gay friend, Mason, and they met for coffee. She ranted about how low a man could go, passing himself off as straight.

"Oh, are all straight men of high moral character darlin'?" Mason, in his aristocratic southern drawl, answered his own question. "I think not. Now let me help you out here in case you should find yourself in any type of doubtful situation. If your man friend looks in the mirror more than you and has more personal hygiene products than you, start looking elsewhere. You know you should really think of this as a happy accident," Mason said, "I mean that you found out so soon. He had you under his spell sweetie and it might have been weeks, months or years before you caught on. I would hate to think that I might have had to be the messenger of doom. Picture this: we are at your wedding rehearsal dinner and I whisper in your ear that your gaydar malfunctioned. The groom's shoes have left footprints by the beds of half the men in West Hollywood."

They both cracked up. Mason could always make her laugh. He reminded her so much of her beloved cousin Dix. She had tried calling Dix first but he didn't pick up and still hadn't called her back. She just couldn't get through to him lately. He seemed to be on a downward spiral and she didn't know what to do.

CHAPTER 5

Gia and Dix

Gia Thomas and Dixon Brown were cousins and had both been born in Gaffney, South Carolina. Gia was older by three months and they were in the same kindergarten when Gia's father decided to move his family to Southern California. Gia was devastated at the thought of losing her best friend. Dix lived only two blocks away and they spent most of their waking hours together. She didn't really know what moving to California meant until her mother opened up the Atlas and attempted to explain where their new home would be. Gia was miserable for days and there seemed to be an unending stream of tears cascading down her cheeks. Finally, the promise that she and Dix could spend the summers together was the hope she needed. But it would be Dix who suffered the most over the years.

Gia had been a wild child who loved exploring the woods and shallow stream nearby. She and Dix would make forts and play 'hide and go seek' for hours at a time. It was always Gia who initiated the out of doors play. Dix was secretly delighted when inclement weather caused them to stay indoors where they could play house or dress up. One rainy day Dottie, Dix's mom, came by Gia's house to pick Dix up for supper. Dottie, a thin woman with tight, curly black hair, would frequently look as if she were pondering some troublesome secret. She entered the house and her big brown eyes were horrified to see Dix in full makeup parading around in one of Gia's Sunday dresses.

"Dixon Brown you go in an change your clothes right now! Then come out to the kitchen sink," said Dottie.

Maggie, Gia's mother, thought it was funny and couldn't understand the extent of Dottie's annoyance. When Dix had changed, Dottie proceeded to scrub his face with a nervous energy, ridding him of all traces of femininity. Dix wriggled and cried that she was scrubbing too hard and hurting him. Gradually, she calmed down and sent the kids to play on the porch until she was ready to go.

"Please Maggie, don't let this happen again," she begged. Dix was perplexed by his mother's agitation. He peeked through the screen door and heard his mother say, "If Bobby Joe were to see Dix dressed–like that–he would skin him alive."

The next day Dottie and Dix came by Gia's house and, while the kids were out on the swing set, Dottie confided her concerns to Maggie. Dix had said on two occasions that he thought he should have been a girl. The first time Dottie laughed and didn't take it seriously. The second time Dix made the mistake of saying it in front of his father, Bobby Joe. Dix had been slapped so hard he lost his balance. Bobby Joe's big calloused hands must have felt like a two by four. Dix was stunned having no idea why a simple statement would provoke such a horrific response, he had never been hit before. He cried inconsolably until, exhausted, he fell asleep.

Bobby Joe had stomped out of the house and there was no sight of him until he staggered home in the wee hours of the morning. He had a bloody nose, a black eye and the stench of a dirty bar room brawl. Bobby Joe was a muscular man, just about six one, who had done manual labor since he was a teenager. Dottie hoped the recipient of his rage was alright. It didn't cross her mind that Bobby Joe might have lost the fight; she knew how powerful he was when his anger took control. Dottie had dutifully left a few bandages, ointments and a baggie for ice on the kitchen table in anticipation of his return. She hated that this had become his pattern for dealing with stress, but was thankful that they were rare occasions and she had never been his target. She was angry too and vowed that she would never let him hit their son again. She prayed that, in time, he could accept his son with unconditional love. For Bobby Joe that was not likely.

Bobby Joe's father was a preacher who connived his way into the homes of the faithful, generally at supper time. Reverend Calvin Brown had mostly survived on day labor jobs until he found an old Bible and decided his silver tongue could work up an audience as well as the phonies he saw on TV. Calvin's eighteen year old wife had died in childbirth and Bobby Joe was raised by his maternal grandmother, Big Betty. They were poor but Big Betty was a great cook and loving grandmother. She made sure Bobby Joe went to school, attended church and had the manners of a good southern boy.

Bobby Joe was twelve when she died and he was devastated. His father was practically a stranger who came by, on occasion, when he was passing through. He did see the notice of Big Betty's death and showed up at the funeral to claim his boy and teach him how to work. But there was no love lost between the two.

Calvin thought having his motherless boy by his side created an air of sympathy, especially amongst the widow ladies at his revival meetings. Plus, there would be another pair of hands to pitch the tent as he made his way around the country, preaching and encouraging donations for him and his boy "to carry on the Lord's work." Calvin had no idea, nor would he have cared, that Bobby Joe was harboring an increasing resentment toward him. Big Betty had taught him well and all the "please", "thank you", "yes sir" and "no sir," of polite speech, concealed the disgust he had for Calvin and his con games. Bobby Joe remembered, when he was eight, sitting on the porch with a puzzle, Big Betty didn't realize the window was open. She was telling her best friend that "no good son-in-law came by" and how she suspected her daughter would be alive today if that "lying good for nothing Calvin" had been there to get his wife to the hospital on time. He showed up stinking of whiskey and another woman's perfume.

23

They lasted two years and during that time Bobby Joe had hoped to find some redeeming quality in his father. He watched for signs of basic humanity but there just didn't seem to be anything except the abhorrent behavior that Calvin actually preached against each week. The greed of taking money from the poor for "God's work" became intolerable. Then there was the way Calvin flirted shamelessly with the widows and treated his son like a slave. Bobby Joe started noticing that his father would sometimes brush up against people, on their way out of the tent. He came to realize that Calvin was not only a liar, hypocrite, womanizer and con man, but also a pick pocket.

Bobby Joe, at fourteen, had a growth spurt that gave him the appearance of a much older boy. He was disassembling the tent one day when he heard someone say they were desperate for construction workers at a new shopping center a couple of miles away. Bobby Joe dropped everything and, without so much as a 'good bye', picked up his few belongings and started walking away. Calvin noticed when Bobby Joe was about eight yards away, walking toward the road, and started yelling, "Get back here and finish your work Bobby Joe, where do you think you're going?"

Bobby Joe just kept walking. Calvin ran after him and grabbed his arm, but Bobby Joe swung his fist around catching Calvin's chin. He did not wait to see what damage he had done but, with a smile on his face, he walked away. He was free.

This was the background and baggage, that Dottie would remind herself, came with the whole package. He had his faults but he was a good man, her Bobby Joe, and she would make it clear to him that he would never hit their son again. They had to face the reality that their son's penchant for the feminine side would never change.

The day finally came when Gia's family were packed up and ready for their departure to the Golden State. It was a difficult day for both families but especially for the ones left behind. The children hugged and cried, promising to be best friends forever. Bobby Joe was obviously uncomfortable with the emotional display but he too was saddened by their departure. He had looked on his in-laws more like the brother and sister he never had and promised to allow Dix to visit in the summer. It was then that Dottie made a commitment to herself that she was going to make sure those summer plans would work out. Bobby Joe was sincere, at the time, but construction work was not always a reliable source of income and one could never be sure the money would be there for a luxury. Dottie was determined. She and her sister were very close and she too needed to look forward to a California vacation.

Dottie took inventory of her possibilities and proceeded with a vengeance. She made the most of the next ten months. She had a great reputation for her pies and added cookies and cakes to her roster of delicious desserts. She sold these at the Farmer's Market, giving out a flyer with her phone number for special orders or midweek snacks. The fruit season had been especially good and her canned jams were selling well too. Bobby Joe admired Dottie's energetic pursuits but she knew where he would draw the line. He would be gone for several days at a time, on his job, so it was only then that Dottie would sometimes take in laundry, do ironing or babysit for the wealthier folks in town. Dottie had been so successful with her numerous jobs that, ten months later, all three Browns were in an air-conditioned bus on their way to California. Dottie knew that both she and her husband would feel better about Dix, being so far away, if they could picture his surroundings. Bobby Joe took ten days off work to allow for the bus ride and time in California, but he would need to fly home. Dottie would stay another week and take the bus back. Then, at the end of the summer, Dix would get to fly home. This was one of their happiest times together and their California trips would become Dottie's main focus the rest of the year.

Chapter 6

Sharon and David

Sharon had been leaning across her 6' by 4' table, in her garage studio, working on a diorama and a few sketches for an upcoming Indie murder mystery. The soap opera she worked on was her bread and butter but the show wouldn't need any set changes for a few weeks. She loved the challenge of a new project and, when she got an assignment, she would mull over her ideas for an hour or so. Then she was like the "Little Engine that could." Starting out slowly then fueling up the motor until a flood gate of ideas were pouring out. Even Sharon sometimes wondered how she pulled these concepts from the back stage of her mind. She suddenly realized she was stiff and had tensed up her body. She took a break to stretch and do a few yoga poses. She happened to be in the downward facing dog pose, with her butt facing the door, when David walked in.

"Hmmmmmm, nice view from here-or should I say bootylicious?" David laughed.

"Can't you make some noise when you come in a room?" said Sharon as she slumped to the floor. She realized she was a little shaky, having been surprised, but then she was always a little off kilter when David first entered a room. He reached out one of his strong hands and helped pull her to her feet. She couldn't help but admire the strong leg muscles in his tight jeans as she rose. He couldn't help but think, in her cut off shorts and tank top, she looked delicious.

David was five ten with a solid build and wavy ginger hair that was a wee bit too long, by disinterest rather than design. Today his hazel eyes were reflecting the green in his plaid shirt.

"Hey, I'm wearing boots not ballerina slippers," he retorted, "How would I know that you would be going deaf at the tender age of thirty something?"

"Very funny, now let me show you my latest creation," as she led him to the table that he had actually made for her two years earlier. "I have a meeting at three o'clock on Monday. The writer/director wants a safe room in the middle of a second story family room. If they want the usual bookcases with a secret door I can give them that, but I really like this alternative," she said.

David could see, in miniature, a room with a cube structure in the middle. Sharon explained that on one side was a shallow gas fireplace and the other three sides were shelves. Behind the shelves would be mirror to help deflect the eye from realizing the size of the cube. There would be a four inch mirror molding on the bottom to camouflage the rollers that helped open the cube. The space inside had a firemen's poll leading to a small room below that could hold whatever was deemed necessary by the writers. Then Sharon suggested that it could actually be an elevator to a basement with a secret tunnel that led to a small clump of trees on the properties edge.

"Hey, aren't you getting a little carried away?" asked David. "Indie film makers usually have budget constraints. Show him what you've got and, if he wants anything more exotic, you can take the conversation in that direction." David was not a negative person and Sharon always listened to him with an open mind. She realized he was probably right.

They had been kicking around ideas for an hour or so when Sharon's stomach started gurgling and she suggested making them lunch. David said that was a great idea and he would work on a side table he was making for her. He couldn't help but watch her as she seemed to glide and swagger toward the back door.

Fifteen minutes later David bounded into the kitchen.

"Oh my god, I didn't realize the time. I've got to go pick Lexi up at preschool and take her home to the housekeeper. Thanks for making that," he said looking at the sandwich.

Sharon didn't give away her disappointment and wrapped the grilled cheese and tomato on rye in napkin for him to eat on the way.

"Atta here boy. I'll call you Monday and let you know what happened at the meeting," she said. The gentle scent of his aftershave diminished as she watched him walk away and thought, 'that will never happen.'

CHAPTER 7

Sharon

Richard and Calle Pruit started their married life at twenty and nineteen and were devoted to each other. Richard had worked and attended night school until he was sufficiently confident to apply and be accepted to the police academy. The union of his African American father and Native American mother produced a ruggedly handsome man with high cheekbones and regal posture.

Callie Pruit was a hairdresser at Marcel's, the most popular black salon in town. She was proud that, after having two of her six kids, she had studied and obtained her license. Callie was also the product of a diverse background; her mother was Puerto Rican and her father was half black and half French. The six Pruit children, their mixed genes fighting for recognition, were all rather ethnically ambiguous looking.

The Pruits were Catholic and, although the money was tight, they sent all the kids to Catholic School. St. Cecilia's Church, Elementary School and High School were located in their home town of Englewood, New Jersey and were an integral part of Pruit family life. Besides Sunday Mass, the whole family would attend sporting events where the three oldest Pruits were cheerleaders. The older girls had choir practice on Friday night and Sunday night dances in the Cafeteria from eight to ten p.m.

Sharon was the fourth child, seven years younger than her oldest sister. She wanted to do everything her sisters did and she would watch them practicing their calisthenics for hours, always trying to learn and imitate their every move. She was in the third grade and the youngest two, twin boys, were in kindergarten.

Sharon was a little girl who rarely caused any problems. Her mother would laugh and tell the story about how Sharon was shocked, the first day of Kindergarten, that not all the children listened to the teacher and some of them would talk or giggle during prayers. She couldn't understand how anyone could be disrespectful of the God she loved so much. Callie, in later years, would also describe Sharon as a very independent little girl. But, in reality, Sharon's sweet, quiet way went rather unnoticed in a noisy bustling household. Callie ran an organized home and everyone was required to help, but with both parents working to feed six kids, there were times when they were barely keeping their heads above water. Sharon's so called independence may have been wishful thinking, on the part of her busy parents, and more the result of emotional benign neglect.

Young children are rarely aware of appropriate moments to approach their parents. Sharon told her mother that Brother Ed was having tryouts for a cheering squad the next day, and there was going to be an examination. Callie was removing a particularly clumsy roasting pan from the oven and said, "Oh yes, that's nice dear. Will you please set the table, dinner is almost ready."

Brother Ed was a Carmelite brother who did many of the things the priests did with the exception of administering the sacraments. He was given the responsibility of organizing the elementary school sports and activities for the after school program on Monday, Wednesday and Friday. But he could often be found walking around the school ground, at lunch time, like the pied piper. He was tall with dark brown thinning hair and a benevolent smile that reminded Sharon of the statue of St. Francis in her classroom. The children adored him and would gather around hoping to garner attention from their most beloved authority figure.

Brother Ed had told a group of girls that they were to meet at the Old House at three-ten p.m. The Old House was a turn of the century clapboard house, on the school grounds, that was used for sports meetings, Girl Scouts, Brownie and teacher meetings. On this particular day it was not being used from three p.m. to seven p.m. So 11 little girls, ranging in age from eight to twelve, ran and skipped to the old house with the great expectation of becoming cheerleaders.

It was a three story, dreary brown with cream colored shutters. Over the years many of the Church members volunteered their services and removed wall partitions, updated plumbing, electrical wiring and painted, but it still seemed to maintain the sad appearance of something that should have been discarded a long time ago.

Brother Ed lined the girls up in the main room on the first floor that had stacks of folding chairs, a chalk board and about a dozen collapsed tables. He advised them that he was not only a brother but also a doctor and, if they wanted to be cheerleaders, they needed to have an examination. They each grabbed a chair and waited their turn. The lavatory, on the first floor, had been added a few years earlier and was only a couple of feet from the side exit. The girls were told they would enter the bathroom, one at a time, and they were to leave, directly after, by the side door. It seemed like a very long time before Sharon saw the second girl leave and it was her turn. She wasn't the least bit nervous since she had regular check-ups and knew what to expect.

She entered the bathroom where Brother Ed was sitting on a stool. He told her to take her clothes off and she did, leaving her uniform neatly folded on the floor. She stood in front of Brother Ed as he started out slowly; running his hands up and down her arms and legs. That seemed strange to Sharon since it wasn't the way Dr. Ridley examined her, and he didn't have that thing around his neck to listen to her heart. Then, he pulled her panties down and started feeling between her legs, it was like a lightning bolt. Sharon didn't know what to think, but as she looked at her beloved Brother Ed he had a very peculiar expression on his face. He was hurting her now and she knew something was very, very wrong. She was frozen in place and, in her mind, she was screaming. She felt like her head was exploding She looked at the pile of clothing on the floor and tried to concentrate on that while he continued exploring her body; her mind went somewhere else. Abruptly he stopped and told her to dress and send in the next girl. His tone was harsh and her heart was shattered. She left without looking at him again, running all the way home.

For the rest of her life, without knowing why, she could never stand to see clothing on the floor.

Chapter 8

N.C. and Kevin

N.C. had been spending lots of time with her horses, Blue and Lady Jane. Her husband, Kevin, was a writer enjoying the fourth season of one of the top rated comedies on TV. Money was not an issue at their sprawling ranch house in Hidden Hills. Kevin knew that his creative, energetic wife might have to spend a couple of weeks unwinding from the frenzied pace she had known, but he secretly coveted their time together and only feigned disappointment when her show was cancelled. He knew his feelings were selfish but his love for N.C. had never wavered and only increased as the years passed.

They had met when she was producing a segment, for Entertainment Tonight, on up and coming writers. The chemistry was there from the first few moments and it was obvious to everyone who knew them; this petite blond and burly redhead had something very special and marriage was soon to follow. They nurtured their relationship through the usual trials and tribulations of a new couple coping with busy lives and divergent schedules.

However, ten years later, they had anticipated their union would have resulted in more of a family. Three miscarriages and several years of fertility treatments had not produced the desired result.

They felt they had exhausted all resources for natural procreation and were now ready to adopt. This, they found, was not an easy feat. There had been the laborious effort of contacting numerous agencies and getting scores of references only to be told that, due to the many younger couples attempting to adopt, they were rather far down the list. Friends and relatives recommended attorney's who might help with private adoptions, but to no avail. Apparently N.C. was one of the many modern women who had, willingly or not, postponed childbearing and were now scouring the country for a baby to call their own. There had been one hopeful association with a young woman who had pledged her child to them but, in the end, she had changed her mind.

Then one afternoon, almost as a fluke, N.C. found a website on the Internet that looked very promising. It was for an "Attorney Seeking Parents". A young woman, who had three healthy children, found herself pregnant and abandoned by her husband. She would not consider abortion, for religious reasons, but she felt physically, emotionally and financially unable to care for a fourth child. She desperately wanted to find a loving couple to provide a home for her child and help lift the financial burden imposed by the departure of her husband. She gave descriptions of her three children, two boys and a girl, and assurance she had never abused drugs, and only had an occasional drink-but never when pregnant.

The Web site looked official and the attorney, Samuel J. Cohen, stated he was just helping someone in need and would only be a go between for Mrs. Elsie Blake. He would run background checks on prospective parents but it would be Ms. Blake who would make the final selection and come to terms with the perspective parents. Anyone interested could submit their name, address, phone number, and occupation. Mrs. Blake was soliciting thirty thousand dollars to be disbursed in increments of ten thousand dollars over the last three months of her pregnancy. Her plea included an explanation that the money was to reduce the tremendous monetary stress she was under, and ensure adequate care for all her children until she could get back to work. She did not want the money to be construed as payment for her child, but as a donation for the considerable gift she would be giving. This made perfect sense to N. C. who realized they had spent more on their latest BMW then the "donation" this poor women was requesting. N.C. vowed that, if all this came to pass, Elsie Blake would get a considerable bonus.

N.C. approached Kevin about her latest internet find. Kevin had come to grips with the realization that they might remain childless and that was quite alright with him. He was thirty five when they married and now, at forty five, he was very comfortable with their lifestyle. His love for his wife was not predicated on producing offspring. So when N.C. introduced him to this new plan he was far more cautious about the possible ramifications of dealing with a stranger who, as he put it, "was willing to sell her child over the Internet." But the mere sight of N.C.'s crushed expression was enough to conquer him and he reluctantly agreed to check things out. So N.C. started another journey to motherhood.

CHAPTER 9

Lynn and N.C. The Class

Lynn ran into an old acquaintance, Carol, at the grocery store and mentioned that she and another friend were interested in painting. Carol excitedly grabbed her purse and pulled out two applications for a painting class by the world famous Carl Bindes. Carol was Carl's American representative and was thrilled to help out an old friend with two tuition receipts for Carl's class tomorrow night. There was a no refund policy and two Europeans had to cancel. Lynn accepted saying, "Thanks, this must be my lucky day."

So the next evening Lynn and N.C. sat in an overcrowded studio, in Culver City, that used to be a train station. This hadn't been a convenient location since Lynn's home was over the hill in Studio City, about 30 minutes away on a good night. N.C.'s place was another 25 minutes west on the Ventura Freeway. But they were determined to be taught by the best and continually heard people touting Carl as just that.

Carl's niece and assistant, Tammora, who he was rumored to be having an affair with, greeted his disciples and attended to the mundane tasks of setting up materials and assigning easel space to each participant. Her large grey eyes betrayed an almost angelic devotion to her duties, as if she were grateful for a special vocation.

It was a good 20 minutes before the tall blond creature bounded into the room in what seemed an explosion of energy. His pallid complexion almost appeared as a canvas itself; a back drop for his chiseled features to shift and roam in animated confusion. His approach to teaching was unconventional, if not amusing, as he theatrically flailed his arms about while explaining his color and light theories. Clearly, this was a man enthralled with his own opinions in front of an audience equally enthusiastic. N.C. and Lynn both felt out of the loop of adoration and tried to focus on the information. Carl finally instructed the class in an exercise meant to develop awareness of the use of the left and right sides of the brain. There was a poster hanging in front of the studio, a still life. He turned the poster upside down and told the class to draw what they saw. So as the evening wore on it became apparent that this was a prerequisite and there would be no actual painting that night.

On the way home both expressed a little disappointment, "I don't know N.C., he may be a little too esoteric for me," chuckled Lynn.

N.C. laughed, "And you'd have to be deaf, dumb and blind not to think he was having an affair with his niece. The way they flirt with each other, icky."

"I just hope she's a niece by marriage, it's just creepy thinking otherwise," Lynn interjected, "she's just totally mesmerized by him."

"Well, different strokes I guess," said N.C. as she mimicked one of Carl's extravagant gestures and said, "we just don't have the proper appreciation." Both friends broke up in belly laughs.

They decided to stop for hot chocolate and N. C., for the next half hour, confided to Lynn her decision to pursue yet another endeavor of adoption. Lynn had witnessed N.C.'s other disappointments and fervently hoped this would not be another heartbreak for her friend.

It was 11:30PM by the time Lynn quietly unlocked the back door and swore to herself that tomorrow she would apply some WD40 to the squeaky hinge. Lynn hadn't really admitted to her daughter what she and N.C. were doing on their ladies night out. Lynn felt disloyal about seeking help elsewhere when she had praised Amanda's instruction so highly. She was sheepishly tip-toeing down the hall, assuming Amanda to be in bed, when her daughter bolted out of the bathroom and they collided in the hall.

Lynn's smock over her arm and painting supply box in her hand were a dead giveaway. Why hadn't she left the box and smock in the car?—was screaming in her head. Amanda, more than anything else, registered the guilty look on Lynn's face.

"Oh you'll never guess what N.C. and I did tonight, honey," she began nervously, "You know that famous painting teacher, Carl Bindes, well N.C. has a friend who got us into one of his classes. It was a last minute thing and I didn't want to say anything until we were enrolled. Sometimes too many people show up and they literally turn people away at the door." Why am I babbling and sounding like such a hypocrite?—thought Lynn.

Amanda headed for her door, turned, and with a glare made "good night" sound like, 'go to hell' in Lynn's ears.

Chapter 10

N.C and Kevin-
The First Encounter

They sat in a large red booth, eagerly awaiting Elsie Blake. It was not quite 3PM, on this unseasonably warm California afternoon, and anticipation was heightened with every passing minute. Then a young woman with strawberry blonde hair entered Mimi's café. She wore a pair of jeans and a pale yellow checkered maternity blouse. The crowd was sparse at this time of day so Elsie spotted the awaiting pair with no difficulty. Clutching her black leather purse, she walked strait to their table. Kevin stood and stepped toward her, shaking her hand and making excited hasty introductions. There was a moment of awkward silence and then they all started talking at once. Laughing, with their discomfort eased, Kevin suggested Elsie tell them a little more about herself and they in turn would do the same.

Elsie's speech exposed her southern roots as she explained, "Well, you see it's like I was telling N.C. on the phone, I think things got to be too much for Jeb, he's my husband, and he just up and left one morning. He had lost his construction job over an argument with the contractor. That was the night before I told him about this one," she said gliding her hand over her stomach. "I guess some men just can't take the pressure. Then the rent was due and the bills were commin' in and I just didn't know what to do. My mama sent me some money but that's just about gone now. I thought Jeb would come back, but now I'm afraid I'll be homeless and the state will end up taking all my kids. My friend gave me the idea, about adoption, and it seemed like the only thing to do. Well, just as long as I know the baby's goin' to a good home a' course."

Kevin asked, "Elsie, what would you do if Jeb were to come home tomorrow?"

"I don't blame you for your concern," Elsie went on, "but it's been six and a half months. My mama didn't raise no fools, I'm goin' home with my other kids and start training at beautician school. I've got it all worked out. Mama said she would help with the kids, but she doesn't know about this one," patting her belly. "She never liked Jeb and I'm sure we'll have a few 'I told you so' moments, but eventually I'm gonna be free and independent of any man. That's what I want."

It was Kevin who thought it odd that Elsie didn't insist on seeing their home. She had told N.C. she wanted to meet in a restaurant where they could talk without the other children interrupting. A friendly neighbor was babysitting but her time was limited. Once again it all made perfect sense to N.C. who was becoming more and more like a runaway train just speeding ahead. Kevin commented that Elsie did have a car and their home was only an hour from where she lived but he realized that whatever he might say, at this point, would be interpreted as negative thinking. Once again he indulged her and just stepped out of her way.

Elsie wrote down mailing instructions for their first "donation" and said a P.O. Box was safer than mailing a large check to the house. There had been someone "messin" with the mailboxes in the neighborhood and she didn't want to take any chances. She gave them her address too and Kevin felt better at that. He resigned himself to the situation and, as N.C. and Elsie were talking, he was trying to picture how closely the offspring of this young woman would physically resemble he and N.C. Elsie had the same clear blue eyes and light completion of N. C. but was two or three inches taller with a bit heavier bone structure than the sinewy limbs he had become so accustomed to holding.

N.C. gave Kevin a reproachful look when he asked Elsie about her husband. Elsie charmed him with the news that Jeb was about his size, six foot, lighter brown hair with similar navy blue eyes, but not as good looking as Kevin. Elsie had said this all in a very matter of fact tone that sounded all the more sincere. Kevin was inwardly softening in his attitude, what else could he really do.

CHAPTER 11

The End of Gia and Dix

Everything had gone so well and all his dreams seemed to have come true when he moved to L.A.. So, why was Gia staring at the body of her beloved cousin? His head was leaning on the back of the bathtub, with arms outstretched, he looked like he had just finished a prayer—maybe he had.

They hadn't exactly grown apart but the business of life had whittled away at their time together and, in the last six months, their contact was reduced to an occasional Sunday brunch and a few phone calls a month.

Like many talented and creative young people in Los Angeles, Dix and his muse, Carrie, had found themselves invited to all the "best" parties. They had both smoked weed since high school but now had the opportunity to investigate other "mind expanding" vehicles. The pattern had formed and Dix and Carrie would work hard all week at their respective endeavors. On Friday, if Carrie didn't have a show, they would meet at a club and decide where the evening would take them. More often than not they would party late in the evening, then Carrie would meet up with other friends and Dix would find his one-nighter at a gay bar or even on the street. He never seemed to cultivate a real relationship.

Carrie adored Dix and would never even look at another designer. She would envision a vague concept about the theme of her show and Dix would set out to interpret her idea and transform the idea into reality. Dix was able to design the costume and stage atmosphere far beyond Carrie's expectations. Carrie was grateful that she could leave that part of her performance up to Dix and concentrate on the music and vocals. They had a good run, and then things started falling apart.

Carrie grew up. She had always been interested in yoga, nutrition, health and spirituality. This detour into the world of hard drugs and parties was, for Carrie, a youthful experiment. She had a good self image and didn't like the results of this recent lifestyle. The late nights and lack of sleep had taken a toll on her voice and appearance. The people she was meeting seemed to be on their way down rather than up. Creativity had been clouded rather than expanded and she decided to cleanse her body of all chemicals and get back to work.

Then, about the same time, she began worrying about Dix. His work ethic was slipping and he began being late for meetings, if he showed up at all. He hadn't lost all his talent but the brilliance was fading and he was losing his attention to detail. Carrie was wrestling with decisions about what to do and then Dix made the decision for her. He came to her studio for a meeting, grabbed a cup of coffee, and proceeded to pass out on the conference table. It was the last straw. Carrie took him out for a decent meal and gingerly gave him the ultimatum; he had to go to rehab or quit his association with her. She emphatically declared her love for him as a person, artist and friend but could no longer witness his self destruction.

Dix tried to deny the extent of his addiction, but to no avail. He knew she loved him but couldn't shake that old familiar feeling of rejection; the addict's self loathing and self pity.

Gia had a brunch date with Dix and when he didn't show up she got worried. He had sounded strange on the phone the day before and she just had a funny feeling. When she reached his apartment, and saw his car, she thought he might have had a late night and overslept.

The door knocking went on long enough for a, "What's going on," from a neighbor. Gia was starting to become frantic and quickly told the neighbor her concerns. He hurried to get the manager. A tall body builder type appeared a few minutes later with a huge ring of keys. Gia's stomach ached as the seconds passed while he fumbled for the right one. Finally the door opened and Gia went running through the apartment. The sight of Dix in the bathtub, his eyes staring vacantly and his skin a translucent bluish tinge, was too much for Gia's mind to assimilate; she went blank and hit the floor.

The initial shock, especially seeing Dix in the bathtub, had totally knocked the wind out of Gia. She looked and felt like a walking zombie. Then, at home, she became angry and drank herself sick until she thought she would wrench up her internal organs. How could he possibly do this to all the people who loved him. We all go through pain. Why couldn't he just tough it out? Why couldn't he reach out to her or anyone of his friends? But, in her heart, she knew the answer to these questions. Dix had been in pain all of his life. He couldn't manage the struggling and trying to prove himself. He kept thinking that success was the answer to all his problems. He didn't realize that money and accolades from strangers didn't fill the void created, at first, by his father and then reinforced by homophobes.

He had sought peace, when he was seventeen, at several churches. They either wanted him to denounce his sexuality and 'find a good Christian girl' or they didn't want to speak to him at all. How devastating to be rejected by his father and then by the people he thought represented god. He had expressed to Gia that even his friends in LA would not have given him the time of day if he wasn't at the top of his game. He claimed that only Gia, his old friend, from back home, Callie and Carrie knew him and accepted him. His gay friends were never aware of his dirt poor roots and he never had a comfortable love relationship, only one night interludes.

Gia felt mournful and lethargic, not wanting to do anything. She had the agonizing responsibility of telling Dottie, Bobby Joe and her parents. Then arrangements had to be made for a service in Los

Angeles. Phone calls were made to friends and associates, many of whom volunteered to contact the people Dix had worked with that Gia didn't know.

She called Dix's favorite caterer who was so shocked, she ended up consoling him. He would take care of the refreshments after the funeral for a nominal fee. One of the last calls she made was to arrange transportation for Dix back to South Carolina. That's when Gia broke down again; it would be the final destination for Dix.

Chapter 12

N.C. and Elsie

Most women get a nesting urge toward the end of their pregnancy and, even though N.C. was not the birth mother, she was manic about preparing for the arrival of her baby. She would wake up in the morning thinking about the perfect comforter or whether she wanted a rocking chair or glider in the baby's room. An old friend 'in the business,' who was a gaffer, volunteered his time to arrange the perfect lighting ambiance.

A neighbor, who N.C. had helped with emergency babysitting, was a local artist and she insisted on painting a mural of all the Disney characters on the nursery wall. It turned out better then N.C. had expected and she posted a dozen pictures on her Facebook page. "That should get you some business," she told her friend.

N.C. got a call from Elsie reminding N.C. to meet her at the Doctor's office on Tuesday afternoon. "Of course, I'll be there," said N.C.

N.C. arrived on time but Elsie was already sitting in the waiting room. They exchanged pleasantries and Elsie commented on how "this little one has been very lively." She took N.C.'s hand and placed it on her expanding girth.

"Oh my god, I can feel the movement, was that a kick?" N.C. asked excitedly.

"Oh, yeah, but it's not so fun in the middle of the night," Elsie said flatly. N.C. wished she could experience that feeling anytime—day or night.

The doctor was pleasant and the visit routine for Elsie. N.C. was fascinated with the sonogram, seeing the tiny human they thought was a girl. This was Elsie's last month and she would now be on a weekly office visit schedule until the birth.

N.C. had invited Elsie out to lunch and handed over the last check. They chatted pleasantly and N.C. told Elsie that she and Kevin were enrolled in parenting classes, thinking this would please her. Elsie didn't seem to have any reaction but appeared anxious about the time. She was obviously ready to leave. So they made plans to meet the following week at the next scheduled appointment.

Chapter 13

Lynn

Lynn was wondering why it seemed that when her professional life was going well her personal life seemed to hit a wall. The wall was Amanda. Lynn couldn't confront Amanda about why they were not talking, because they were talking, but there was no substance to their conversations. It was a "yes" or "no" or "can I" from Amanda. Lynn spent several hours at the book store, scanning all the self help with teenagers information she could find, to no avail. She wondered if any of those authors actually had children of their own. Her friends, who had older kids, would just smile that annoying 'we've been there' smile and reassure Lynn that it would all clear up in a few years—probably when Amanda's frontal lobe was fully developed.

Lynn had landed a job in a new pilot that was somewhat based on her show "Hans and Kahn Cook." It was a comedy about two similar characters, on a cooking show, but had more to do with what happened to them off camera. Lynn's friend had watched "Hans and Kahn" when he was finished with his last project. He was having writers block, while working on another idea, and decided to veg-out on the couch and watch his friend Lynn's show. He got the idea, after ten minutes, and went racing to his computer where the words just kept flowing.

Lynn was elated but they wouldn't start shooting for a couple of months. He needed to polish the last script and the director he wanted was on board but not available for two months. That was perfect for Lynn. Maybe she could mend fences with Amanda or at least have time for the attempt; and help N.C. with the new baby.

Chapter 14

N.C. At the Doctor's Office

There were five other women in the waiting room, in various stages of pregnancy, when N.C. arrived at the Doctor's office. The weeks seemed to be dragging now that the end was drawing near. N.C. had several conversations with the women in the room but, twenty minutes later, she started getting concerned and approached the receptionist.

"Hi, I'm waiting for Elsie Blake and I'm getting concerned. I believe she had an appointment at two and she is usually prompt. Have you heard from her?"

"Hmmm, let me see, yes that's right, but I haven't heard from her. She probably just got caught up in traffic," she answered.

Two hours later N.C. was on the phone with Lynn. Lynn had just taken the Cornish game hens out of the refrigerator and was sprinkling salt and pepper in the cavities when the phone rang.

"Oh Lynn, its four twenty and Elsie is still not here. I know I'm starting to panic but I don't know what to do. I've called her cell phone and it's no longer in service. Kevin is on a location shoot and

I know it's a busy time for him, I just don't know what to do," N.C. said, sounding breathless and frantic.

"Listen to me. Sit down and calm yourself. Have a glass of water and, when you feel composed enough, go home and I'll meet you there in a half hour," Lynn said, "but take your time and be careful driving."

Lynn had a lump well up in her throat. She couldn't believe it, not again. She just knew how terribly heart-wrenching this must be for N.C. She put the hens back in the refrigerator and scrawled a note to Amanda and Chuck apologizing. The beautiful dinner she had planned would have to wait until tomorrow night.

"I have an N.C. emergency. I will explain later. Order pizza or Chinese and I'll call in an hour or so. I'm going to N.C.'s house. XO L." Grabbing her jacket and purse she was out the door and on her way in record time.

Lynn drove up N.C.'s winding driveway reminding herself not to give her any false hopes that everything would be alright, it probably wouldn't. She had a bad feeling about this Elsie from the start. What pregnant mother didn't ask more questions and not insist on seeing the home where her child would be raised. Her excuses were flimsy but Lynn did not want to be the one to rain on the parade. She took a deep breath and rang the door bell. N.C. answered, her eyes red and swollen, and gave Lynn a big hug.

"Thanks so much Lynn," she started, "I'm just beside myself thinking of all the terrible possibilities. Could she have been in an accident? Did her husband come back and was he angry about the adoption? Is she hurt?"

N.C. didn't have Elsie's address on her at the Doctor's office but found it when she got home. She and Lynn set out to find Elsie. It was close to six-thirty p.m. when they pulled into the Blake's driveway. The house was dark and only a broken tricycle on the lawn, that looked like it had been run over, stood as testament that a family had once lived there. The small tract home had a picture window with no drapes, revealing no furniture inside. Its vacancy seemed to be mimicking N.C.'s own feelings of emptiness. They decided to take a chance and ask the neighbors if they knew anything. The house to the left had two cars in the driveway so they decided to try that one first.

A man, about thirty, came to the door and suggested they talk to his wife, who knew the neighbors better than he did. She came to the door with a baby, about nine months old, bouncing against her hip.

"Sure I know Elsie, I've baby sat her kids a few times," said the neighbor, "but it's Clark, not Blake. They lived here, oh, about seven months. They have a little boy, Jeb, just like his daddy." She was friendly and chatty. She yelled down the hall, "Lenny, will you please go watch Andy and Matthew in the back while I talk to these nice ladies?" She gave the impression it was a treat to talk with adults.

"Did Elsie have any other kids?" asked N.C.

"No, just Jeb, and the one in the oven," she smiled.

"Do they get along well, Jeb and Elsie? We heard he might have run off," N.C. continued.

"No way, those two love birds. Hey, are they in some kinda trouble? she asked.

"Nothing like that," said Lynn. "We represent the owners. They're paid up for the month but we owe them a security deposit. We just wanted to make sure everything was alright. Do you know how to locate them?"

"No, they didn't even tell us they were leaving. It was about a week ago. I was just back from taking my Lenny to the dentist. Elsie and Jeb were packing up one of those small u-Hall trucks, just about ready to take off. Elsie said Jeb got a job offer from a cousin in Texas. But why were you looking for somebody named Blake?"

"Oh, Don't mind me. It's been a long day. Our next stop is with someone named Blake," said N.C.

"You know, now that I think about it," she said, "it was exactly a week ago, almost to the minute."

Lynn suggested they stop and get a something to eat on the way home. She figured Kevin would be home about nine and didn't want to drop N.C. home to an empty house.

"I've been so stupid. I feel so bad. The last time, when that other girl backed out, I think Kevin thought I would give up. He seems perfectly content with just the two of us. I just have such a longing to have a baby and I can't seem to shake it," admitted N.C.

Lynn proposed meeting for brunch the next day to ensure N.C. would be out of the house and not under her covers.

Chapter 15

Sharon, David and Lexi

Sharon liked to arrive early for her meetings. She was well-prepared but liked to sit in her car and meditate a few minutes before a presentation.

Two hours later she was back on the freeway headed home. She had wowed the director who continually repeated, "That's how I see it too." She felt like he was a little too patronizing but, other than a few short meetings, she would most likely be dealing with his underlings anyway.

Now she couldn't wait another minute, she had to call David. He was not surprised and suggested they meet for dinner to celebrate. Her heart took an elevator drop to her stomach and it took a moment for her to sort out her conflicted feelings. They had never been out to "dinner," just sandwiches while they were working on a project, but not a "date."

"Hey, are you there," David asked. "Sure, I mean yes. I'm driving and had to change lanes."

"I'll pick you up at seven. Clean up, no jeans or tacky flip flops tonight," he ordered.

"Ok, ok see you at seven," she agreed.

"And Sharon, for the sake of everyone on the road, stop talking and driving, You know it's illegal now," he said.

Sharon thought, had they been in a romantic relationship, that remark might have annoyed her, but she had too much excitement running through her veins for anything to bother her.

David rang her door bell at seven sharp. Ten seconds later he saw a vision of loveliness. Sharon stood before him in a turquoise dress, with just a hint of cleavage, a multicolored shawl and black sling back heels.

"Hmmm, you do clean up well," David said, staring.

Her eyes were drinking him in as she attempted to be nonchalant, "Well back atcha."

"Do we have time for a glass of wine?" she asked.

"No, we're toasting with Champagne tonight and I don't want them giving our table away. Let's get going," he said.

Sharon felt a difference in David tonight. He was sounding much more in charge, nothing tentative in his voice. She liked this confident side; he always seemed to surprise her.

Le Sanglier was crowded but, within five minutes, they were seated in a very high-backed booth looking over the menu which was written on a chalk board and propped on an easel. The ambiance was romantic and the acoustics allowed for patrons to actually hear one another without difficulty.

"The Rack of lamb is very good here, well just about everything is good here," David commented.

"Do you come here often?" inquired Sharon. Both knew the real underlining question 'was this a favorite place for you and Abby?'

David responded by saying, "You know I grew up in Encino. Whenever there was a family celebration my parents would bring us here. It became a family tradition."

Abby was David's wife. She was a lovely brunette and an only child used to getting what she wanted, and that included the handsome baseball player, David. They had been high school sweethearts and both attended UCLA. He had been an engineering student and she was a psychology major. They had been sleeping together since senior year in High School and they took it for granted they would one day marry. The plan was hastened when, in their junior year of College, Abby got pregnant. Both of them were Catholic, Abby's family was so in the strictest degree, and abortion was out of the question. Well, Abby would have considered it but her timing was off. She was already in her second trimester and felt she was too far along. So they married.

Abby was pregnant for another two months when complications caused a miscarriage. She was devastated and depression soon followed. She became resentful that her life had changed so dramatically. Her dreams of being a psychologist had been abandoned and replaced by motherhood, but now there was no baby and she felt shattered. She didn't consider David's altered situation. He too had made life-changing decisions.

Their parents had helped to get them started, financially, but it still required David to quit school. He was lucky enough to get a job, through his father's friend, as a carpenter's apprentice with the studios. The remainder of the college fund, his parents had put aside, helped supplement his income. Six months later David had invented a new type of cabinet hardware and a tool that would work with it. It would be three more years before he would see any money for his patent. But this was a start and he was happy, he had other ideas too.

David, after the first miscarriage, was working long hours and Abby wasn't back to school yet. She was 'too depressed' to think about cooking and, rather than fight, David fell into the routine of making dinner and cleaning up, which continued through their marriage. Abby's mother would occasionally send her housekeeper over to 'help' Abby, but it was David who did most of the laundry and vacuuming.

Abby eventually got over her depression and went back to school. She received her Bachelor's Degree and then went on for her Master's Degree. She was weary of taking more classes and decided to postpone a Doctorate. She set up a Marriage and Family counseling practice. Six months later she was pregnant with a little girl.

David was happy with his work now and, with the income from his patent, he was able to afford his own workshop and do what he loved best: woodworking, carpentry and design. So when Abby complained of morning sickness, cramps or backache he tried his best to comfort her. Deep down he felt the marriage should have ended a long time ago, but with this pregnancy he would try to work things out. If motherhood didn't change her, he just didn't see spending the rest of his life in a loveless marriage.

David and Abby both welcomed the pregnancy, this time, and hoped it would renew their marriage. The past few years they seemed to be going in different directions. David would inquire about Abby's progress but Abby never really seemed interested in what David was doing. David eventually admitted to himself that, although he cared for his wife, there were times he just didn't like her. The spoiled child had morphed into a selfish, demanding adult. Abby managed to do it in a very low key subtle way, but it was there.

Abby's water broke about eleven thirty on a Friday night. They had everything ready by the door. David grabbed the suitcase and Abby's favorite pillow. The hospital was only five minutes away so there was no rush. They were two blocks away when a drunk driver passed out behind the wheel and hit them while they sat at the red light. The impact was at an angle that sent David's car in a circular motion careening against a telephone pole, and Abby got the worst of it. Thankfully, the baby was delivered and was fine. David had a concussion but Abby was in a coma and continued in a vegetative state hooked up to machines that provided her with the basics of existence.

David didn't feel Abby would have wanted that but they had been young and never had that, "what would you want me to do if," conversation. Her parents held the hope for a miracle, against all odds, and he didn't feel he could insist on taking that away from them.

His other consideration was his daughter, Lexi. She had met Sharon a few times and understood that Sharon was a friend who daddy worked with sometimes. But every once in a while she would ask about Sharon and say she was "nice" and how "pretty" she was.

David just knew Sharon would make the kind of mom Lexi hungered for. He was also concerned that if he waited too long, little girls start to get very possessive of their daddies and his window of opportunity was closing.

David had arranged for a bottle of Champagne to be brought over as soon as they arrived. They happily toasted their own prosperity and leisurely looked at the menu. David made some small talk and asked more about the earlier meeting. He sensed Sharon's nervousness and wanted to let her relax for a bit. They ordered dinner and had another drink as appetizers were served. They continued talking about different aspects of the job and David related some stories about acquaintances they had in common. Dinner was served and the Champagne was flowing.

Neither one was much of a drinker so they were enjoying a little buzz when David slid closer to Sharon and took her hand. "We need to talk," he started.

"Isn't that what people usually say when their breaking up," Sharon said with a little nervous giggle.

"Well I've always been a little backwards," he smiled. "Listen Sharon, My marriage wasn't very good, for a long time. I was hoping it would get better when the baby was born, but that was doubtful. Abby is never coming out of the coma, she's brain dead. The life support machines are really for the benefit of her parents. I think I've waited long enough. I want you with every fiber of my being. I'm hoping you feel the same way."

Sharon felt almost faint. She could tell there were beads of sweat forming on her brow and her hands were getting clammy. This was her dream come true but it was also a shock.

"I hate to sound like a cliché, but this is so sudden. You never led me to believe you had strong feelings for me," she blurted out in a hushed tone. "I don't even know what to say or what I'm feeling," she said, almost to herself. "Of course I've been attracted to you but I always held that in check, knowing your situation. Now, all of a sudden, I need to make a 180 degree turn–about in a few minutes. I have so many questions whirling about in my head. You're Catholic first of all, what will your family say, and what about her family?" asked Sharon.

David had always been a straight arrow and, although he had been attracted to Sharon early on, he never made inappropriate advances. They had recently dabbled in a little innocent flirtation, but it was becoming unbearable for him to be so physically close without actual touching.

"My family will be overjoyed," he said emphatically. "They want to see me happy and they've hinted about how I need to get on with my life. I just wanted it to be with the right person at the right time. You know me Sharon. You know how I get a little methodical about getting everything clear before I can continue, then there's no stopping me. And I can't really believe all those church rules. What god would stand in the way of the happiness of two good people? And I don't really care about what anyone else thinks, except you."

"Aren't you forgetting about what Lexi might think? I've only met her a few times," responded Sharon, "I don't want to traumatize her."

David took something out of his jacket pocket and opened a small box revealing a beautiful diamond ring. "First of all, if you could manage becoming her stepmother, I'm sure she would love you as much as I do. She's asked me several times about 'the nice lady' I work with, so I think she likes you already."

Sharon didn't really hear anything after David said 'love you as much as I do'. She leaned over and gave him a long loving kiss. When they finally broke away she started softly laughing and said, "I don't think most people have their first kiss after they become engaged, at least not in this century."

"Technically you never said yes" was David's response. "I know this all sounds a little crazy, and I come with baggage, but I just couldn't keep it to myself any longer. I love you and I want to marry you and spend the rest of my life with you," and he punctuated his declaration with another hungry kiss. When they pulled apart he said, "Well?"

"Well what? Oh, YES," said Sharon.

Twenty minutes later they were in Sharon's house making love for the first time. Slowly, cautiously and tenderly they explored each other in a matching rhythm. They could feel each other's heat and their lust could not wait any longer. Then, with an urgency they had never known, they climaxed and collapsed in each other's arms. Ten minutes later, the second time, was not so gentle. They pounded against each other's bodies with all the vigor and abandon of their pent up sexuality until their cravings were exhausted. They were quiet for a while, and then they laughed and hugged until David had to leave. His housekeeper usually left on Friday but she agreed to babysit for this special night. Sharon was not sorry he was leaving; she had a lot to think about.

Sharon had left the Catholic Church at twenty two, finally making the conscious decision that she was not a believer in their chauvinistic doctrine. But she still had the residual effects of years of indoctrination and she had a nagging feeling that she wasn't sure she was doing the right thing.

The next night they had dinner with Lexi. She was so cute Sharon could hardly stand it. She had insisted on wearing her pink princess ballerina tutu and her purple Dora the Explorer sweat jacket. Little strawberry blond ringlets framed her face with the bulk of her thick curls secured in a thick ponytail. Her grey green eyes seemed to absorb everything.

Lexi loved going out to dinner and she asked some very amusing questions.

"Sharon, why do you have three earrings in one ear? Do you have children? Do you want to come to my birthday party? Can I touch your bracelet?"

Sharon had a thin silver chain link bracelet on. She unfastened the clasp, slipped it off and as she wrapped it around Lexi's wrist a few times said, "How about this for your birthday gift?"

David started to protest but Sharon spelled out 'bribe' quickly and said, "sometimes girls just need something a little special." Of course Lexi was delighted. So much so she decided to invite Sharon to see her mommy sometime.

"She's not like other mommies cuz she's sick and has to stay in a bed, and she can't talk or see. But her room smells pretty. Grandma brings her flowers every week"

Sharon had to fight back tears, this sweet little girl was so innocent, Sharon wanted to grab her, hug and kiss her, but she knew that might only frighten Lexi.

David wasn't sure if they were overwhelming Sharon and thought they had better wrap this up before Sharon went screaming out of the restaurant. This was their only dinner until next week. David had been contracted to design and supervise the building of an elaborate stage, in San Francisco, for the memorial tribute to a recently deceased rock star. The money had been too good to turn down and now he would be working twelve and sixteen hour days for the next week. Sharon was busy too, and the following week she had committed to a long weekend with the girls, thinking it couldn't have come at a better time.

Chapter 16

Gia, Sharon, N.C. and Lyn

Lynn's husband had read about Dix's death. He always read the obituaries and had met Dix at Gia's Halloween Party last year. He brought it to Lynn's attention and she was shocked. She was very aware that Gia and her cousin were as close as siblings and knew this would be a heart breaking time for her friend. She called Gia, who apologized for not telling her sooner. She had been so depressed she just wanted to get through making all the arrangements before she could really talk to her friends. So Lynn called N.C. and Sharon and they all went to the memorial service to support Gia.

We expect death to steal our older family and friends but when someone dies, at an early age, it seems to take a strange toll that creates a temporary inertia. Sharon, Lynn and N.C. were going to take turns, discreetly, keeping Gia busy. But for now the friends agreed to meet at the Aroma Café the next day for lunch.

N.C. picked Lynn up to go to the café. Both of them had huge sunglasses on. As Lynn got in the car, N.C. pulled off her glasses to read the parking ticket she got while buying a sympathy card. She passed the card to Lynn who took off her sunglasses to read it. That instant, they looked at each other and started laughing. They both had been crying and rubbing mascara laden eyes, now looking like raccoons. Lynn knew that N.C. was still upset about the baby.

They both went in the house to clean up and Lynn went on to explain that she thought Amanda was shutting her out. The last straw was when Lynn asked about an upcoming school trip, that she had volunteered to chaperone, Amanda told her they had plenty of volunteers and she wasn't needed.

"I think its hormones," Lynn said, "Amanda has too many and I don't have enough. I know it's silly to take this all so seriously. I know that Amanda needs to explore her world and assert some independence. I just thought we would have a little more fun time before I became irrelevant." N.C. reminded Lynn of her own teenage years and said, "Trust me, in a couple of years your relevance will return." Then the two went off to meet Sharon and Gia at the Café.

It was a quirky place in Studio City, half indoors and half outside with a canopied roof and heaters intermittently dispersed between tables. Patrons ordered and paid at the main counter where fresh bakery goods and desserts were displayed in glass cases. Sharon was third in the queue when she got the call from Lynn. Lynn said to go ahead and order them a couple of cheese and avocado omelets, orange juice and coffee. They would be there in five minutes. Gia came in just as Sharon got to the counter to order. The place was jammed. They finished with the counter-waitress and were given a number to place on their table. Luckily, they managed to secure a booth inside as N.C. and Lynn walked in. Hugs went around and they sat down to commiserate on their situations.

Death takes priority and Sharon started commenting on the beautiful service that Gia had arranged for Dix.

"You created a wonderful memorial for Dix and you should be proud of yourself. Dix would have loved all the attention and eulogies," said Sharon.

Gia's eyes welled up a bit but she managed to control the tears as she said, "Oh he would have thought it wasn't over the top enough. Cirque du Soleil should have been performing while Gustavo

Dudamel conducted Mozart for the service, then Jay-Z and Beyonce back at the house," Gia mused squeezing out a smile while they laughed and agreed.

They talked a while about what a character he was then listened as Gia told stories about the funny things they did as kids.

Lynn briefly repeated her tale of woe about Amanda, secretly not knowing if N.C. was ready to share about the baby. "I think god is punishing me for all the grief I gave my mother," she said laughing, trying to lighten up the conversation.

Gia, innocently asked N.C. how close it was to the baby's birth. N.C. had cried all her tears and knew she just had to let it go.

"Soon, but it's not going to be my baby. Baby mama flew the coup with her dead beat husband and their little girl. I would like to blame him, but she was just as culpable." The others tried to console and encourage N.C.

"I feel sorry for their children, having grifter parents can make for a very insecure childhood. Meanwhile, Kevin has been so good to my miserable self. He wants to take me on some European excursion when they go on hiatus. I really don't deserve him," she declared.

A waiter spotted the number on their table and came to distribute their order. Conversation resumed when plates and cups reached the designated consumers.

"I found out we're not the only gullible ones. I made a police report and the investigator said he received three other complaints describing Elsie down to her sweet southern drawl," said N.C.

They all had comments then stopped abruptly when a mutual acquaintance approached. She told them her new assignment for 'Relax and Retreat." It was a start up, small company and they are doing a few long weekends to work out any kinks in the program.

"The setting is lovely," she said, "the Serendipity Ranch in Santa Barbara. They will be doing painting, massage, yoga, hiking and, best of all, great food. There will be no pressure so you can be involved as much or as little as you like. Oh and there's a hot tub too!"

They knew this woman well and she was never involved with anything that wasn't top notch. They all agreed it sounded wonderful and inexpensive. They had planned on a girl's weekend anyway, so each one received a two page application and was advised to read it carefully.

"There are a couple of ground rules: no electronic devices, you turn them in when you get there and they will be put in a safe. And you stay at the ranch—no shopping trips," she added. "But wow, I wish I could go. Four days to relax sounds like heaven to me." Then she moved on.

PART II

CHAPTER 17

Mamie and Jan

Mamie had been angry at God, nature and the world. What kind of legacy was this for her girls? She didn't think much of it when her routine mammogram showed an irregularity. It had happened to her before and several of her friends; a misread x-ray, a benign tumor or maybe a fibroid cyst. No one, on either side of her parent's families, had ever had breast cancer.

A pleasant, pudgy, young nurse, wearing purple scrubs, escorted Mamie to a seat in the radiologist office. She said, "The Doctor will be with you in a few minutes." Mamie thought she must get tired of saying that all day. Then the anxious welling in her stomach began. She had never been called in for a consultation before, how could she not realize how serious this was. She began to survey the room, trying to calm herself down, but the sterile atmosphere left her cold. She loved black and white photography but the three photographs, hanging above the credenza behind the desk, looked amateurish. She was mentally redecorating when Doctor Singer walked briskly into the room. He leaned down to say hello and shake Mamie's hand before retreating to his chair behind the desk. Mamie sensed that his neutral expression was a camouflage for his task ahead.

"Well there is just no easy way to say this Mamie, your biopsy was positive for cancer cells. Luckily, from what I can tell, it is at the beginning stages and we feel the prognosis is very good. I'll give you some information and a referral to an excellent surgeon, Doctor Silverman. I think he's the best in Southern California."

Mamie felt like a bomb had exploded in her head when the doctor gave her the bad news. She felt incredibly isolated, like the world was melting away. She couldn't focus on what he was saying as she watched his lips move. She wanted to strike out at this messenger of doom and call him a liar. But years of practiced appropriate behavior surfaced and she quietly accepted the written information he handed her and the surgery referral. Her movements seemed ethereal, as if somehow the cancer invading her body caused her to float home with no recollection of how she got there.

Mamie was relieved that it was Friday, the day her mother, now called Nana, routinely picked the younger girls up from school and took them to the roller rink, then for ice cream. Jules, the oldest daughter, had cheerleading practice and was rarely home before five p.m.. The luxury of having time for herself was rare, and now it was precious. She needed to put this all together in some order in her mind; figure out how to tell family and friends. She decided to take a bath. Filling the tub, half way, she sank in leaving the hot water running. She turned the cold tap off so she could gradually withstand the intense heat. She wondered if the extreme heat might be good or bad for her "condition," reminding herself that it was cancer. She realized that for the next few months she would wonder about lots of things: causes, cures, and consequences.

Mamie had always been health conscious and had her regular checkups. How could this be happening? It wasn't fair. Her family didn't deserve this and she desperately wanted someone to blame. Mamie's emotions were in a frenzy. She had only told her mother that she "didn't feel well" and thought she was having some "female trouble." But she was just buying time and knew she needed to get over the shock before she could tell her loved ones. Mamie thought of her best friend Jan, yes, that's where she would start. Then she had a good cry.

Jan was having a very hectic day and almost didn't take the call. She looked at the caller ID and thought to herself that it was very unusual for Mamie to be calling at five-forty-five p.m. Mamie didn't normally call her at the office, knowing the amount of trouble shooting Jan did throughout the day. She knew there was something wrong as soon as she heard Mamie's voice. Mamie was insistent that everything was ok but she really needed to talk as soon as possible and would explain when they saw each other. They were both glad the next day was Saturday and agreed to meet at Marmalade Café, in Agoura, for breakfast.

Mamie didn't wallow too long in self pity; it was too foreign a territory for her. She had asked her husband, Bill, to put the kids to bed and told him she might be coming down with something.

"I'll go in the guest room so at least one of us can get a decent night's sleep." It was only a white lie, she told herself; let them all have a few more hours of peace while I sort things out.

The overcast sky made the morning feel particularly chilly. Jan and Mamie arrived at Marmalade almost at the same time, early enough to get one of the coveted tables by the fireplace. Mamie's eyes betrayed her sleepless night as she pictured a multitude of scenarios on how she would tell the family. She finally settled on a couple and thought she would run them by Jan; but first she had to tell Jan. So, over the omelets, coffee and toast she calmly started with her routine visit to the OBGYN.

Of course Jan could tell what was coming and started biting the inside of her mouth. She had not done this since she was a child. It was a way of concentrating on a minor pain to avoid thinking of something that might cause an emotional outburst of tears. It had been helpful during confrontations with other kids who would cruelly say her mother was in the crazy house. But Mamie needed her comfort now and she honestly couldn't imagine a world without her dearest friend.

Jan was going to have to reverse roles and be the grownup for once. She knew her own emotions would have to wait and she couldn't just babble hollow reassurances. There wasn't anything Jan really needed to say; she just needed to be there, the way Mamie had always been there for her.

Jan's head was swimming a little but she was determined to concentrate on Mamie's words. Mamie was talking about her part time job as a highly overqualified receptionist. She would probably have to quit as soon as they could find a replacement. For the last few years, now that the kids were in school, Mamie liked getting out of the house and earning a little 'mad money'. It was only 15 hours a week and during that time, over coffee breaks, she had become the unofficial romantic mentor for several of the young women working in the real estate office.

"You wouldn't believe what these young women put up with from their boyfriends," she would tell Jan. These young women had learned to love Mamie for the same reason Jan did. Mamie could listen to anything and never betray, scorn or criticize unless it was directed at the young women's object of affection or rejection. She had a way of finding just the right words to cushion your fall and boost the ego at the same time. Her friendship had such a feeling of unconditional love that Jan thought, if she went to the top of a building with a machine gun and mowed down everyone in sight, Mamie would comfort her saying, "those people probably did something to deserve it, and they should have known you had PMS."

They both ordered second cups of coffee and talked about how Mamie would break the news to her family. Then they went on to look over the oncology information. Jan was insistent about taking Mamie to her doctor appointments saying that, even though she had a busy schedule, she had more flexibility than Mamie's husband, Bill. Mamie admitted she hadn't told Bill yet and Jan came up with a solution.

She had Mamie call her husband to meet her for lunch. Mamie hated to interrupt Bill's work day with such bad news but Jan had said the sooner the better and there was never a good time for bad news. She needed to tell him now and realize this was not something she could deal with on her own. She needed the support and help of everyone around her. Then, in the evening, Jan and Mamie would go to a movie and let Bill take the kids out to their favorite restaurant, Red Robin, for dinner. He could give the kids a talk about Mamie having cancer. This way the kids could ask questions, without inhibitions, in a festive, familiar environment.

"You know you have so many people who love you," said Jan, "and you caught this so early—we just need to get through the next few months." So, by the end of their breakfast, they both had a spark of hope that things would work out.

Chapter 18

Jan

Jan was a blond, energetic and wiry 5'6" whose slow articulate speech seemed to be in opposition to her quick brusque movements. She once explained to a friend that, as a child, her thoughts seemed to be quicker than her ability to express them. She had trained herself to slow down her mind, while speaking, and avoid stuttering or tripping over words. Jan had been a free spirit who had lived a much more unrestrained life than that of her best friend. Mamie had accepted her college diploma and an engagement ring on the same day. Six months later Jan was the Maid of Honor at Mamie's wedding and, 12 months to the day after that, she became godmother to Julie, affectionately known as Jules, Mamie's oldest.

Jan felt like Peter Pan losing her best friend to the world of adults. She loved Mamie's husband, Bill, like a brother, and wanted nothing but the best for both of them. But she missed their long phone conversations and the way Mamie could mimic anyone. It didn't matter what the crisis, they could always make each other laugh. Jan knew, especially after the baby was born, that Mamie was too busy for a lot of her nonsense.

She then gravitated towards a party crowd of young professionals and it would be ten years before Jan would disengage herself from a shallow existence of parties, booze, recreational drugs and men she didn't love or didn't love her.

A year of therapy later, Jan was ready to face the social world again. Jan had picked a good therapist who did not believe in lifelong sessions. After a little background of the "why" in her past, they focused on what were her goals and the behavior that would be useful in attaining those goals. She felt she had overcome her commitment phobia and she was much more selective about the company she kept. She was much improved but, against the wishes of her therapist, discontinued sessions.

Fortunately, throughout her problematic years, her work flourished and Mamie would tell her she evolved into an A type personality. She was now the Marketing Director for a software company in downtown L.A. and, in the last year, had developed some healthier recreational activities. Skiing was now a passion of Jan's and, luckily, she had met an attorney last winter on the slopes of Sun Valley. The relationship seemed to be developing nicely. It was ironic to Jan that she traveled a thousand miles to meet someone who worked two blocks away from her office. Jan had come to the realization that she needed to love someone. Most women might feel they needed to be loved, but Jan understood, that to love someone else meant giving. She needed to give to someone.

Tony James had appeared at a healthy time, she thought. Or, maybe, because she felt better and now knew what she wanted, she was attracting Mr. Right. Tony was the strong silent type. At 5'11" he could be lean and mean in a courtroom, but when he would strut up and down in front of a jury he was unaware that some of them preferred concentrating on his wavy black hair and his crystal blue eyes then the content of his presentation. The aggressive personality he displayed in the courtroom seemed to gradually vanish as he descended the court house steps.

Jan felt she had met an old soul in Tony. He was "much more centered and secure" than anyone she had ever dated, she would tell friends. He seemed devoid of pettiness or jealousy and she appreciated his lack of concern for her past. Jan had not introduced Tony to Mamie for months, fearing he was too good to be true and might only pass through her life briefly. But the time came when Jan was ready to see herself as part of a couple.

Jan and Tony went by with dinner, for Mamie's family, on a Friday night. They hadn't planned on staying since Jan was never sure how Mamie would be feeling after chemo. As it turned out, it was a good day. Jules answered the door and gave Jan a thumbs up before ushering them down the hall to the kitchen. Mamie was delighted and welcomed the company. Introductions were made and the red wine was uncorked.

"Oh this is great," said Mamie. "Bill look, Lasagne, Antipasto Nuovo, and Eggplant Parmigiana from Maria's. You know Maria is the only one who could compete with my nonna's recipes."

She unpacked the bags as Bill started getting out the silverware and plates and Jules called her little sisters. They set up the kitchen table as a buffet. Everyone made their own selections and then entered the dining room and chose a seat at the long formal table. The kids sat at one end, allowing the adults to cluster at the other and get to know Tony.

They liked him right away. Tony's easy manner and straightforward approach to life was refreshing to Mamie and Bill. They had noticed recently that a lot of people felt awkward or uncomfortable around them and assumed cancer was a difficult subject for everyone. During the evening Tony revealed his mother was a breast cancer survivor, of seven years. He told Mamie that, according to his mom, having a good relationship with her oncologist was very important. He seemed genuinely pleased when Mamie said she did. The conversation moved on to lighter subjects and Tony already seemed like an old friend.

Jan realized, as they were leaving, that Mamie was giving her that all encompassing wink of approval.

They had been dating for eight months and now she was actually going up to San Francisco for Thanksgiving dinner. And, by now, she knew that all wasn't perfect. Tony came with some baggage too. He was the father of a twenty-one year old boy who was now applying to law school. Tony, when questioned about his marital status, would usually say he had been "married for about 5 minutes" when he was 19. It was a marriage of 'doing the right thing' by the young girl he had gotten pregnant; neither one of them truly wanted the union to continue. It lasted about a year and, although strained at first, eventually they just wanted their child to grow up in a psychologically healthy environment.

Tony was well aware of the sacrifices his ex wife, Sheila, had made for the sake of their son. No matter what help he had given, she had been the one up in the middle of the night with the childhood ailments and attended all the school conferences when he was away in law school. He owed a great debt to Sheila for picking up his slack with a generous spirit, and not tainting his relationship with his son.

Jan was somewhat taken aback to find out the other guests at Thanksgiving included Tony's ex wife and her boyfriend. Tony was truly unaware that this might be considered an unusual arrangement. Sheila had been a part of his life for so long that the situation just seemed normal. He was pleased that Sheila had a man in her life and realized that neither one of them had invited anyone to Thanksgiving before. Maybe it was serious on both their parts.

Chapter 19

Mary and Sheila

Tony's dad had died about two months after his son, Chris, was born. His dad had not been a wealthy man but had been prudent in his spending and wise with his investments. He left enough money for college, law school and support for Tony's wife and child for several years after the divorce.

Sheila, his ex, would reflect that she actually had an idyllic situation compared to most single moms. She was able to stay at home with her son for the first two years and then attend nursing school without financial worries or emotional guilt. Tony's mother, Mary, was always there for Sheila and little Chris. After her husband's death, Mary needed to keep busy and welcomed the opportunity to be her grandson's nanny. This position became permanent when Sheila started nursing school. Mary would go to Sheila's house at 8am and stay until 4pm Monday through Friday and refer to herself as 'Nana Nanny.' Sheila would often times refer to Mary as "my son's other mom" and Mary's face would swell with pride.

Sheila was always grateful for the help Tony's family had given her. Her own family had taken a cold view of the union and all but ignored them for Chris's first 5 years. Initially, Sheila had asked for some financial help from her wealthy parents. They made it clear that the only help they would consider was to pay for an abortion. Sheila would have considered that except her periods had always been irregular and she felt she was too far long for that to be an option.

Sheila's parents had also withheld emotional support, which was typical behavior for them. Had it not been for her sweet spinster Aunt Laurie, she would never have learned the loving, caring and nurturing behavior she was able to give to her own child. She had embraced Tony's family as her own, and had even named her son after his paternal grandfather. Over the years she and Tony developed an almost sibling-type relationship. Sheila actually spent more time with Tony's mother than he did. She became the daughter that Mary never had and Mary was the mother that Sheila had longed for as a child. They were always there for each other.

Sheila had several long term relationships over the years but never seemed able to get past the level of comfort to that of commitment. She didn't think she could handle a man, other than Tony, acting as Chris's father. Now, at twenty-one, that was a moot point and she had been dating with a freer outlook on her future.

Sheila had met a cardiologist at the hospital where she worked. A forty-year-old widower, Jim Stewart, who had an excellent professional reputation. He was the right age and, most important in the workplace, was gossip-free. They had been dating for four months and both appeared giddy with delight when in each other's company. It was obvious, to all the staff at the hospital, that these two were in the initial stages of infatuation, if not love. It was no surprise to Mary that Sheila wanted to invite Jim for Thanksgiving. When Chris was a little boy his parents had always had Thanksgiving at Nana's house, and that grew to be an expected tradition. Sheila wanted little to do with her own parents and secretly wanted Mary's approval of Jim.

Chris had met Jim on several occasions and Sheila was relieved that he appeared to have no objections. They were both avid sports fans, so Sheila had planned their first meeting to be a brunch, but really being a prelude to a football game she knew they would both want to watch. Their favorite munchies on hand, Sheila had set the stage well and was more than pleased while listening to the ease of their banter as they compared player stats.

Sheila smiled and thought to herself that ten years ago this scene would never have taken place. Boys can be very protective of their single moms and they can find fault with any man seeking to become head of their household. But Chris was grown up now and had long ago given up fantasies of a parental reunion. He had a girlfriend and understood that his mom not only needed but deserved the companionship of a good man.

Chapter 20

Thanksgiving

The first thirty seconds went well. Mary, Tony's mom, answered the door with a bright, cheery smile. Her shock of orange hair took Jan by surprise and was later explained as a horrible hairdressing debacle, meant to be a tame strawberry-blonde.

The weather had been somewhat overcast with intermittent drizzling and Jan had worn her long trench coat. She carried a large bowl of bean salad, protected only by clinging cellophane wrap, that they had transported in a cooler. Tony was toting bags of chips, beer and wine.

Jan soon discovered that even two inch heels can be hazardous when she entered the hallway and took a stride toward the living room. Somehow her heel caught in the hem of her coat and she splayed across the hall towards the living room. The recognition that the oil and vinegar, from the salad, were riding airborne on the beans and would soon wreak havoc on the living room Persian carpet, prevented Jan, that instant, from realizing that her trench coat had flown up and her thonged buttock was greeting the rest of the company. Adding insult to injury, the little tattoo of Mickey Mouse winking, that her grandmother warned her she would regret, also greeted the guests. And things went downhill from there, yes it got worse.

Mary, normally a gracious and warm hostess, had prided herself on her ability to choose beautiful and unique antiques and artfully display them with more contemporary pieces. Her home was considered her showplace. Although Tony had heard her say, many times, as he was growing up, "People are more important than things," she was visibly suffering some inner turmoil over the prospect of her irreplaceable Persian rug being ruined. A hubbub of activity ensued. Mary's special solutions and clean rags were employed with diligence but the final judgment of damage would have to wait until hours later.

The pleasantries of meeting had been postponed during cleanup and now Tony, Jim and Sheila attempted to liven up the atmosphere with introductions and libations. Jan's complexion was slowly losing its embarrassing red luster as she tried to regain composure.

Mary's house was built in the 30's and had a rather typical entrance, of that era, with a short hallway facing the formal living room, framed by an archway. Beyond the living room was another archway leading to the kitchen and above that archway was the doorbell. It was suspected that the former owner had difficulty hearing in that it seemed several decimals louder than necessary. But Mary was accustomed to it and, although annoying if you were in the kitchen, she liked that she could hear the ring when she was in any other part of the house or on her back porch tending her flower pots. The far side of the kitchen had a butler's pantry with Dutch doors that, during the holidays, was set up as a bar. Once everyone had their drinks in hand, Mary suggested they all get out of the kitchen and relax in the living room while she checked the turkey.

As they moved through the kitchen, Jan had been just before the archway when the second disaster happened. She was complimenting Sheila on her lovely winter white pantsuit when the doorbell screeched, directly above her head, and Jan's red wine found its way to the white suit. Tony, not knowing what to do, rushed to answer the door as Mary ran to grab the seltzer water. Sheila and Jan, simultaneously, bent over to dab the excess wine with their cocktail napkins and managed to ram heads, hard enough to leave subsequent lumps where none had been before. So this was the chaotic scene that greeted Tony's son Chris, and his girl friend, Katie.

The entrance of the young couple and ensuing introductions served as a welcome diversion for Jan, who by now was hoping the earth would open and swallow her up. Once she decided that odds were the rest of the day couldn't get worse, she relaxed and actually had a good time. She made a mental note to buy Sheila a new suit, if that stain didn't come out, and prayed the carpet wasn't destroyed.

Chapter 21

Jan and Mamie–
Café Lunch

J an called Mamie saying "This is a red flag moment, can you meet me for lunch?" They had used this code to mean they needed a serious talk when one or the other had something on their mind. Jan had reflected that Mamie had omitted this ritual the day she called to make a date to tell her about the cancer. She guessed it was part of Mamie's downplaying the situation.

They met at the Aroma Cafe where they both ordered the house salad with chicken and hot Earl Grey tea at the counter. It was a bit chilly so they opted for the indoor room and were fortunate enough to seize a table just as the former occupants were leaving. They had been given a number to display on their table for the waiter to recognize and serve their food. Jan asked Mamie about how she was getting on and what time she should pick her up for the next doctor visit. Mamie seemed to be progressing well and she was glad her oldest, Jules, had not been too inconvenienced by all this.

"After all this is her senior year. But enough about me, this is your Red Flag," Mamie insisted, "what's going on?"

Jan proceeded to describe the Thanksgiving fiasco. By the time she got to the spill across the floor revealing her 'Mickey Mouse' they were both hysterical laughing. Then, after the head butting incident, they were laughing so hard tears were rolling down their cheeks and Mamie feared incontinence. The neighboring tables looked like they wanted in on the joke.

So what seemed to be the worst day of Jan's life was now her best story. This is how it happened over the years: whenever tragedies, humiliations or breakups occurred, after a brief mourning period, they could be reduced to laughter between best friends.

Mamie suggested that Jan have a few dinner parties, inviting Tony's mother and son down for the weekend. "They will get to know you and see how fabulous you are," she assured Jan, then adding, "but don't be surprised if they come in a suit of armor with a food-taster."

Jan felt a great cloud had been lifted, just by Mamie's calm reassurance. She had no doubt that Tony loved her, so why did she constantly avoid any inferences about commitment and marriage when she loved him too?

They were pulling out credit cards when Jan saw Tina Matthews walking toward them. Tina had done some PR work for her firm and she was just hoping Tina was not going to try to do an impromptu meeting. Jan had to be downtown in an hour. Tina literally swooped over to their table with a load of fliers in her arms.

"Hey Jan, I'm so glad I ran into you," she said with enthusiasm.

Introductions were made and Tina explained her mission. She was contacted by a new company, Relax and Retreat, and they were planning a special long weekend, "Thursday through Sunday at the Santa Barbara Serendipity Ranch." Tina went on, "They have painting and yoga instruction for all levels, plus massage, facials, acupuncture, hiking, a hot tub and gourmet meals. The rooms are double occupancy and it's by far the most reasonable deal you could find. The catch is that you fill out the forms I submit and they pick the guests," she concluded.

"Well you certainly tickled my curiosity," Jan admitted. "So what exactly are they looking for and how much is it?"

"For all that it's only three-hundred dollars. They said it's a pilot program but I have no idea how they pick the participants. It may be random for all I know," she added.

"Let's do it Mamie, and keep our fingers crossed. I could use a relaxing weekend and I'd love to try some art work," said Jan.

"Can I apply?" inquired Mamie, thinking Tina may have had other people in mind.

"Of course," said Tina as she handed them application flyers and advised them to fax the finished form, to the number on the bottom, in the morning."

"Oh, by the way," she added, "they are very emphatic about no electronic devices or leaving the premises during your stay, you should read the whole thing. Good luck," said Tina as she moved on and they gathered their things to go.

They were squeezing by tables and Mamie noticed the same flyers on the table of an acquaintance, a casting director named Gia. Jan waived to N.C. who had produced a commercial for her company a few years ago.

"Wasn't that Lynn Kahn at that table?" asked Mamie.

"Yes, I met her only once, she seemed very nice. I've got to run now, I'm afraid I'm going to be late," and after hugs they went off in their own directions.

CHAPTER 22

Jan and Mamie-
The Ride

M amie and Jan were both excited when they received the faxes notifying them that they had been chosen to participate in the first Relax and Retreat weekend in the United States. The text was impressive. Mamie wondered how they were 'selected' but she was also not one to look a gift horse in the mouth and was happy just to get away. Everything at home was running smoothly and Mamie almost felt like she wasn't really needed. Her doctor had been encouraging but she was tired and had some doubts. Yet Mamie knew this wasn't her real self. She was not one to give in to depression or self pity, or was she? She was looking forward to clearing her head and maybe getting a fresh perspective on her future. Mamie lived the farthest so she was picking Jan up.

"Hi there kiddo," Jan said throwing her bag in the back seat then sliding in the front, "How's the home front?"

"In a minute, I have to see the ring," Mamie said as she grabbed Jan's left hand, "it's magnificent, a great guy and he has good taste too—in women and jewelry. I'm so happy for you."

Jan had called Mamie the night before to tell her the good news. Tony had proposed and presented her with a beautiful engagement ring. She had an idea that this was coming but she was still secretly glad she had this weekend to think a few things through. She didn't understand how she could be so happy and yet somewhat apprehensive at the same time. Mamie had been busy with the kids so they didn't have much time to talk the night before.

"And on my home front, actually everybody is doing really well," said Mamie, "Jules decides on a different college every day, but she'll figure it out soon enough. We'll start visiting schools in a couple of months. So what else is going on with you?"

"Well, you are not going to believe it," started Jan, "Sheila and Mary are going to be there too. The yoga instructor in Northern California, where they both take classes, was hired for this weekend at the Ranch and, of all her students, they were picked. What a coincidence is that, I mean what are the odds?"

"What, that's unbelievable," said Mamie, "How do you feel about them going?"

"I really like both of them, but I haven't had a chance to fill you in about when they came down last weekend. I don't think I made too many inroads into their hearts, if you know what I mean. We ended up having an unexpected Monday deadline at work. It makes this week a little easier for getting away but I probably annoyed both of them, my cell went off practically nonstop."

"You have a secretary and an assistant, why not try giving them more responsibility?" questioned Mamie.

"You know what they say about 'when you want something done right, do it yourself,'" Jan responded.

"You can still check their work, oversee what they're doing. You are a real control freak my dear friend, I say that with love. You can't keep that pace up forever and still have a life. I didn't think you would actually go this weekend unless they excluded you from that cell phone ban," said Mamie.

"Oh I have that figured out. I have two cell phones. The one I keep I'll turn off until I'm ready to use it and they can have the other, safely locked away," she said pleased with herself.

"Well smarty, did you read the fine print. I believe there's a hefty fine involved," reminded Mamie.

"Oh they'll never know, but I'll deal with it if it comes to that," Jan said with her sly smile.

"How is Tony, by the way? What was he doing while you were being rude to his ex-wife and mother?" Mamie chuckled.

"Weaving and bobbing, if I hadn't been so nervous myself it might have been fun to watch. Like a master game player, he cajoled and distracted, trying to keep them entertained and somehow not notice me on the phone, like a dad would do with kids. I think they must teach that in some kind of secret parenting school. He really is so good, I don't know what I did to deserve him but I'm not going to question it," admitted Jan.

"Do they know about the engagement?" Mamie asked.

"Yes, Tony called his mom and she tells Sheila everything," Jan said, exaggerating "everything." "They both have called to wish me well and tell me how happy they are to have me in the family and I believe them, they really are good people. Hey, I think we turn here."

CHAPTER 23

Lynn, N.C., Gia and Sharon

Lynn had Chuck's van for the weekend so Sharon and Gia met at Lynn's house and they picked N.C. up on the way. They were all chatting about how great it was to get away, and catching up the way friends do.

Sharon had been ruminating over David's proposal and couldn't hold it in any longer. She blurted out, "I'm engaged!" The other three broke out in hoots and hollers. Then Sharon gave them a brief rundown of recent events demanding that, "you guys must have known I had feelings for David."

"I think we all thought you were crazy if you didn't have feelings for him. What took you so long?" asked Lynn.

"You all know his story," said Sharon, and they nodded heads in affirmation.

"Sure, this is really a small town when it comes to work gossip, but hasn't it been three or four years since his wife went into a coma?" Gia asked.

"Almost four, Lexi's birthday is coming up in a week. The accident happened the night she was born, on the way to the hospital," said

Sharon. "It's just that I have been craving this man for three years without an inkling that he had feelings for me. Now, all of a sudden, he's ready for a divorce and marriage and he, well he just overwhelmed me," she admitted.

N.C. chuckled, "Be careful what you wish for, they say."

"Come on Sharon," said Lynn, "We've all seen the way he looks at you, you can't be that shocked."

"I just thought, well I don't know what I thought, but believe me I was totally surprised. You would think he would want me to be around Lexi a little more," Sharon said.

"That's not the way men operate," said Gia. "Give the man credit. David knows you and the kind of person you are. He knows you'll be good for Lexi," she insisted.

"Thanks for the vote of confidence," Sharon said. "I guess I'm being a little insecure."

"You know, Chuck has a good friend who works a lot on the same projects with David," said Lynn. "I remember when the accident happened, everyone was talking about it and how terribly sad it was. I remember Chuck's friend said he was surprised that those two were having a baby instead of getting a divorce. They didn't seem to get along that well and, at parties, she was a big flirt, inappropriately so. I'm not going to repeat anything else but you get my drift. Everyone thinks David is a great guy, a real mench."

"What do you think of Lexi, would you want to be her mother?" asked N.C.

"Oh she is precious, adorable and she likes me. But I don't know how she would feel in the long term; it might be awfully confusing for her. She loves her housekeeper, and has a great routine. I'm sure David wouldn't expect anything to change, I mean work-wise," she said. She really hadn't thought about that though, they would have to have a talk.

"Oops," Lynn made a sharp right turn, "I think this is the private road."

They reached the top of the long, winding driveway and arrived at a large, circular graveled area with several cars being evacuated and trunks yawning with luggage. There were trees surrounding the left side of the driveway and directly ahead was path leading to higher ground. To the right they were looking at what was actually the back of the ranch. Windows with curtains flanked the back door and there were several potted plants, at intervals, an either side. Five women in casual dress, one with white hair and an apron, stood waiting for their guests.

PART III

Chapter 24

The Hosts–
Earlier Thursday

Five ladies were gathered in the room they decided to call the Great Room. Walking from the dining room, through the heavy double doors into the Great Room, revealed a huge expanse with almost floor to ceiling windows at the far end. French doors opened to the front patio where the hot tub sat to the far left. The walls on each side had a compliment of windows adding further light to the interior. Floor to ceiling draperies hung patiently for a time when it might be necessary to cut any glare. The view was magnificent, stretching beyond the shoreline to the open sea.

Grabbing chairs and forming a circle the cook and leader of the group, Julia, asked for their attention. She was a generously proportioned woman, with short white hair and twinkling blue eyes that confirmed there was a bit of mischief about her.

"Maddy," she started, "I want you to show Rose 'the ropes' as they say, and have you checked that all the linens and cleaning supplies are in order?"

"Everything is in order," answered Maddy with an equally well educated sounding British accent. She turned toward Rose looking as if she had smelled something foul, her pale eyes wide. Julia and Maddy both looked to be in their early seventies, Maddy being the taller of the two with short cropped salt and pepper hair.

"By the look of you, there's something on your mind, come on, speak up," insisted Julia.

"No problem exactly, but I think you should get a few things sorted out with Rose, she is constantly asking questions and it's a bit, well, annoying," replied Maddy.

"She's supposed to ask questions, that's why you are her mentor here. You have made almost as many trips as I have, you should be able to instruct her," Julia retorted, rather annoyed at the obvious.

Rose looked to be about twenty-three with large brown eyes and long wispy lashes. She was a petite brunette with Mediterranean skin tone but, even so, the color in her cheeks seemed to be rising.

"Well, some of them I'm not sure I can," said Maddy indignantly. "You've not always been clear about how much to reveal at what stage of the process. The ones I've mentored before weren't as, um, curious. And actually there are things I haven't thought to ask you. For instance, why are we English in America? And just once in a while I would like to be trim, stylish and in my thirties. Is that asking too much? Why senior citizens?" she huffed.

"They give senior discounts here," said Barbar. She was the slim, fifty-ish painting instructor with yellow cats eyes, and curly auburn hair.

"There are several reasons. You know very well," said Julia and she turned her attention to Rose. "We try not to interfere with most of the earth's routine and we like to present ourselves in a manner that will make our subjects comfortable. I'll explain a little further for you, Rose. We borrow the recently deceased for a few days and have them back for their memorial services before anyone realizes they are missing. Maddy and I, for example, are wearing two very popular British actresses who have recently finished a revival of a play, in Los Angeles, called Arsenic and Old Lace. It was quite a success and they will probably receive a posthumous award for their performances.

Unfortunately, they were both on their way to the airport, returning to England, when they were in a horrific car accident; both died instantly. Now, by the time they are shipped back home we will be finished with them and no one will be the wiser. The details are not important and that will be explained at another time, but I can assure you it is a seamless transition," explained Julia.

"Did you have anything to do with the unfortunate accident?" Rose asked sheepishly.

"Oh no my dear, absolutely not," said Julia indignantly. "I told you we keep interference to a minimal and do not terminate life. We may tweak things a bit and, I must say, sometimes it's awfully tempting," she said with a wicked smile.

"There have been many times I have had difficulty restraining myself from terminating the likes of Nero, Custer, and Hitler—oh I could go on—but Julia would have had a fit," Maddy chuckled. "And some of those little tarts like Cleopatra and Salome, the trouble they stirred up," Maddy said shaking her head and making a tisk, tisk sound as Julia gave her the 'enough' look.

"Where did this come from," Rose said indicating her body.

"Oh, don't feel slighted, yours was very famous too. Actually it was quite sad that a talented young woman, Raphaella, was killed before her time. She was a very popular singing star, known worldwide. Unfortunately she had a soft spot for the bad boys," Barbara told her, "typical of abused women, 'Oh but he really loves me and promises never to do it again,'" she mimicked in a sweet voice. "It broke everyone's heart when the bastard punched her for the last time. She might have lived but he was so drunk he passed out and slept for seven hours while she lay on the floor dying, with a concussion and internal injuries," concluded Barbara.

"I must say Julia, you did a wonderful clean up, she looks great," said Vivian, adjusting the sleek bun at the back of her head. She was a sturdy looking tall, black woman. "I'll help with the questions too, Rose. Just follow our lead and you'll get the hang of it," she encouraged.

"Now Vivian, have you all the massage tables you requested, towels and such?" Julia asked.

"Yes, and I have plenty of oils and aroma therapy for the massage rooms. I thought a little soft classical music in the back ground would be nice too, I don't want to be listening to any babbling brooks and waterfalls this time," Vivian said adamantly. "There will be plenty of musical selections for other times of the day too. Oh, by the way, we have all the tonics, herbs, potions and medicines necessary. Rose helped me set up, she's excellent in that department."

"I'd like to use some of the music you've chosen in the Great Room for the painting class too, if you wouldn't mind," said Barbara.

"Not at all, I'll help you set up and we'll have music during dinner too," Vivian said.

The next two days were a hubbub of activity. Everything was cleaned, dusted, polished or waxed as needed. Windows were washed and beds made. Sound systems were set up under the jurisdiction of Vivian, who was a stickler for perfect treble and bass.

Barbara sectioned off part of the Great Room, by the front windows, to catch the best light. Easels, canvases, paints, brushes, pallets and turpenoid were lined up, ready for use. The other side of the Great Room would be used in the evening for card games, backgammon or scrabble. Small tables and folding chairs leaned against the wall waiting to be summoned for the games to begin.

They were all doing last minute organization when the hall clock chimed. It was four PM and Julia called the ladies for Tea. She liked being in character and had always enjoyed the little rituals of every society. They gathered in the dining room that was adjacent to the kitchen. Julia had made finger sandwiches and biscuits to tide them over until dinner.

"Well Ladies, now that we all know every inch of this place, what do you think?" asked Julia as she passed around a plate of cucumber sandwiches.

They all agreed, though not luxurious, it was quite adequate for their purposes.

"I find it lovely and peaceful," said Barbara, "City noises can be quite irritating."

"Even though I miss some of the more formal customs of olden days, and the fashions, I do love the fresh smell of things in modern times. Oh remember Julia, that Henry VIII, the stench of his open sores became more and more difficult to camouflage until you could smell him before he even entered the room," sighed Maddy as she recalled the unpleasant odor of his abscessed flesh.

"I don't have much sympathy for a man who kills his wives," Vivian stated flatly sipping her tea.

"Not very polite conversation to be having during a meal," interjected Julia, "but I do agree the medical and hygienic advances in the last hundred years have made visiting a much more pleasant experience."

Rose had a quizzical expression on her face and asked tentatively, "Why exactly are we here if we don't interfere?"

"We listen, we observe and we try to gently steer the individuals we gather to resolution of their problems. Not on a grand scale, but the results can be grand. Like the little tweet heard around the world. Or the ripple of water that becomes a wave. We try to cause momentum of thought that starts out slowly in a small group and becomes a collective consciousness," said Barbara picking up a biscuit. "It's not that we never interfere, but we try to avoid it."

"Nicely put," said Julia, "and I must say, after our last trip, we've made significant progress on the issue of smoking cigarettes, at least in the United States. We need to go work on that in Europe."

"It doesn't always happen as quickly as we would like," Maddy said reaching for another sandwich, "and then some things work a little too quickly. Hmm Julia, these are delicious."

"What was too quickly?" Rose inquired.

"Humans have a great capacity for many things dear," Maddy said, touching the corners of her mouth with a napkin, "but emotional change is not always 'neck and neck' with mechanical or technological change."

Vivian, seeing the befuddled expression on Rose's face, went on to explain, "For example: children here now have access to powerful communication devices, but they are children. Their parents are as lost as the children when it comes to appropriate restrictions or supervision of computers and, many times, they don't have the good sense to be 'The Parent.' Children are often bullied on the internet to the point of suicide and the parents on both sides of the bullying are clueless. Then, of course, there are the predators looking for innocent kids to corrupt. It can even lead to murder or suicide."

"If you don't mind ladies, I would like to finish my tea without further discussion of unpleasant odors, murder or suicide. It's most disagreeable for the digestion," Julia chastised, "and while we have these borrowed bodies we need to take good care of them."

"You said she has to learn and they will be here tomorrow," said Maddy. "I think that body you're wearing is having a bit of a Patrician effect on you," she addressed Julia, and then Barbara spoke up.

"Patrician, oh don't remind me of the Romans," said Barbara. "They are a perfect example of what we are trying to avoid here. They had so much, and then depravity, arrogance and egotism crept in. The Senators were greedy, catering to their own self-serving desires, not unlike today. Oh, don't get me started," as she grabbed the tea pot.

"I think you already started. Simmer down woman or that borrowed body of yours is going to explode," Vivian laughed, "but I know what you mean. They haven't learned from the past and they don't pay enough attention to their own politics. They marry a party and, no matter what that party does, they keep on defending it."

"They don't know how close they are coming to a Code 13," said Barbara.

"What's a Code 13?" Rose asked.

"Now is not the time for that discussion Rose, as I said, I'm trying to enjoy my tea," said Julia.

"Well why the painter, masseuse and yoga teacher?" Rose asked the group, "Is that just part of the ruse to get them here?"

100

"Yes and no," said Barbara. "A true artist enables people to understand what they might have been feeling but couldn't verbalize on a conscious level. I use paints to help them see in a new way," she explained.

"Some of those canvases can give way to some pretty scary subconscious," laughed Vivian and the others, except Rose.

"Why, I remember that German painter," she started.

"That's enough of that," interjected Maddy when Julia gave her a quick look. "We try to give people an 'Ah ha' moment of sorting things out for the first time."

"I relax them with massage," said Vivian, "it helps them abandon thinking of everyday problems and opens them up. We encourage them to get in touch with their core and meditate to silence the mind. Please pass me the tea pot, Barbara. It's amazing how touching people while talking can open a floodgate of emotion. Hairdressers and manicurists experience that all the time."

"You see, over the centuries, many humans have lost their connection to nature and their own power," said Maddy. "So much about the curative powers of herbs and plants was lost when the superstitious minds of the early settlers, from Europe, burned witches at the stake. Many of those women were just knowledgeable about curing illness with the things nature provides, and it's only a relatively small number who have gone back to recapture that knowledge."

"The yoga instructor has a twofold role here," Julia commented, "Again we are trying to give tools to calm down the mind and allow clarity of thought, the goal being moral choices that benefit the individual and society. You know, that ripple effect we were talking about."

"What's the other role for the yoga teacher?' Rose inquired.

"She doesn't know herself," Maddy started, but Julia cut her short.

"Oh let's just let that one unfold as it may, you'll see for yourself, if it works. Now it looks like everyone is finished so we will go through the rooms and put on the finishing touches."

They all began to rise and move the chairs back in place. There were boxes of candles, incense, bath salts and complimentary robes lined against the wall.

"Maddy, you and Rose take the rooms on the north side; Barbara and Vivian the south. I'll do the public bathrooms and kitchen. Now Rose, tomorrow you are in charge of collecting the cell phones and other electronic devices as we receive our guests. The wall safe, in my office, will be open. Just put everything in there and, once you close the door, spin the knob around a couple of times," said Julia.

"Maddy, you are in charge of the Force Field switch. Make sure everyone is here before turning it on, as you well know, remember" Julia was saying when Maddy cut her off.

"Of course I remember Babylon. How many centuries will it take for you to stop reminding me about that one," said Maddy annoyed.

"Someone has a missing sense of humor," said Julia indignantly, and then smiled.

"What happened in Babylon and what's a Force Field switch?" inquired Rose

"Not now Rose," said Maddy and they all moved on to complete their chores.

CHAPTER 25

Thursday–
Late Afternoon

They stood outside the front door lined up like eighteenth century servants waiting to greet the arriving guests. The weather was magnificent and, as all the cars and vans drove up, everyone was awed by the view. It seemed like they all converged about the same time, had a moment of silence, and then an explosion of activity. Exiting the vehicles they grabbed purses, suitcases and jackets. Rose was quick to greet and ask for their electronic devices which she deposited in a basket, under her arm, while the others acknowledged friends and acquaintances.

Most of the women were gathered by the door as the last person, the yoga teacher Donna, drove up.

"Ladies," Julia addressed them in a louder than usual voice, "I am Julia and this is Maddy, Vivian, Barbara and Rose," as she indicated each with a touch on the shoulder.

"We welcome you all to the Ranch and trust you will have a pleasant relaxing weekend. Barbara and Rose will show you to your rooms. If you would like to freshen up, dinner will be served in one hour and I hope you are all hungry, early birds get cocktails."

One by one they introduced themselves.

Julia went in to finish preparations. The others walked through the door as Vivian turned to Maddy and said, "Well she knows how to get them there on time."

They approached Donna who was finishing empting her car and struggling to pull a small and a large suitcase and a third bag over her shoulder.

"Are you planning on permanent residence here my dear? You were only hired until Sunday night," smiled Maddy as they each grabbed one of her bags.

The petite brunette, from a distance, had looked small and frail. However, up close, one could see the definition of muscle in her arms. She had clear brown eyes that smiled along with her mouth.

"I have mats, I hope enough, and do you have towels? I'm Donna and you are,"

"Maddy, I'm in charge of housekeeping, supplies and such, Vivian is the Masseuse. We have plenty of towels. I already have a pile of them in the Great Room. I thought you would like to do a class tonight. I posted a schedule in the hall but I'll leave it up to you to fill in the time. You can talk to the group at dinner if you want to get some kind of consensus," she added.

"Sounds great, if you point me to my room, I'd love to dump this stuff and wash my hands," said Donna.

"Follow me honey, it is double occupancy but I think you will be very comfortable," said Vivian.

Inside the door was a small mud room with a deep closet to the left housing outdoor supplies. There was a large bell overhead with a sturdy cord that Maddy pulled vigorously.

"Ladies, may I have your attention please," said Maddy. The bedrooms were on either side of the long hallway and, as heads poked out, Maddy continued, "In twenty minutes Vivian will give you a tour of the ranch house and then you should be ready for cocktails and dinner."

The guests found their rooms were identically furnished, only varying in color combinations. The beds were situated to the right of the entrance, the bathrooms to the left with the door positioned between two closets. Two wooden side tables, set against pale green walls, held wrought iron reading lamps topped with yellow and white striped shades. There was another small table, in between the beds, holding a bowl of potpourri. Crisp white spreads with yellow piping and matching shams were accented, across the bottom, with folded pale green and white checked comforters. Various botanical prints dressed the walls in simple light wood frames.

CHAPTER 26

Dinner Thursday Night

The long bedroom hallway opened to a large dining room with a rustic wood table that seated fourteen comfortably. A sideboard-table hugged the wall to the right. The adjacent wall, half of which was parallel to the table, turned into a serving counter for the kitchen beyond. Jan, Mamie, Sheila and Sharon were the first to the dining room.

"I suppose you four are in need of libations," Maddy smiled. "Help yourselves to the liquor on the side table, if anyone would like, Barbara makes a mean Martini. We're having Minestrone soup, garlic bread, crab ravioli in a basil, mushroom, tomato sauce and roasted vegetables. There's chocolate cake, ice cream, cheese and fruit to choose from for dessert."

"Hummmm, sounds yummy, my favorites," Sheila declared. "I'm starving."

Barbara was mixing a batch of Martinis and the ladies were nibbling on the cheese and crackers that had also been set on the side table.

"Hey Sheila, so sorry Mary couldn't make it, what happened?" asked Jan.

"Well you know that rock star, Raphaella, whose boyfriend literally knocked her lights out, poor thing, she's from San Francisco and the memorial service had hundreds of people tied up in traffic. Mary ended up having a fender bender and when she got out of the car she twisted her ankle. I was going to stay and take care of her but she insisted it wasn't that big of a deal and I should go. So here I am, ready to relax," said Sheila.

The other ladies had come in and were milling around. Vivian and Julia were asking who would like red or white wine with their meal and placing bottles on the table as Barbara was offering the Martinis around. Barbara had noticed Rose making a quick exit to the adjoining kitchen and went to see why she appeared alarmed. She heard Maddy addressing Rose in hushed tones.

"Oh not to worry my dear, among these ladies Julia and I would be far more recognizable. You see, Julia can adjust the brain recognition. Just a little tweek and we may resemble those dearly departed but they will see us a shade differently. For instance, my eyes may appear smaller. Your nose may look larger. Why one time I overheard someone say my ears were so large I could probably hear 10 miles away. That was one of Julia's little jokes," said Maddy as Julia and Vivian walked in the room.

"I do have my moments," Julia said with a wicked grin. "Now let's get the rest of the plates out there."

Rose and Maddy had already distributed the soups on the table while the women enjoyed their cocktails. Now all five hosts carried bread, ravioli and vegetables to the table as the ladies commented on the fabulous Martha Stewart table settings and the Ina Gartin food presentation. The white plates popped against the light orange linen cloth. Three short vases with yellow roses, daisies and baby's breath sat at intervals on the table.

"I would have been happy with just the soup," exclaimed N.C., "this all looks wonderful."

Julia picked up a glass of wine and made a simple toast, "to good food and good company."

Plates were passed around as they all made small talk. Maddy suggested they go around the table and each say what they would like to get out of the weekend.

"Let's start with you Sharon and go clockwise," urged Maddy.

"This is so good," said Sharon, after swallowing a mouth full of stuffed ravioli. She smiled timidly saying, "I thought this would be a good opportunity to think things through, get a different perspective on things away from home."

"Oh, but you say that with such sadness in your eyes," Maddy pointed out. "It really doesn't tell us anything specific and it seems that something is weighing heavily on you. You are among friends and we want you to feel comfortable enough to say anything. What's worrying you?"

"Now Maddy," said Julia, "don't be such a nudge."

"I guess I'm not ready to share," said Sharon, who was very good at avoidance tactics. Changing the subject and perking up a bit she addressed Julia saying, "May I watch you cook tomorrow night? I love cooking and I'm always interested in the way other people do things."

"Certainly dear, but I warn you, I'll put you to work," Julia smiled and turned her attention to the yoga teacher.

"Donna, other than your yoga classes, you are free to enjoy the facilities. What would you like to get out of your stay here?" inquired Julia.

Donna put down her wine glass and said, " Get away from this," as she rolled up her long sleeves revealing massive bruises on her well toned arms in a rainbow of muted colors. A hush and then quiet gasps circled the table.

"Oh, I just like being dramatic, they look worse than they feel," she said, now feeling a little embarrassed.

Sheila, looking horrified, said "Why didn't you say something, did Syd do that?"

"Yes, but the problem is solved. I didn't tell you and Mary because I was too ashamed, but I'm moving to L.A., actually, as we speak. My aunt agreed to meet the moving van for me, when this job came up, and the timing could not have been better. I watched the memorial service on TV for Raphaela and the commentary on abuse. I could just see that happening to me one day and I finally knew what I had to do. I found out I would be seeing you this weekend and I thought it would be better to tell you in person. I never want to see Syd again. I start work at the Yoga Center in Studio City on Monday and I'll be staying with my Aunt until I find a place of my own, but I'll really miss you and Mary. Hey, let's move on, I didn't mean to blurt all that out, guess a martini turns me into Miss Loose lips," she said trying to lighten the mood.

"Thank you for sharing, that's just the kind of thing we want to know. We have a few helpful tricks up our sleeves," Maddy said glancing at Vivian.

"Rose and I have perfected a cream that will heal those marks on your arms in a couple of days, and tomorrow I'll give you a massage, without hurting your arms," declared Vivian.

"Deal," said Donna.

The elephant in the room was what they all wanted to know and Lynn was the first to bring it up.

"We are curious about one thing," said Lynn looking over at Julia and pouring a little more wine into her glass. "Why was this group of women picked? Obviously we all have some kind of connection, first or second degree."

"Oh sorry dear, I thought I had addressed that earlier," said Julia. "We wanted to start with a small group of women who would feel comfortable enough with each other to use the time and facility to the best advantage. In the interest of full disclosure; the five of us are qualified therapists. We use several techniques aimed at releasing psychological and subconscious blocks. You are our first group here in the United States. Vivian and Rose are holistic healers who can do acupuncture as well as massage. They have extensive training in herbs, vitamins and minerals. Barbara uses art and dance Movement Therapy, I think you will have fun with that. And we are all knowledgeable about different tinctures, poultices, household remedies and, of course, meditation. So ask for whatever help you need, we are here to serve."

Jan looked quizzical and said, "Wait a minute, I don't understand, I signed up for a relaxing weekend, not for psychotherapy. What is this?"

"We're not forcing anything on you dear," said Maddy, "We're just letting you know that there are more things available than meets the eye. You can take advantage or not. Stay in your room and sleep if you want. You can do as you wish."

"Ok," said Jan, "I guess I didn't understand what you meant."

"Can you do anything for allergies?" N.C. asked.

"What kind of allergy?" Rose responded.

"Well, cat dander for sure and I think maybe pollen too," N.C. replied.

"Let's hope so, those are easy. I'll have your eyes, ears, nose and throat free of irritants in no time," Rose said enthusiastically, then demurred as all eyes were upon her.

"How about cancer?" Mamie said with a hiccup. Jan remembered that Mamie hadn't had any alcohol for months. Her doctor had okayed having a glass of wine with dinner but her previous abstinence must have enhanced its effects. Mamie was not usually one so quick to share. The table went silent and Jan was hoping she wouldn't be sorry tomorrow for blurting out her condition.

Mamie went on to explain, "I just don't have my energy back, I get so tired and my stomach is just not right."

"I think we may be able to help you with that," said Vivian. "Come to the massage room first thing in the morning. There's something I want you to take on an empty stomach."

Lynn asked, "Is there anything I can take home to cure my daughter of being a teenager?" They all laughed and sympathized; the mood picked up. Julia was in the kitchen spreading out the deserts on the counter between the kitchen and dining room. Maddy suggested Lynn should sign up for a chat with Julia who had some very good ideas about parenting skills. "What the hell, I'll try anything at this point," she responded.

"Is there anything you would like to work on, Gia?" Julia asked.

"Peace of mind," she said quickly, seemingly without censoring herself. Then, looking self conscious, she smiled and addressed Julia who was now back in her seat, "Ok, I'll sign up for a little chat." Gia was thinking that it might not be bad to talk with someone she would never have to see again.

Maddy looked at Sheila and said, "Sheila, you have been rather quiet this evening, anything on your mind?"

"Oh no, just mellowing out. Can't think of anything, but I'll let you know," she smiled pleasantly.

"That's fine dear, no pressure here," she commented.

They continued chatting and toasting. Jan and Donna were the only ones Sheila knew, so they explained how the other women were connected.

"Ladies, it looks like we're ready for dessert. If you wouldn't mind taking your dishes and stacking them by the sink, Julia has set the goodies out on the counter," announced Barbara.

They all were rewarded with sweet treats, bumping into each other as they made their selections.

"Nobody said anything about the five pounds I'll add before going home," said Gia as she selected a nice hunk of chocolate cake and capped it with a small mountain of ice cream. "I think I just lost all will power."

"You don't look like you have anything to worry about," Donna assured her.

"Not to worry, Julia insists there are no calories in anything she serves," smiled Vivian.

"That's right," Julia chimed in.

"Oh, if only," said Lynn, who was the last to sit back down, savoring a bite of cake.

"Julia and Maddy, I see you two picked the fruit, how do you resist that luscious cake?" asked Sharon.

"Actually, I usually eat fruit by itself since it breaks down quickly and eating it, on top of a meal, is really not the best thing for digestion," Julia said. "But fruit is delicious and far better for you than empty calories."

"Yes, Julia is right," said Maddy. "Just notice how you feel after you eat. If you are sluggish or tired then that's something you should avoid."

"You make it sound so simple," said Jan.

"People underestimate their capacity for change," said Julia. "'There is never a right time to do a difficult thing,' that is according to a man named John Porter and I believe he meant you either do something or not. It is simple, perhaps not easy. But if you clear your system of sugar, I promise, it does get easier."

Donna waited for a moment then interjected, "I know I could really use a yoga class tonight after the driving and plane ride. I feel like I've been sitting all day. I'll be in the Great Room in fifteen minutes. Or maybe we better let our stomachs rest, let's say in half an hour, if anyone would like to join me."

"Now I know what you mean Julia," said N.C. with hands on her tummy. "After the cake and ice cream, on top of dinner, I feel like I swallowed a basketball, but I'll get over it, I'm in, Donna."

The rest of the group agreed and were vacating chairs, stretching and starting to clear the table. As they grabbed the remaining dishes and piled them in the kitchen Maddy said, "You're not here to do dishes ladies, run along and get ready for your class. The towels and mats are waiting for you in the Great Room."

"Donna, when class is over would you come to the massage room? I want to give you that cream." said Vivian. "And Mamie, don't forget to come to me, first thing in the morning. N.C. you can meet with Rose after yoga. She'll take care of your allergies."

They all went to their rooms to change into more comfortable, loose clothing.

"I want to call Ross and make sure he gets prepared for the budget meeting Monday," Jan told Mamie.

"You mean he doesn't know about it? Mamie asked.

"Of course, but this is a very important meeting, and I don't want him to forget anything," Jan insisted. She tried calling but couldn't get a signal. She turned to Mamie and said, "I'll have to go outside for reception."

"Ok, I'll make some excuse and tell them you'll be along in a few minutes," said Mamie.

They took turns in the bathroom and slipped into comfortable pants. Mamie started off to the Great Room as Jan quietly walked to the back door. The way the ranch was set up, you actually drove up the driveway to the back door. The front door was accessed by a walkway around the side of the ranch to the front of the Great Room. Jan felt like a kid again, trying to sneak out without her grandmother knowing. She was outside and a few steps from the door when Julia seemed to appear from nowhere, Jan was taken aback, letting out a surprised, "Oh."

"I didn't mean to frighten you dear, did you leave something in your car?" inquired Julia.

"You startled me. Yes, I think I left my hair brush in the car," said Jan, always quick to supply an answer.

"Have you seen a cat running about?" asked Julia. "There is a stray that seems to have taken a liking to us and I didn't want to lock the doors before giving him a little something. Run and get your brush dear, I'll look a bit longer and then lock up. If you hurry you can still make the class," said Julia.

Jan had the funny feeling she got caught and, as she went through the motions of pretending to look for her brush, she felt Julia was going through the pretend motions of calling, "here kitty, here kitty." Something was not quite right. She went back into the ranch house and got to class just as they were starting. She leaned over to Sheila and whispered, "Have you seen any cat around this place?"

"No, why?" she whispered back.

"Oh nothing, really," Jan said as they began rolling heads from side to side.

CHAPTER 27

Yoga Thursday Night

"I think we will need to keep a close eye on Jan," Julia said to her cohorts.

"What was she doing?" asked Rose as she was just walking into the kitchen.

"She was trying to make a phone call and thought she might get better reception outside," Vivian informed her.

"I collected the phones as they walked in," Rose said quickly in a defensive tone. "I know I took Jan's phone and there's no way she could have gotten it out of the safe."

"Don't worry, no one is blaming you, Rose. I'm sure she had an extra phone," said Julia.

"So much for the honor system," Maddy said indignantly.

"I think it was less complicated in the old days," Barbara mused. "Before advanced communication it was easy to isolate a small group of people without their constant expectation that something would ring, vibrate, tweet or poke," Barbara complained as she placed a glass dome over the remainder of the cake.

They were all in the process of cleaning up the kitchen when a dark grey cat jumped up on the stool in front of the counter. Julia took a bit of extra crab from the refrigerator and, placing it in a custard cup said, "There, there Sammy I promised you something nice," as Sammy purred like a motor boat.

"I thought you didn't like animal distractions," said Vivian as she finished drying the pots.

"Oh Sammy is special, and I needed an excuse for being outside when Jan was sneaking around. You'll see, he can be very helpful," Julia added.

Vivian looked at Rose, "Let's go to the massage room and make up a batch of cream for Donna."

"Sure, and I'd better mix up N.C.'s allergy drink, she's going to need it soon," said Rose.

"Its nine-twenty and they will be out of class in ten minutes. Shall we get them to bed early tonight?" asked Maddy.

"Well, by the time they shower and all it will be after ten," Julia surmised. "I'll give them hot chocolate at ten-fifteen to ten-thirty and they'll never know what hit them. They'll be in bed by eleven and I'll have them up by seven, bright-eyed and bushy-tailed," she said.

"I haven't heard that one in forty or fifty years," Maddy said rolling her eyes.

The class was enjoyed by all. Donna had extensive training and every possible yoga certification available. Her normal conversational tone was somewhat blunt and occasionally a little rough around the edges, but once a class began Donna seemed to channel a yogi like no other. Her voice was calm and well modulated. She was patient and caring, noticing every nuance of movement and correcting postures with encouraging sincerity.

They finished with the Indian salutation, 'Namaste,' and a few seconds of silence. Then they slowly began thanking Donna for such a wonderful session. Those who hadn't done yoga before, N.C., Lynn and Jan, were sworn converts; those who had strayed from the practice, Gia and Mamie, were glad to have renewed enthusiasm. The experienced, Sheila and Sharon appreciated Donnas' expertise.

They picked up their towels and deposited them in the bin by the door, leaving the mats on the floor for the morning class. Then they heard Barbara on the intercom.

"Ladies, if you shower quickly, you will be rewarded with the best hot chocolate you have ever tasted, at ten fifteen, in the dining room. N.C. and Donna, if you would, please go directly to meet Rose and Vivian in the massage room."

Rose had been busy with her mortar and pestle. She had a lovely china teacup waiting on the side table with the herbs she had ground up. The electric tea pot had made its final hiss and she was pouring the steamy liquid into the cup when N.C. and Donna walked into the room.

"Ah, perfect timing, Rose was just finishing up and I have your salve ready," Vivian said addressing Donna. "Now, honey, after you shower, put a generous amount on any bruise or sore spot you have. It absorbs quickly but wait five minutes before putting on your pajamas."

"Are results guaranteed?" said Donna smiling.

"Like death and taxes, they say. Money back if you're not satisfied," Vivian smiled. "You'll be all fixed up by, hmm I'd say tomorrow afternoon."

Rose had added a small amount of cool water to the cup to make it drinkable and handed it to N.C.

"Ok, bottoms up, drink all of it," she said with uncharacteristic authority.

N.C. did as she was told, to the last drop.

"How was it?" Rose asked.

"Not horrible, but it wouldn't be my beverage of choice," N.C. made a twitching face.

"Fair enough, I put a little stevia in to help the taste," she revealed. "Just wait twenty minutes before eating or drinking anything. By the time you're finished washing up you can enjoy Julia's hot chocolate."

The pajama-clad guests started wandering back at about ten-fifteen. Julia filled their mugs with the steaming hot chocolate as they filed by the kitchen counter. Lynn and N.C. were the last ones to walk in the room. As soon as they came in Sammy jumped up on one of the empty chairs, as if announcing himself, and N.C. let out a yelp.

"What's the matter dear?" Barbara asked.

"I forgot my allergy pills and, if I don't get away from that cat, I'm going to be a mass of hives in about five minutes," N.C. warned.

"Nonsense, Rose knows what she's doing in the herb department dear," said Julia. "Please trust me and don't get yourself upset."

"Are you sure? I've seen what happens and it's not a pretty picture," Lynn said.

"Absolutely, now relax, you can even pet Sammy if you like," Julia added.

N.C. was not about to go that far and she did not look happy, but with strong reassurances from Julia, Barbara, and Vivian she sat down, looking like a criminal waiting for the hangman.

They all reiterated praise for Donnas' instruction and she reminded them they would have a class in the morning at nine-thirty. Rose suggested that she lead a group hike before breakfast. There were some affirmatives and some maybes, as they were all getting a bit drowsy.

"Julia, I had my doubts, but this is really the best hot chocolate I've ever tasted." said Gia. "What's your secret?"

"I use real chocolate and a combination of almond and coconut milk, but that's all you're going to get out of me," Julia laughed.

"Why not regular milk?" Sharon asked.

"Cows don't even drink cow's milk after they're weaned, it just doesn't make sense dear. And of course they are full of injected hormones. Even the organic have hormones—meant for cows, not people.

The small talk went on until suddenly N. C. said, "I don't believe it, it's been twenty minutes and nothing; no runny nose, itchy eyes, hives or swelling extremities."

"Told ya," Rose smiled sheepishly.

"Normally, if I didn't have my pills, I would be on my way to a hospital by now. Thanks so much Rose, I can't tell you how much I appreciate that. Now where can I get it, or can you mix me up a vat of that stuff?" she added.

"Oh that won't be necessary," said Rose.

"I mean for when I go home. How long will the effects last?" N.C. asked.

"You can throw away your pills, you're cured," Rose said in a matter of fact tone.

"Wow, I'm amazed, I want to come back for another consultation doctor Rose," N. C. insisted.

"Sure, we'll find some time tomorrow," Rose said, pleased that she was building her reputation.

The yawns were getting the better of everyone and, almost at once, the room seemed cleared of guests and Sammy was purring contentedly.

"Anyone up for a game of backgammon?" asked Julia.

CHAPTER 28

Friday Morning

Their eyes all seemed to pop open at about six-thirty. Refreshed and energetic, the hallway was a hubbub of activity. You could hear them asking, "Who's got tooth paste?" or "can I borrow a brush?" Someone yelled, "Look under the sink," and they were pleasantly surprised to find everything they could possibly need in a lovely basket.

Soon they started wandering into the kitchen to find beautiful crystal glasses, seemingly standing at attention in front of decanters of orange, pineapple and cranberry juices, maintaining their chill in champagne buckets.

Rose was ready, in her walking shoes, to lead the ladies in exploring nature. Those who seemed the most resistant, the night before, now appeared the most anxious and ready to go.

"Hey, what was in that hot chocolate? I haven't slept that well in years," Gia addressed Julia.

"You'll never get Julia to tell you her secret ingredients," said Barbara.

"That's not true, dear." said Julia. "If you really want, I'll have my recipes printed out before you all leave Sunday night, with full disclosure."

"I've heard that before," Barbara claimed under her breath.

"Oh hush now, you're still blaming me for that cake you made for," Julia started, but with a quick look from Barbara continued, "Oh, who was that, anyway that was a long time ago."

They had some juice while waiting for Mamie who was in the massage room with Vivian.

Chapter 29

Vivian and Mamie

Vivian was saying, as she filled an empty pill casing with a grayish white powder, "Now last night Rose and I compounded several herbs and plant extracts that should do the trick. You can start taking one now and don't have any food or drink for an hour. This should always be in your system a good hour ahead of a meal."

"I don't know Vivian. Maybe I should talk this over with my oncologist first. I don't want to do anything counterproductive to my treatment. I thought you were going to give me something for after my treatment," Mamie said, seriously concerned.

"First of all, I would never do anything that would hurt or interfere with your medical advisors. Herbs can be powerful and dangerous when used by people who are not fully knowledgeable. I have studied for thousands of ye, of hours," Vivian quickly corrected herself. "This is an art that must be cultivated and I really do know what I'm doing. I have worked with many Doctors over the years and I promise you this can only help. The pills I have given you work best when they accumulate in the body. They are very safe, when taken as directed, and the results have been consistently positive. One in the morning on an empty stomach," she said with great authority.

Mamie took the pill and swallowed it as Vivian added, "You know, one of the ingredients comes from the Venus Fly Trap, in case you get the urge for a little bug protein." But, seeing Mamie's eyes grow wide, she quickly added, "Oh, just kidding, a little apothecary humor, honey. Let's go, they're waiting for you in the dining room."

The group headed out with water bottles on hand and Rose in the lead.

CHAPTER 30

While They Waited

J ulia, Maddy, Vivian and Barbara had breakfast warming, chilling and waiting for their guests. They sat down with their tea for a chat.

"I think it's a lovely group. Each with their own unique story, trying to do the best they can. They really all want the same thing, peace and love," said Barbara.

"Yes, but still, They carry around the criticizing voices of parents, teachers, guardians and religious advisors. They have heavy emotional shackles that are so difficult to shed. You can't blame them for getting discouraged. Would you pass me the tea Barbara, please?"

"Yes, I imagine it's frustrating; always looking for something outside themselves for some type of salvation, not realizing that they have all the answers themselves. Why, Jesus told them that there is god in all of us. They just didn't listen," Julia sighed.

"That's organized religion for you," said Maddy. "Make people feel they need you, need to support you financially, and then get them to use politics to further your agenda. That's become the way to power."

"Now Maddy, don't get your knickers in a bunch," said Julia.

"Oh, I think it's too late," said Vivian, "there she blows," and she threw a wad of napkins into a trash bin against the wall.

"Can you blame me?" Maddy pleaded, "It's just gone on too long, when will they ever learn, look at the Christians?"

"I know you're still angry about the Inquisition, but they also provide hospitals and schools," Julia added.

"And gave the pedophiles a safe haven," Maddy cut her off. "Look at the good Christians who burned witches at the stake or hung negroes from a tree and could be found the next day warming the pews in their churches with a clear conscience, believing the bible justified them."

"Will you pull the soap box from under Maddy, Barbara," said Julia, "we all agree. Jesus never wanted the Church to become a political machine. He never wanted the Popes to live in luxury and protect 'the Church' rather than its people, its children."

"Then we have those Protestant extremists. They go around preaching the 'will of God' and condemning homosexuals, quoting from the Bible as if it were meant to be taken literally," said Maddy.

"Give it a rest, Maddy. It's not all Christians, most are good people struggling to do the right thing; the same as the good Jews or good Muslims," said Barbara.

"The Jews sure haven't had a very decent time of it," said Vivian. "It seems like someone is always trying to get rid of them."

"My theory is that saying you are the chosen ones, and being exclusive to your own people, unknowingly invites a strange type of jealousy, like a private club," said Barbara.

"I don't know about that, there are many reasons people develop prejudice," said Julia.

"Remember how the Jews were forced to collect taxes, 'back in the day', as they say," added Barbara. "Tax collectors are always hated. Then the Jews became proficient at handling money and were hated for that. They just couldn't win."

"I've always wondered why people say, about different religions, that it's all the same god. One god is vengeful, another merciful," complained Vivian, "the Jews say 'an eye for an eye,' the Christians say 'turn the other cheek' and the Muslim extremist think that their seventy-two virgins will be waiting for them—a heavenly porn fest," and they all laughed.

"The majority of Muslims are lovely," said Julia, "but people seem to demonize whoever they think is the opposition, it makes them easier to kill. And both sides use 'the will of god,' as their mantra," she added. "It's the people at the top, not the churches, synagogues, temples or mosques."

"Well, if you were an American and had money in a well respected bank, but didn't trust the president of said bank, would you maintain an account there?" asked Maddy.

"No, Maddy. I see your point, but there are people who find comfort in religious organizations," said Barbara.

"If it gives comfort and does not become contaminated with self interest and loss of integrity," said Vivian, "I'm all for it."

"Yes," agreed Maddy, "but what does one give up? Is it comforting to be told, as a woman, that you do not have domain over your own body? And that's most of the mainstream and the extremist religions. How hypocritical is it to belong to a religion that claims only god has the right to judge and then proceeds to judge anyone whose ideas do not conform to theirs? Why can't they leave other people alone and let their god judge?"

"Oh we know why dear," said Julia. "Their displaced anger over their own shortcomings finds a home in condemning others, they get to feel superior. Then what starts out with altruistic motives often times evolves into political agenda."

Sammy had run in and was rubbing his head and shoulder against Julia's ankle, purring enthusiastically.

"That Jan is at it again." said Julia. "I think we are going to have a very heavy rain storm after breakfast. That may deter her from going out."

Chapter 31

Hike

The ladies on the trail were delighted that Rose was so knowledgeable about the local fauna and flora. She seemed to have superman eyes, pointing out little lizards as they basked in the sun before scurrying off the trail, or a rabbit in the distance, examining the group. Just after Rose had pointed out some wild berry bushes Lynn asked, "Where are you from Rose?"

Taken by surprise she said, "Oh here and there, military family, never too long in one place." Rose did have a back-story but preferred to say as little as possible on the subject.

N. C. said, "You know about so many things, but you look so young."

"I'm twenty six, but I've always been a nerd and I've studied nature all my life," she told them, hoping that would satisfy their curiosity.

Meanwhile, at different intervals, Jan would hold back a bit and stand behind the group trying to get service on her phone. Even if she couldn't talk in front of Rose she could text, but no luck. How could she not get service out here, in the open space?

It had been lovely and cool, but after walking a couple of miles, they started to shed a layer or two of jackets, sweaters and scarves.

Mamie turned to Rose and said, "I just can't place who it is Rose, but you remind me so much of someone," her voice trailed off.

"Oh, I just have one of those faces." Rose answered. "I get that a lot." Rose was relieved when she was asked a question.

"Rose, what are those little yellow flowers?" said Sheila.

"That's sticky monkey flower or Mimulus Longiflorus," Rose informed them. "It's such a prolific blooming shrub; I've seen a whole hillside look like a volcano dripping sherbet."

Sammy all of a sudden appeared out of the brush and was walking beside Jan. She looked down and his eyes met hers for an instant. She felt like she was being chastised and his mental communication was, 'I know what you were trying to do.'

Gia bent down to Sammy and he purred at her slow petting touch, then looked at Jan as if saying, 'yeah, you know that I know.'

They were a few yards from the back door when Jan suggested that they take a ride into town after breakfast.

"Oh, that's forbidden," Rose responded, "I mean I don't think Julia would like that. You ladies are here to totally relax and forget the outside world. I think that was in the contract you signed."

Jan was dumbfounded, "Contract, what contract?" she said.

"Oh, I mean the agreement," Rose corrected herself.

They were at the door and Jan walked in, somewhat indignant, followed by the rest of the hikers. The group all disbursed quickly to clean up before breakfast.

Mamie and Jan were washing hands in their bathroom when Mamie said, "Is everything ok? You look a little," she paused, "puzzled."

Jan wasn't sure herself but said," I think something is a little funny about this place. I can't explain it, just odd."

"Oh you're just having cell phone withdrawals." Mamie told her. "Didn't you text out there?"

"No, there was no signal, how could that be in open space?" Jan asked.

"Maybe there is a power line tower out there," answered Mamie, "they really interfere with reception."

"If there is, I sure didn't see one," she answered while drying her hands on a beautifully, luxuriant towel.

Chapter 32

Friday Breakfast

They gathered in the kitchen and were wowed by the spread they saw before them. Cold cereal, fruit displayed in beautiful bowls, hot steel-cut oatmeal kept warm in a crock pot, an egg casserole and plenty of whole grain and Ezekiel toast with several varieties of jams and jellies. Even Sammy had a variety of delicacies in his bowl. On the side table were brightly colored plates and bowls, a caddy with silverware, a coffee urn, an electric tea pot and stacks of cups and saucers. It all looked like a richly painted canvas. Barbara was just finishing up with a basket of different teas and placing three small flower arrangements at intervals on the table. The group wasn't shy and attacked the table with gusto.

"Well, I hope you all had an enjoyable outing and worked up a good appetite," said Julia. "It should be a lovely day and I know you'll enjoy Barbara's class this afternoon."

The hustle and bustle around the table continued as cups and saucers clinked to a lovely symphony Vivian had playing in the background. Rose was lavished with praised for her knowledge that kept them interested, and entertained, to the point of being oblivious as to how far up, and around, the modest-sized mountain they had circled in the rear of the property.

Everyone was seated when Jan decided to bring up a trip into town.

"Oh dear, that would spoil everything. The critical point here is to extricate everyone from the norm to pursue calm relaxation," Julia answered rather dismissively as she turned her attention to Vivian.

"Vivian, have you made up a massage schedule, I think some of the ladies would enjoy that after a hike and yoga today."

"Yes, yoga is from nine-thirty until eleven. I can see someone from eleven-ten until twelve-ten. We have a light lunch planned until one and then Barbara's class will go from one to four. There will be tea and scones in the dining room for an hour from four to five and dinner will be served tonight at seven thirty. I've listed the time slots on the massage door. Of course, I'm available if anyone is not attending painting class, but I strongly advise everyone to go. Barbara is quite an amazing teacher," Vivian added as Sammy abandoned the bowl he licked clean and was now rubbing against N.C.'s leg.

N.C. leaned down and scratched his head exclaiming, "It's still working." She caught the attention of the group and said, "I know you guys must think I'm crazy to be so excited, but I've never been able to go near a cat and I still can't believe it. Rose, can I see you after breakfast for a few minutes?"

"Sure, whenever you're ready," Rose answered.

Vivian looked over at Donna and said, "Donna, before your class, come by my office, I'd like to take a look at your arms."

"Sure" she said, "but honestly, there's not much to see." Her long sleeved tee shirt was tight on her arms but she did her best to push up her sleeves saying, "Well, I'll show you later but the color is almost normal and that sore feeling is gone. That's probably why I almost forgot about it. This is the first time in weeks I haven't had sore arms. Really, thank you so much," she said sincerely.

Gia and Sheila were both chatting about how pleasant the music sounded. Lynn admitted to be a hardcore rock and roller but said she was enjoying the change of pace. Mozart had just gone off and a more spirited tune was playing.

"What is that?" Sheila asked.

"That's the Four Seasons by Vivaldi," Barbara answered. They were all getting up and taking plates and cups to the island when Barbara started moving to the rhythm of the music. It wasn't really dancing, more like a kind of staccato marching and elbow movement. The rest followed suit and they made a festive job of clearing the table until Julia shooed the guests away saying they didn't come here to clean. So Julia, Barbara and Maddy continued the cleaning as Rose and Vivian went to the massage room and office.

N.C. came into the office where shelves lined the walls with potions, herbs, extracts and tinctures. Rose chose to sit down in a comfortable chair, ignoring the desk, and indicated that N.C. should sit in the other comfortable chair about two feet across from her. N.C. was tentative at first, not really wanting to admit to this twenty six year-old how naïve she had been. Then figuring what the hell, I need help, she launched into the full story. How she and her husband had planned on adopting a baby, then at the last minute, the mother changed her mind. She continued with her humiliation at the hands of Elsie Blake and realized quiet tears were rolling down her cheeks. Rose asked N.C. if she and her husband had been to a medical doctor.

"Yes." replied N.C. "That's why it was so puzzling."

They had both checked out as healthy specimens with no physical or mobility issues, but that biological clock was ticking away. Rose told N.C. that she wanted Vivian to give her acupuncture treatments but she would also mix up an herbal potion that should help increase her fertility.

"I can't make promises but sometimes a few small changes of body chemistry can make a world of difference," Rose encouraged and handed N.C. a tissue from the desk to wipe her face.

Donna was in the massage room, shirt off, with Vivian examining her arms and back.

"Everything looks good and I'd say all the marks will be gone, maybe in a few hours," she said.

She continued more soberly, "I think, after listening to you talking last night, you realize the sick and dangerous nature of this abuse."

"Yes, I know," said Donna. Her head had been down and now she looked straight at Vivian saying, "But it wasn't always like that. When we first got together it was great. The jealousy and anger were very gradual and I let it go on too long, I know that."

"Your class should be starting in a few minutes," said Vivian, "but I'd love to talk more a little later, when we have more time, I think it's important. Would that be alright?" Donna agreed and thanked Vivian. She met N.C. in the hall and they rushed off to class.

Most of the group was warming up. Jan was in the back, next to Mamie, talking and stretching while waiting for class to begin. Jan leaned over to Mamie and whispered that her new plan was to slip out the back door, after lunch, and walk down the hill to see if she could get cell phone reception. Jan could be stubborn when she felt restricted and was determined to get her way.

"Oh for god sakes, give it up Jan. You're supposed to be relaxing, so just relax," was Mamie's uncharacteristic response. Mamie would usually have laughed and plotted with Jan, but that spirit of camaraderie was absent today. Mamie felt Jan was acting like an annoying child. Donna and N.C. came in and class began.

Five minutes later the sky was dark and a thunderous rain began pouring down. It was startling to the group and interrupted the flow. They were shocked at the contrast from their pleasant hike in the sun to the angrily-spitting sky. They ran a few minutes over the allotted time and everyone was anxious to clean up, but Jan was the first one out the door on her way to her room.

Mamie got back to the room, wanting to make up for her earlier irritation, she smiled and said, "Well, it seems the gods are against you on this one."

Gia and Donna were walking back to the rooms together chatting and Donna was saying, "Your doing great, you're very flexible."

"Oh I have done yoga for years, off and on, but the past few years mostly off. I definitely want to get back to it. Please write down your studio address and schedule. You are the best yoga teacher I've ever had and Sherman Oaks, where I live, is just one town over from where you'll be staying," Gia told her.

"Sure, I'm going to be staying with my aunt for a month so I can get my bearings and figure out where I want to be. If you want, we could make a deal. You show me or advise me about the area and you can have a free trial week of yoga."

"Deal," said Gia. "I bet you'll like it. People complain about the traffic in LA but I think you'll find everything you need in a three mile radius. Now heading downtown is a different story. Los Angeles is not a visitor-friendly city, but my friends have talked about it and we decided that was probably good, or the rest of the east coast would be out here too."

"I feel better just knowing somebody nearby, closer to my age than my Aunt. Thanks so much. It has been a crazy few weeks for me. Syd, aside from being my lover, was my best friend too. It's kind of like cutting off a terribly infected limb, you know it's got to go but it still hurts," Donna confided with an ironic smile.

The guests had a little free time to relax, take a nap, read or take advantage of the steam shower in the public bathroom.

CHAPTER 33

Friday Lunch

The ladies started meandering about the kitchen and commenting on the unusually loud thunder storm. Some of the group expressed annoyance while others thought it made being indoors cozy.

"I just love a good storm, and in California it clears the smog out of the valleys," said Julia. She had arranged a buffet in the kitchen. There was a huge pot of butternut squash soup simmering on the stove top. On the counter, sat Ezekiel bread, toasted, and cut into strips. There was a large bowl of salad boasting several types of lettuce, herbs, seeds, garbanzo beans, grape tomatoes and small pieces of red and yellow peppers. A large platter of chicken, tuna and turkey sandwiches sat on the table with two bowls of coleslaw on either end. The side table, held a generous platter of cheese and fruit nesting by two apple pies and a plate of coconut macaroons. The ladies lined up with a plate and bowl in each hand, appreciating the aromatic fragrance of the soup wafting across the room.

Lynn turned to Sharon behind her in the queue saying, "Ok, now I'm sure we died and went to heaven, I love not running to the market and cooking. And this is their 'light' lunch."

Once they were seated the table was hushed for a moment while they savored their first few mouthfuls of food. Sharon was the first to break the silence.

"This soup is delicious Julia. Don't forget we have a date for me to hover over you preparing dinner."

"Oh I haven't forgotten dear, and I hope you remember my promise to put you to work," Julia smiled.

"Would you like your massage at twelve-ten Donna?" Vivian asked.

"Sure," Donna declared. "I have a few knots in my back if you're looking for a challenge."

"I don't mind if you need to come to the painting class late Donna, it's not a problem," said Barbara.

"I love to paint," said Donna, "I was an art major in college. I'll come in as soon as we're finished."

Lynn asked Donna what style of painting she preferred.

"There are so many that I love, but if you mean what style painting I do, I would say representational. I had a wonderful teacher who once said that since the invention of the camera it was silly to do realistic painting, just take a picture," said Donna.

"I agree with your teacher," said Barbara, "when you take liberties with reality your subject can actually reveal more intimacy. Look at Edvard Munch's 'The Scream', it exudes the terror he was trying to portray much more so than if he had painted a realistic person screaming. The right teacher can make such a difference when you're studying something new."

"That makes sense," said N.C. "You know Lynn and I went to a Carl Hines painting class. I don't know if any of you know him but Lynn and I were not impressed. It seemed more like going to a fan club than a class."

Most of the group had heard of the famous artist. Lynn went on to say that it was a fluke that they even got in the class, and explained how it happened

"I'm just glad we didn't have to pay. You wouldn't believe the way the women were acting, it was like Elvis came back, I thought they were going to start throwing their panties at him," she laughed and reached for a chicken sandwich.

"I didn't care for his work at all," Donna said, "and you're right about the women. I think he is even more famous for his Casanova reputation. I attended a lecture of his in San Francisco and honestly, I don't know how anyone could learn from that man. I know that we should love ourselves but I think he is 'in love' with himself."

Sheila changed the subject looking at Barbara and asking, "Can you do anything with someone who has no artistic talent?"

"Let me ask you something Sheila," Barbara started, "you are a nurse, are you not?"

"Yes," Sheila answered.

"Were you allowed on the floor with patients the first day of school?" asked Barbara.

"Of course not, I'm sure I would have killed someone in the E.R.," Sheila laughed.

"The reason I asked," explained Barbara, "is that most people think that art is an innate talent that you're born with—or not. They don't understand that yes, there are a few people that may have incredible promise at an early age, but most people must learn and practice. The great masters studied for years before painting on canvas. They drew hundreds of sketches of the same subject in anticipation of the painting. Of course we are not going to do that, and we are not going to paint in the same style, my point is that you can learn; just as you learned your job. Put in a little time and effort and you will go home with a good start."

"I'm feeling encouraged," said Gia, "I used to love to draw but over the years I stopped, I'm excited to get back to it."

"I have to do a lot of drawing, for my work, but I would love to try painting again," Sharon said, "I haven't had my hands on a paintbrush since college."

Sammy appeared from under the table and purred as he rubbed up against Julia's leg. Julia turned to Jan, who was sitting to her left and asked, "Jan, you've been very quiet, did you enjoy your hike this morning?"

"Oh, very much," she said in a rather distracted manner. "I think I'll take a twenty minute nap after lunch. If you don't mind Barbara, I'll join the class after that."

"No problem," Barbara responded.

Julia smiled and then addressed the group as her right hand was petting Sammy on the head, "We'll have tea at four for those of you who care to have a snack."

Gia looked over at Mamie smiling and said, "That looks like the map of Italy on your chest."

"Hmmmm, or maybe Florida," Sheila laughed.

"I'd say Baja," was N.C.'s response.

"I'm such a pig; I swear my kids have better table etiquette than me," smiled Mamie, allowing annoyance in her voice. "You can't take me anywhere," as she patted her napkin to her chest where the stubborn remnants of soup refused to depart.

"Nonsense dear, you look lovely in butternut squash," smiled Maddy as she was the first to rise and the rest gradually followed suit.

Vivian had changed the music this afternoon saying she liked up-beat tunes on a rainy day. She turned up the volume a bit as they cleared the table, in a jovial mood, singing and moving to Chaka Chan's 'Life is a Dance' as they exited to prepare for painting class.

Mamie hurried to her room to change her shirt and use the bathroom. When she exited the bathroom she saw Jan rummaging through the closet and grabbing her rubber clogs. As Jan turned around she caught the chastising expressing on Mamie's face.

"You're not really going out in this storm for a phone call, are you?" asked Mamie.

"What's it to you?" was Jan's sharp response. This was new territory for both women. They had been friends for years but their conversations were never harsh or sarcastic.

"I've seen you in a lot of moods but what's gotten into you? You agreed to the rules of the trip but your whole focus has been on a fucking phone call. What's really wrong?" demanded Mamie.

"I thought we were just going to relax. I didn't sign on for a touchy, feely sensitivity fest; and I don't like being told what to do," Jan responded.

"I've never seen you like this Jan. You're acting cold and paranoid and I don't think you should be out there in this weather. Can't you just have some fun?" pleaded Mamie.

"Ok, sorry, I'm going to take a nap. I'll see you in twenty minutes," said Jan, as she pulled off her hiking boots and laid on the bed.

She waited a few minutes until she couldn't hear Mamie's footsteps in the hall. She put her clogs and hooded, all-weather jacket on and headed out the back door.

The wind was blowing and the rain felt like harsh pellets attacking her from all sides. The mud was slushy, sucking at her clogs and hampering her progress even more. She slipped and fell but even dripping mud, she was determined to forge on. She was almost at the end of the driveway when she tripped on a mud-covered log, recessed in a puddle, and her body hurled headfirst into a solid surface.

CHAPTER 34

Julia and Lynn

Julia had been at the sink when Lynn approached and asked if they could have that chat.

"Of course dear," she said and dried her hands on a towel she liked to fling over her shoulder as she worked. They went down the hall and into the office, seating themselves in opposite chairs.

"What's on your mind dear?" inquired Julia.

"Well, all this talk about painting keeps me thinking about my recent mother daughter debacle," Lynn began. She related the story of how she and N.C. had employed her daughter, Amanda, to teach them painting. Then the opportunity came up to be in Carl Hines' class and Lynn got caught, when she came home that night, in a lie of omission.

"It was like rubbing salt in our relationship wound," said Lynn.

"Indulge me, for a moment if you will, there is a technique I like to employ," Julia urged. "I would like you to close your eyes for a moment and picture you and N.C. the day that Amanda was instructing you. Tell me a little more about what you were feeling and what happened; see it in your mind's eye."

Lynn did as she was told, closed her eyes and took a deep breath, relaxing into the chair.

"First of all," she started, "I really wanted to paint a French scene and Amanda said no, I needed to do a still life to concentrate on shapes and how they related to each other. I had my heart set on something else and I was annoyed, and maybe a little difficult. I started fooling around and making jokes."

"Does that behavior remind you, keep your eyes closed," said Julia, "of any other time of your life?"

A few minutes passed as Lynn thought about the question.

"Oh my god, I guess it does. When I was a freshman in high school I was the 'class clown'. I think I reverted to my fourteen year-old self. Amanda was being the adult and I was acting like an obnoxious child. And, believe me, she couldn't have been more professional in her handling of me. N.C. was really impressed, and I acted like an idiot. Then, when we were finished, she told us not to do any more until the next class so we wouldn't mess up and get discouraged—and that's exactly what happened; we continued painting, made a mess of things, and through our own fault were discouraged."

"You're not finished yet dear, keep your eyes closed." Julia reminded her again, "I would like you to examine why you reverted to that behavior and what is making you so uncomfortable in your relationship."

"I think some of this is my fighting the idea that my baby is almost grown up and she's going to leave one day," admitted Lynn.

"You can open your eyes now dear," said Julia smiling. "You're making my job very easy. You seem to know what the problem is, so what are you going to do about it?"

"Oh I don't know, I can't keep her from growing up, now can I?" responded Lynn.

"Nor would you want to I'm sure," said Julia. "Think about it though, don't you honestly have some days when you want to strangle her? Don't you get tired of picking up that discarded sweater, or cleaning up those long abandoned dishes?"

"Now that you say that, I've had a fantasy of putting a lock on my closet door," Lynn said thoughtfully.

"Nature has a funny way of insuring that eventually parents push their offspring out of the nest," said Julia. "Your responsibility, as a parent, is to create an independent human being who has the tools to survive in the world. It sounds like you've been doing a great job, you're almost there. Children appreciate their parents far more when they get out in the world. Of course it will take some effort, on your part, to mend the present situation. May I make a few suggestions?"

"Suggest away, I need all the help I can get," answered Lynn.

"It would be best if you give her the respect you would give a friend or a teacher," Julia advised. "Apologize, and that is a lesson in itself. An 'I'm sorry' can go a long way. People don't realize how powerful those two words can be, and some never learn."

"I think maybe I'm one of those people. My mother's idea of an apology was to pretend nothing happened and move on. I think that's the lesson I learned," admitted Julia.

"Young people live in a different world than we do. Listen up and you can learn from Amanda. At this age, and through her college years, you may find Amanda to be more interesting than many of your own friends," Julia pointed out. "I overheard you telling Sheila you will be starting a new job. I think your anxiety will lesson when your mind is more occupied.

"Promise," Lynn smiled weakly.

"I'm sure you will see a difference," said Julia. "Focus on the positive. There may be some other underlying concerns. You and your husband can have a fresh start too, and that is another adjustment. How is he doing?"

"Chuck, oh he's great, the best," Lynn responded a little too quickly.

"You know this is all confidential Lynn, but if I may be so bold, when was the last time you made love?" Julia inquired.

Lynn was taken aback by Julia's candor and answered almost as if it were a question, "Um, well, I think about a week ago."

"Think again, Lynn dear," Julia said in a serious tone. "I can tell by your hesitation you don't really remember, and that's not good."

Dejectedly, Lynn admitted Julia was right.

"Let me venture a guess here," Julia started, "you've been so wrapped up in worrying about your daughter, and your friends, that the one person who needs you the most is being neglected. He's a good man, but no matter how much he loves you, he is not a mind reader. He needs your attention and affection. Do whatever you need to put yourself in the mood. If you don't give him the love he needs there is always some little wench out there who will. Sex should not be a chore, it should be a pleasure for both of you to renew your love."

There was a loud bang and Lynn jumped to her feet.

"What was that?" Lynn asked.

"Just thunder I'm sure," said Julia, knowing full well that a catastrophe had just taken place.

Sammy had been napping by the desk and his head snapped to attention. Julia gave him a quick glance and he was out the door. She got up and put her hand on Lynn's shoulder staring straight in her eyes. Lynn seemed to come to attention in a trance like manner and robotic tone said, "I enjoyed this, but I would love to go to the painting class now."

"Yes dear, you go on now," said Julia.

Julia reached the back door finding that Rose, Vivian and Maddy were there too. The rain seemed to be lessening and as they grabbed the rain boots, from the small closet by the door, it stopped. They knew what happened and wanted to take care of it before the painting class was over.

Vivian had a large tarpaulin she had grabbed from the storage closet. They started out, covered up in rain gear. It wasn't difficult to find Jan deep in mud and seeming to be lifeless. Julia directed Rose and Maddy to straighten her out and placed the tarp next to her. Then they rolled her on to the tarp and, each grabbing a corner, started back to the ranch house. They used the garden hose outside, by the back door, to get most of the mud off Jan. Rose ran in the house and grabbed a clean blanket as the others took Jan's clothes off and hosed her down again. Then they wrapped her in the blanket and took her to the massage room. Rose left and brought back a clean pair of pajamas.

"This hasn't happened since Lazarus, and we were just trying to help out a friend," said Maddy, as each began cleaning an appendage.

"See what happens when we interfere?" said Julia. "The Force Field is supposed to make people want to back away when they get to close, not kill them.

"I thought we didn't interfere," said Rose quizzically.

"Occasionally, but if we do it can sometimes drastically change the course of history. In this case, I think we can get away with it," Julia surmised. "Now make sure you get under the nails."

Jan was cleaned up, combed and in fresh pajamas when they each placed hands on her and closed their eyes to concentrate. It took about a minute and then Jan seemed to convulse back to life. She looked bewildered and opened and closed her hands, as if to make sure they were still working. Julia looked at the others and signaled them to move back and leave so as not to frighten her.

"Where am I? What happened?" asked Jan as she looked around, trying to get her bearings.

"Well I'm afraid you did a foolish thing my dear. You went out in the rain and had a very nasty fall. You hit your head and passed out. Of course we took the liberty of taking off your dirty clothes and cleaning you up a bit. I suggest you take it easy for the next few hours and rest. I do not believe you have a concussion, and your eyes look good. Sheila is a nurse so we can have her check you out too. How are you feeling?" Julia asked.

"Ah," it took a moment for Jan to answer. "I know it's crazy but I woke up angry that I had to come out of a beautiful dream. I saw a glowing white light and, as I moved toward it, I could see my grandmother. She was the only one I felt truly loved me, and she was smiling at me so sweetly. Then, she shook her head slowly from side to side and blew me a kiss. I loved her so much. She was my only anchor in a family of chaos and I just wanted to run to her, but I couldn't."

"A terrible fall, like you had, can sometimes, how can I put it, shake up things in your head and bring some strange thoughts to the surface," but before Julia could go on, she could hear the house phone in her office ringing and she knew there would be other concerns. She asked Jan if she was feeling well enough to go back to her room and helped her off the massage table. Maddy came in and, as both women helped her to the doorway, Julia explained she had something important to take care of.

"Get some rest and I'll look in on you in a little while dear," Julia said as she entrusted Jan to the care of Maddy.

Julia went to her office, listened to the message, and called the City of Santa Barbara. They advised her that Saturday morning the access road to the property she was renting would be used by the Society for Cancer Research. They were sponsoring a Hike-a-Thon and didn't want the ladies to be alarmed at seeing people pass by the ranch to reach the open space. It would start at eight A.M. but the volunteers were going to be putting up trail markers this afternoon.

Julia realized that it would be necessary to turn off the Protective Force field but was sure Jan wouldn't be wandering off any time soon.

CHAPTER 35

Friday Painting Class

Barbara had created a lovely fruit bowl still life for the ladies, not unlike the arrangement that Amanda had made for Lynn and N.C. They were going to do two paintings; the first to help understand shading, using only black and white paint. If they completed that, to their satisfaction, they could do the second in color. Barbara went on to explain how they should look at these objects not as fruit but as lines, shapes and shades of different light intensity; observe the relationship between the objects and the negative space.

N.C. turned to Lynn, her eyes wide and whispering with a big smile said, "Gee, where have I heard that before."

Barbara reminded them that this was a much abbreviated class but, if they listened closely and followed her directions, they would be pleased with the results.

They each had a work station equipped with an easel and canvas; next to the easel was a small tray table with charcoal, several differently shaped brushes, and black and white paint. The table against the back wall held hair spray, clean rags, turpenoid and a number of small containers for clean up. The ladies were told to sketch with their thin charcoal until they were satisfied with their drawing. Barbara would be walking around checking their progress and they could call on her whenever they wanted.

Those familiar with drawing and painting started and Barbara went over to Sheila, who was the least experienced. She demonstrated how to hold the charcoal lightly and move her hand continually, even when not touching the canvas. Some of the less experienced walked over to Sheila's area to watch. Barbara kept her whole arm moving as her eyes darted quickly from the arrangement to the canvas. They were mesmerized at how swiftly the images appeared. She explained that eventually they each would find their own rhythm of movement. Then, taking a rag from her pocket she removed the traces of her demonstration and handed the charcoal back to Sheila. The others moved back to their own space and enthusiastically began.

Donna came in about twenty minutes late from her massage and got right to it. Having been an art major in college, she had no problem catching up. Barbara had some classical music playing softly and they all seemed to be in the zone. When the drawings were done, it was time to spray their drawings to fix the charcoal. Barbara had explained that a lot of artists used charcoal fixative but Aqua net hair spray worked just as well and was much cheaper. They each took turns on the far side of the room spraying. When that was done they started the black and white painting and were reminded to pay attention to the shading and contrasts.

All of the ladies were so involved that, when a loud thunderous bang occurred, they seemed to spasm at the shock. Sammy appeared at the door and then Barbara walked over, closed the door and said, "Oh, it's only thunder," and they proceeded to have a few minutes discussion about how it was more like an eastern storm and how unusual for Southern California. Then it was back to work

Barbara went around to each student and was delighted to see they had been listening and were doing well. She noticed Gia and Donna had been commiserating about the shape of the apple next to the pear and stopped by them to see how they were progressing.

"You know, I have found that painting in a group of compatible people adds so much to the experience and can make it a wonderfully rewarding time. You get to use not only your eyes, but those of the people around you. Someone might say that 'maybe this is too round, or this is too bright' and, if you are open to constructive advice and agree with the suggestion, it makes the work so much easier. Of course I should stress 'compatible' since there are some egos, I'm sorry to say, who could never work in that atmosphere. You may not listen to everyone, but you will figure out the people whose opinion you trust and eventually you will come to your own style. Then, with Donna's permission, she showed how lowering the edge of the bowl, just a tiny bit, gave a better, more balanced view of the contents.

"It's amazing what a silly little millimeter can do," observed Donna, whose painting was quite good.

Sharon was helping Sheila and encouraging her saying, "All you need is a little confidence."

Mamie was near Lynn, who turned to her and said, "I guess Jan must have fallen asleep, I thought she would be here. Is she ok, she seems a little, um, stressed."

"She has been really busy at work, maybe she is just tired. You know how those A-types sometimes burn themselves out," said Mamie.

They continued until Barbara heard Sammy whining at the door. She let him in and then announced, "Ladies, we ran a little late. Its four-ten and I'm sure that Julia has tea and a snack for us in the dining room, let's cleanup now."

CHAPTER 36

Julia and Jan

Julia had alerted the others about the phone call and asked Maddy to turn off the Force Field. Then they all proceeded to put out the tea and scones with jam, a plate of fruit and some coconut macaroons. Julia then went to Jan's room with a tray of snacks and tea.

"I think it would be best dear, if you rest until dinner, is that alright with you?" she inquired.

"I owe you an apology. Really, I'm not always such a little bitch. I don't know what got into me and I know you and I got off to a bad start," Jan admitted humbly.

"Nonsense dear," Julia responded generously, "sometimes that happens when we have things weighing on our minds. I sensed that about you and perhaps I was a bit too aggressive approaching you."

"You were nothing but kind, I guess I just wasn't ready to listen." said Jan. "You know the dream I had, it was just so real. You see my grandmother was the only one in my family who could care for me and who really loved me. I was euphoric when I saw her and I just wanted to be with her. When she shook her head and waved goodbye to me Tony flashed in my mind and I wanted to be here for him."

"Is it Tony you were worried about?" Julia asked.

"It's more than just Tony. I come from certifiably crazy stock and he doesn't know anything about it. He knows my parents died when I was young, but not the details. I've always liked kids but I'm afraid that the genes I carry are probably defective. Do you have a few minutes?"

"Certainly," Julia assured her.

"You see, my mother was a paranoid schizophrenic. She and my father were high school sweethearts who made the mistake of conceiving me after the prom. Mother was eighteen when I was born and hadn't showed signs of her disease until I was about a year old. Apparently, she was hearing voices and my father came home to find her attempting to bury me in the backyard. She didn't want to kill me. She had put me in a big box, cushioned with small pillows, and had a lid ready to cover it. She was frantically digging a hole when my father found her. She showed him a piece of plywood she wanted to use to camouflage the hole and pleaded with him to help her. She was terrified that "they" were coming to get me and she had to hide me.

My grandmother stepped in to care for me and took me to her home, fearing my mother might inadvertently harm me. My father never found out who she thought "they" were and I think, in her mind, he became part of the "they." Granny said my father was devoted to my mother and went into debt trying to help her. He finally agreed to shock treatments but, after that, she wanted nothing to do with him. Then my dad started drinking.

I saw my father often enough, but I think he always associated me with the onslaught of mother's illness. She was institutionalized when I was two and he visited her every week. Somehow the shock treatments took away her memory of me, and Granny thought that was a blessing for both of us. The intense fear and hypersensitivity were gone but she lived in a different world than ours. I never saw her. Granny didn't feel an institution, especially in those days, was the place for a child to visit."

"My father would occasionally take my mother out for a drive, always hoping for a few minutes of normalcy. When I was ten they were killed in an automobile accident. It must have been in the newspapers because I overheard some rumors and Granny decided to tell me the whole story. The people driving behind them said it appeared that the passenger moved over to the driver's side of the car and grabbed the wheel, turning it quickly to the right. The driver lost control and careened into a retaining wall. They were both killed instantly and, as young as I was, I somehow felt ok about it. Granny said mama would be cured in heaven and I thought they would both be happy now. Granny had impressed on me that love had brought me into this world and I should always remember that I was not responsible for whatever happened with my parents. I would have really been screwed up if it weren't for her. She gave me a loving supportive home. She died about three months after I graduated from college and I had long periods of self destruction. But I was lucky enough to have good friends who pulled me through. I don't know where I would be without Mamie, and I was even nasty to her this weekend."

"Losing parents is one of the greatest traumas anyone could have and I think you have survived very well," Julia pointed out. "You have at least two people who love you very much. You have a very good job, and friends. Don't you think that Tony's love for you can overcome the events of your life that you had no control over?"

"It's not as much that as the problem of having children. I have successfully skirted around the issue but I'm not sure how he feels about it," Jan admitted.

"Didn't I hear that Tony has a son?" asked Julia.

"Yes, he's a wonderful boy. Sheila is his mother and Tony's ex wife," Jan informed her.

"I would think that the pressure is off. Tony has a son and, if he hasn't mentioned procreation before, I should think it is not a priority with him. It would seem more important for you to know, yourself. Let's not put this on Tony right now, do you want a child?" asked Julia.

"I, uh, I don't know. I've always liked kids but I'm afraid of my mother's disease," Jan admitted.

"I would suggest you make up your mind what it is YOU want. There is no crime in not having children but, if you decide you want a child, there is always genetic testing or adoption. If Tony really wanted another child, I would think he would have chosen a younger woman. You only have a few fertile years left so you had best make up your mind. Think about how your life would be impacted with or without a child and I think things will fall into place. It seems we are all our own worst enemy, at times. I think you know, in your heart, that Tony would do whatever you choose. He is not the problem here," advised Julia as she stood up. "Remember it is not the load that breaks you down it's the way you carry it."

"Julia, you are profound," said Jan.

"Oh, not me dear, that was Lena Horn," admitted Julia. "I'm going to go out to tell the ladies you are resting and I'll come back in a little while. Enjoy your tea."

CHAPTER 37

Snack Time

The women were all in the dining room and, once assembled, Maddy called them all to attention. "I have a couple of things to tell you ladies. Now please, do not be alarmed, Jan is fine but she did have an accident. She went out, in the height of the storm, fell and hit her head. Her eyes look clear and Julia was sure there was no concussion but she would like Sheila to look at her to double check."

Mamie and Sheila went to Jan's room as the others sat down. Julia came out and joined them for tea.

Mamie and Sheila walked into the room of a much more serene Jan then they had seen in the last twenty four hours. Sheila checked her eyes and told Jan if she were to feel the least bit nauseous to let her know at once. Jan proceeded to tell them about her dream and seeing her grandmother.

"Funny, that's what people who are revived from death say, I've seen it in the ER," Sheila said.

All three started making jokes that Jan was probably a zombie since their hostesses didn't seem to be carrying a defibrillator around.

Jan apologized to Mamie for being so bitchy and said she had a nice talk with Julia. Sheila said that Jan should get some rest and they would see her later. Walking down the hall Sheila repeated, "That is strange, really, it is exactly the way I've heard people describe the near death experience." She made a mental note to ask how it was that they even found Jan.

Mamie and Sheila reported to the group that Jan looked to be in excellent condition. Sheila said there was no sign of concussion.

"Jan seems to be in a much better mood and I think you had something to do with that Julia," was Mamie's conclusion.

"Sometimes accidents can shake things up a bit, and we look at things with a new perspective," Julia explained.

They were making comments and inquiries as to why Jan was out in the rain, only Mamie knew the truth. Julia suggested there might have been something she wanted to get out of her car. Anticipating the next question, she also told them she couldn't find Sammy and thought he was out lost in the rain. When she opened the door she could see Jan's form on the side of the driveway, she must have hit her head on a rock.

"I hope it was something important, I wouldn't have gone out there if there was a pot of gold at the end of the driveway," said Lynn as she reached over and grabbed a macaroon then added, "Oh, maybe I would."

So, after a few minutes of discussion, they continued to jelly their scones and sip their tea and plan the rest of the day. N.C asked Vivian if she could get the promised acupuncture treatment when they were finished snacking. Vivian said they had best get to it in a few minutes since Gia had signed up for a massage at five-fifteen. Maddy made the suggestion that she lead the group in meditation before dinner, at about six-twenty. That would give Gia a few minutes after her massage, to get to the Great Room.

"We'll have dinner at about seven. I'll ring the bell if we are all scattered. I haven't forgotten you, Sharon. I think it will be Mexican tonight and it's a very easy meal," Julia explained, "I'll need you chopping at, oh, let's say five forty-five."

"I'll be taking notes, I'm sure," Sharon responded, "but I warn you Julia, I'm going to get that scone recipe out of you one way or another."

Vivian and N.C. were the first to leave the table for the acupuncture session. Gia went off to shower before her massage. Donna and Lynn planned a scrabble game and Mamie went off to check on Jan. Sheila wanted to read for a while but said she would challenge the winner of the scrabble game. Sharon discretely asked Rose if it were possible to mix up something to calm her nerves a little. They deposited their dishes on the counter and Rose led Sharon to the office to mix up a new concoction.

Julia felt there would be less 'passers-by' if the rain resumed, but she would take it down a notch from the earlier storm. She also made a mental note to give a generous contribution to the Society for Cancer Research. She and Maddy went to the business office to straighten out whatever problems or potential problems caused by both storms.

"It just gets so complicated trying not to leave a footprint here, there are so many things to sort out," said Maddy. "And right now traffic should be the priority. That's another thing that we didn't have to worry about years ago, and I used to think horses and buggies were a problem."

"The population has risen exponentially, but I really think that whether it is chariots, buggies or vehicles, it's more the numbers that cause the cleanup problems," said Julia. "I've been tracking the potential for disasters and I have a team working on accident avoidance. I believe we have it comfortably under control. I have our minions working on the agricultural and animal effects of our deluge, that should keep them busy for a while. No one here would understand the far-reaching effects of interfering with the normal course of things. Remember that old commercial here that said, 'It's not nice to fool Mother Nature,'" Julia mimicked in a high voice, and they laughed until Sammy showed up.

CHAPTER 38

Rose and Sharon

They entered the office where the herbs, various homeopathic medicines and vitamins were stored. Rose was not about to divvy out anything without an explanation as to the need. She invited Sharon to sit in the chair opposite her and asked what seemed to be unnerving her. Rose had noticed that Sharon was a rather closed door and suspected that perhaps Sharon thought dealing with her would require less output of information than with Julia or the others.

Rose started out explaining that what she did required was an understanding of the problem. There might be many substances that worked on the nervous system but there were subtle differences in terms of addressing the cause. A mother's anxiety over a sick child has a different core and affects then say, a student studying for a final exam.

"Think of it this way Sharon. I feel strongly about what I do and I take it seriously. I may look young but I have had a lot of experience. And you can trust that whatever you say here will not leave this room," she said and then added in a lighter tone, "unless, of course you plan on killing someone, then I might have to alert the authorities," and they both smiled.

"You can relax, I'm not planning a murder, unless it's my electrician who didn't show up last week," Sharon answered. Then she relented and told the story of her two years longing for David and finally his abrupt proposal. She should be ecstatic, but the complications just seemed overwhelming. She went on to explain about David's wife, child and his decision to get a divorce even though his family is Catholic.

"Do you always look for problems for yourself?" said Rose shaking her head.

Sharon wasn't sure how to respond and Rose said, "Well?"

Then Sharon asked, "You mean because he is still married?"

"No, I mean because he loves you; he has been beyond reproach all this time; he has a beautiful child who sounds like she could use a mother as kind and lovely as you. So what problems are you looking for here?" said Rose, "You don't know, at this point, what his parents are going to think. They have watched their son, in a loveless marriage, raising a child on his own. Don't you think any 'good' parent would be overjoyed to see their son happy? Honestly, what are you thinking, are you so afraid of being happy yourself that you are willing to deny the happiness of David and his daughter too?"

"Geeze, did someone say they thought you were shy," Sharon said slowly, trying to take it all in. "Actually, I think you made me realize something: maybe I am afraid of being happy. I've gone so many years trying to put a lid on things; contain emotion so nobody can fool me, hurt me."

"Who hurt you Sharon?" Rose demanded.

That statement hit Sharon like a club. The face of her predator flashed in her mind's eye. She began telling Rose the story of Brother Ed. Tears welled in her eyes as she realized that it wasn't his hands penetrating her that had such far-reaching effects, it was the broken love and trust that had weighed so heavily on the mind and heart of the little girl inside. Even Rose had tears in her eyes as they sat in quietly.

Rose broke the silence saying, "That was a lot for you to get out. How are you feeling?"

"Weird, exhausted but somehow I think better. You know Rose, I've never told anyone about that before. That was the worst thing that ever happened to me and I know it's had an impact on a lot of things in my life. That fact that I actually blocked out that memory, for so many years, was almost as frightening to me as what actually happened. Could I be blocking out anything else?"

"Childhood traumas certainly shape part of a life but the mind has a way of protecting people," Rose explained. "You didn't know about sex, much less understand sexual abuse. You didn't even have the vocabulary to explain those complicated feelings. You knew instinctively that something was very wrong and felt, in some way, responsible too; children of that age usually do. At seventeen you were better able to cope with what happened and your mind gave voice to the memory, with a little help from your sisters. I doubt if there are any other hidden traumas but I could hypnotize you and do a little regressive therapy, if you would like."

So, for the next half hour, Rose poked through Sharon's subconscious but found no evidence of further obstructions. That was a huge relief for Sharon. Rose was about to sum things up and said, "Now that you are an adult, you need to let that little girl inside know she did nothing wrong. Do you have a picture of yourself about that age?"

"I have one about the age of six, when I made my first Holy Communion," said Sharon. "My parents only took pictures on special occasions."

"I suggest you put that picture in a prominent place, maybe your bathroom, where you will see it every day. Tell the little girl in that picture that she is doing just fine. She's a good girl who deserves love and a good life. Will you do that?" Rose asked.

"Of course, thank you, Rose," they both stood up and Sharon gave Rose a hug.

"My pleasure," said Rose. "You should go take a twenty minute nap. Emotional purging can be exhausting, and then you're due in the kitchen."

CHAPTER 39

Vivian and N.C.

They entered the massage room and N.C. lay down on the table. Vivian washed her hands vigorously and got her cotton, alcohol, needles and plastic gloves from the cabinet shelves.

"Have you had acupuncture treatments before?" Vivian inquired, as she dabbed alcohol on the spots intended for the needles.

"Yes, a few years ago for my sinuses," N.C. responded.

"I'm surprised you never thought to try this for fertility. It can be very helpful, not a guarantee of course. And I would suggest you babysit. Do you know anyone that has recently had a child?" asked Vivian.

"I have a neighbor who had a child six months ago and I have helped her out a couple of times, but why babysit?" asked N.C.

"Oh, it's complicated honey, but trust me, it can help. It's a hormonal thing. You know how when women live together their periods start to synchronize. Nature can be a real mimic," said Vivian distractedly as she put the last needle in. "In case you have forgotten, the needles need to be turned, three times, at ten minute intervals. Oops, I just remembered, I promised Gia her massage. I'll have Rose turn the needles for you, and we should do this again tomorrow night too." She turned on some soothing music before starting toward the door.

"Don't worry about me, I'll probably fall asleep," N.C. murmured.

CHAPTER 40

Gia and Vivian

Gia lay down on the massage table and Vivian started working on her head.

"How have you been feeling?" inquired Vivian. "Any particular spots you want me to work on honey?"

"My upper back, on the left side, is where I seem to get a lot of knots," said Gia as Vivian's magical hands were moving toward her neck and shoulders.

"And how are you enjoying the ranch?" Vivian asked.

"Great, what's not to like? It's a shame there's been so much rain since our hike. Rose knows so much about nature, I really enjoyed listening to her comments about the plants and herbs. Where are you from Vivian?" she asked. Vivian hadn't expected the question and she stalled a moment.

"Ohio, but then not really. My Daddy was a preacher and we only lived there until I was three. I don't remember much about it. We moved every few years so I think of a lot of places as home for different time zones of my life. I'm lucky to have friends all over. What about you?" Vivian said, anxious to get the attention away from herself.

"I was born in the little town of Gaffney, South Carolina. We moved to California, when I was young, but still old enough to remember lots of it. My cousin, he was my best friend, lived there too. He used to come out here to visit me in the summers and a couple of times we went back for Christmas. Oh that feels good," she said as Vivian was working on her upper arm.

"Are you still best friends with your cousin?" Vivian asked.

Gia explained her cousin's recent passing and that it still felt like a fresh wound. She was grateful that this trip came up and was really glad to get away. She had that picture of Dix in her head and still felt responsible for not preventing Dix's suicide. Vivian asked her to turn over and began attacking the knots between Gia's shoulder blades.

"Did he call you and ask for help, or did you have a big fight?" Vivian asked.

"No," Gia responded, "but I was the closest to him, I should have known how desperate he was."

"Oh honey, you've been holding out on me," declared Vivian. "You're a mind reader and you chose not to read his mind that day, is that right."

Gia picked up her head and looked at Vivian. "What?" was all she could say.

"I think you heard me girl," Vivian challenged. "You have some kind of super power and you're not sharing your gift."

"What are you talking about Vivian?" said a somewhat irritated Gia.

"I'm trying to get at why you think you should have known the kind of pain he was in if he wasn't telling you. And, even if he did tell you, what would you have done with that information?" she asked.

"If I had known I would have gotten him some help," Gia explained.

"I don't usually ask after the fact questions, but I'm curious," said Vivian, as she worked on the other side. "Do you think Dix would have gone to a psychiatrist or psychologist if you had asked him to?

There was a long pause before Gia answered the question saying, "About six months ago we were talking about my uncle, his father. I asked him why he didn't go to a shrink and see what they might say to help him understand, but he wouldn't listen. He said he wasn't going to some stranger and paying a fortune to be told his dad was just a back country, redneck asshole."

"Hmm, I see. So was your plan to drug him, tie him up and force him to a shrink's office, is that how you thought you could help?" Gia was on her stomach now and Vivian was working on her leg. She thought Gia might like to use that leg to connect with Vivian's face. "Then somehow you would force him to talk to the shrink."

"You know that's absurd," Gia blurted out.

Then Vivian's tone went from playful teasing to the stern sound of a teacher with an inattentive pupil.

"Not as absurd as your guilt feelings," Vivian protested. "Honestly Gia, I just want you to understand that you are not responsible for what Dix did. He was in a great deal of pain, for a long time. Now, while that is very sad, he was not willing to go to anyone and seek help, he just wanted it to stop. Do you get that? It was about Dix and his demons, not you. I really don't believe Dix, if he was truly your friend, would want you to go around blaming yourself. I'm sorry if I sound harsh," as she softened her tone, "but I think you need to be shaken up and realize that Dix will become a crutch to avoid thinking about the real issues in your life." She paused then continued, "I guess this wasn't as relaxing as you thought it would be," Vivian smiled, "but I think you need to work some things out about yourself. Maybe things you haven't admitted to yourself."

Gia was teary eyed and about to protest, but did not. Reluctantly, she looked at Vivian and said, "I think you may be right Vivian, I'll think about it," she agreed.

"Now you can relax honey. I'm going to shut up, turn on my Debussy and give you the special lavender and emu oil treatment," and she did.

When Vivian was finished, Gia thanked her and ran off to catch up with the meditation group as Vivian headed toward the kitchen.

CHAPTER 41

Dinner Preparations

Vivian walked into the kitchen and Julia said, "Would you please find Sharon, Vivian? She should be up from her nap and I promised she could help with dinner tonight."

When Sharon joined Julia in the kitchen she was informed they were making fajitas. They started chopping red, yellow and green peppers; then onions. Sharon's eyes were tearing like crazy and she said, "How do you keep your eyes from tearing up, Julia?"

Julia lit a couple of tall candles and placed them near Sharon without really answering the question but saying, "This little trick can help."

Julia had the boneless, skinless chicken steaming in a large covered pot, explaining to Sharon that she felt the chicken would retain more moisture this way for this type of dish. She also told Sharon that she preferred making the salsa from scratch but tonight they were running late so she was going to use readymade from jars, stressing never from cans.

The chicken was finished so they removed the breasts from the pot and let them cool on the platter. They had the onions and tricolored peppers simmering in olive oil for a while and then added the salsa. When the chicken was cool enough to handle, they pulled it apart into bite-sized pieces and added it to the huge pan with the other ingredients. Julia took tortillas from the refrigerator and showed Sharon how to twirl them around the flames of the gas stove top and stack them in the warming oven until just before serving, stressing not too hot or the tortillas would become crispy.

There was a big pot of boiling water and, as Julia got out the shredded cheddar cheese, guacamole, sour cream, cilantro and hot sauce for those with an especially spicy palate, Sharon shucked the corn and placed it in the boiling water for ten minutes.

"The corn is from an organic farmer and has not been genetically-altered. You should be very careful about GMO's, they are in wheat too—and there I go preaching again," Julia pretended to chastised herself.

"Earlier I made more coconut macaroons and chocolate chip cookies, always a favorite," added Julia, "and of course cheese and fruit plates and leftover chocolate cake."

"This reminds me a little of home," said Sharon, "when I was a kid, there were six of us, I didn't have much one-on-one time with my mom, so helping her prepare dinner was kind of our special time together. Did you learn to cook from your mother, Julia?"

"Oh yes, but then from many people. I looked on it as a hobby and a form of relaxation," Julia revealed.

They continued chatting as they put the silverware, napkins and water glasses on the table. Julia filled a round silver container with ice and placed bottles of beer and wine inside. The beer and wine glasses were on the side table and the dishes were stacked in the kitchen since Julia and Vivian would be handing out the plates from there.

Julia was saying, "I don't drink beer often but I do love the taste with certain foods. Did you know that beer was a staple with the Egyptians? Of course, I prefer today's cold beer."

"Oh, so your first beer was with the Egyptians?" said Sharon chuckling. "And were you and King Tut on a first name basis?"

Julia laughed back and, with a twinkle in her eye said, "Oh, I could tell you stories, but you know what I mean, I like refrigeration.

Speaking of which, let's put the guacamole and sour cream back in the frig until the last minute. The others should be out soon. You can go wash the onions off your hands and freshen up. You've been a great help dear, and I've enjoyed our special time together."

CHAPTER 42

Meditation Friday Evening

Jan was resting and Sharon was helping Julia in the kitchen. Rose had finished up N.C's acupuncture session and Vivian had finished Gia's massage. So, with the exception of Jan and Sharon, the guests were now about to have a guided meditation in the Great Room. Maddy had opened a window and turned on a fan to make sure the fresh air was circulating. The chairs were set up in a circle with three lavender and two ylang ylang scented candles lit in the middle to enhance inner balance and well being. Maddy also explained that lavender can be very useful as a spray to ward off mosquitoes saying, "The ancients used it to mask their human scent, and the mosquitoes would move on to someone else."

"And you were there to see that?" teased Lynn.

"Oh, I'm older than I look," she smiled back and added, "folklore my dear. Try it next time you go hiking, although you don't seem to be troubled here, by the little pests, as other parts of the country."

Guests were advised to sit comfortably with their feet flat on the floor and it was up to them if they wanted to leave their eyes open or closed. Maddy told them that this was their time and to allow themselves to enjoy. They were to picture, in their mind's eye, a safe place where they could relax and let all their daily thoughts melt away.

She counted to five and on each number told them to take a deep breath, slowly release and then go deeper into relaxation. They were to concentrate on their breathing and not be too concerned if ideas popped in their heads.

"Just examine the thought objectively, tell yourself you will deal with it later and get back to your breathing."

Sheila was thinking of her son, Chris, and her boyfriend, Jim. They had planned on going to a ball game together. This would be their first outing without her, and she wanted so much for them to get along. She told herself that they had gotten along well when they were with her and there was no reason to think otherwise. She took a deep breath and concentrated on her breathing.

Gia was thinking about Dix. She was trying to put herself in his place and forgive him for leaving her. She felt better after her talk with Vivian. Telling herself to be in the 'here and now,' she took a deep breath and relaxed.

Lynn was doing well until the thought popped in her head that she might have left the coffee pot on yesterday and Chuck was going to be gone all day. This was a recurring fear of hers since she tended to get distracted easily.She decided that either the pot burned, the house burned down or everything was ok and there was nothing she could do about it now anyway. Then she got back on track.

Mamie had reflected, about herself, that she had not been a person 'in the moment' enough. The cancer did have some benefits in that she appreciated more; was aware of more and, when she was feeling good, she let her passion with Bill thrive. She acknowledged this and then focused on her breathing.

N.C. was thinking how ironic that sometimes it is the absence of someone that makes them clearer in your mind. She was appreciating how Kevin had been so supportive of her, even when he had legitimate doubts about the outcome. She decided to do something special for him when she got home; then it was back to her breathing.

Donna was excited about her new life and happy to be making new friends. She didn't know if she had shared too much, too soon and wondered if they would really accept her. Then she went back to her deep breathing.

The time went by quickly and Maddy asked them to open their eyes and suggested they stretch a bit. She turned on a light and blew out the candles. They stacked the chairs, closed the window, and turned off the fan as Maddy assured them dinner would be ready.

CHAPTER 43

Dinner Friday Night

Julia stood distributing each plate with a warm tortilla and then Vivian ladled the fajita mixture in the center and folded the tortilla around the mixture. Rose had drained the corn and, with a strong pair of tongs and heavy drying towel, placed the corn on each plate as the guests passed. Bowls of guacamole, sour cream and shredded cheese were on the table. Flowers were arranged in short bouquets, so vision would not be obstructed as guests chatted across the table. The atmosphere was relaxed as the meditation seemed to have a very calming effect on everyone. Sheila was telling Barbara that she had difficulty clearing her mind and all kinds of uninvited thoughts kept slipping into her consciousness.

"That's ok," said Barbara, "don't try too hard, just see what those thoughts are and look at them objectively, then focus on your breathing. In time it will get easier. Just like anything else, it takes practice."

"Yeah, that's what Maddy told us," said Sheila. "Don't worry, I'm going to keep at it. They say it can help with high blood pressure, my family's curse. It usually comes on at about sixty but I figure if I keep my weight down, exercise and watch the sodium intake, I may avoid medication."

"Excellent plan," Barbara agreed.

They had all picked up their plates and were seated now, passing around the sour cream, cheese and guacamole. After the first few bites that 'hummm' sound could be heard and Gia said," Julia, have you ever owned a restaurant? This is delicious."

Julia smiled as if it were a rhetorical question and spoke up saying, "Well thank you my dear, and thank my sous chef Sharon." The ladies gave a cursory clap, hardly wanting to relinquish hold on their tortillas.

Sharon looked up, smiling and said, "Chopping is my specialty." She went on to say that this meal had been so simple she believed she could recreate it at home; unless, of course, as had been rumored, "Julia might have slipped in a secret ingredient."

Julia smiled and protested that what you see is what you get and swore that the vicious rumor, spread by Maddy, was just not true.

"Some people just can't take a bit of joking and cast aspersions on the innocent," she claimed.

Maddy, chewing and smiling, rolled her eyes as if to say 'who do you believe'.

There were inquires as to how Jan was feeling and she responded positively. The nap was just what she needed.

They continued chatting back and forth until Mamie said, "I know who you remind me of," and mentioned that she and her husband saw 'Arsenic and Old Lace' at the Dorothy Chandler Pavilion in downtown L.A. Julia and Maddy reminded her of the two stars, who were also English.

"That's not the first time we've been told that," Julia commented, "although I do think we are a bit younger and better looking," as she touched her hair and tilted her head with an exaggerated expression, she and Maddy laughed.

N.C. agreed, she hadn't seen the play but knew of the stars since she watched a lot of British TV and they were so popular. "I think their accident was tragic, they still had many good years of work ahead, and I could kick myself for not seeing their last performance."

Julia and Maddy feigned ignorance of the accident claiming they were probably traveling when it happened. They were so busy getting the ranch in order, they hadn't paid any attention to the news. They were sure their countrymen would be morning the loss of such great talents.

Julia was relieved when the conversation shifted as Gia mentioned she had never been to England. Then Lynn, the storyteller, went on to describe an experience she had traveling, with two friends, after college. They were in France, on their way to England, and they met a couple of gay guys on the train. They all got along well and had a lot of laughs.

"The guys said they were going to Mon San Michele for a couple of days and asked us if we would get them rooms at the pensione, or boarding house, where we would be staying in London. We agreed and designated a place to meet them three days later," she explained. "So we found a lovely place, not far from the Garden Museum, and the owner was showing us around. We got to our room, on the third floor, and she turned to me and said, 'have you got any fags?' Not liking the term, I answered indignantly, 'yes, but how did you know?' At which point my friends were hysterical laughing and said, 'she means cigarettes dummy.'" They all laughed.

Julia asked how they were all feeling without their electronic devices. Jan said nothing, still feeling guilty about her recent venture in the rain, and Mamie made a concerted effort not to look at Jan for fear she might start a nervous laughing jag. Most of them agreed they hadn't thought much about it, since they had been busy, and maybe 'out of sight out of mind' played into it a little. The separation anxiety, from their cell phones, was made easier knowing their families had the house number here in case of an emergency.

"People are starting to lose the art of face to face conversation, and the intimacy that brings among friends. Texting and emailing are devoid of the special nuance that is only conveyed with tone of voice, or facial expression. A written communication can be misinterpreted when the emotion behind the missive is lost in translation," said Julia.

A discussion began about how different the world was when they were growing up. Running out to play and being gone for hours until dinner time; parents not knowing exactly where their kids were, but not worrying. They were taking turns telling stories about their parents and siblings.

Mamie told about what happened when her Dad died a couple of years ago. He lived a long, good life but the last couple of years he had no recollection of his family and needed twenty-four hour a day care. Her mother had to place him in a home with medical supervision. Towards the end he was visited by a hospice aide. She and her brother were sitting in her dad's room, the night he died, at three in the morning. She was upset at seeing her Dad's head arched back and his mouth open. Then, for some reason she had a fantasy that rigor mortis had set in and, at any moment he was going to sit up, with his mouth open. That struck her so funny she started to laugh uncontrollably. She kept trying to reign in her emotions but as soon as the attendants in the house came by to pay their respects, it would start all over. Her brother, embarrassed, was elbowing her side and explaining to people soberly, 'we all handle grief differently,' and with that she laughed even harder and wet her pants. Other stories were told for a while then Barbara suggested that they resume the painting class.

"Rather than yoga tonight, since your time with me is limited, if that is agreeable to Donna, as well as the group," said Barbara.

"Sure, you're the boss. Besides I love painting," said Donna.

Gradually they were getting up and finding their way to the cookies, cheese and fruit; some opted for another beer or wine.

"Oh my God, this cookie is a masterpiece," said Sheila after taking a bite of coconut macaroon, "tell me there are no calories in this Julia."

"Of course not, none of my food has any calories," she stood up and with one hand on her hip and the other on her head. "That's how I keep my girlish figure," and they laughed. Julia pretended she was insulted, "You doubt me, ok, just for that the rest of my meals

171

will include calories, you shouldn't insult the cook—she can be quite vengeful."

"Oh Vivian, you're playing 'I left my heart in San Francisco,' could we turn it up a little. I love that song, and Tony Bennett too," said Sheila. Vivian accommodated the request and they started clearing the table and all joined in singing as they moved around the room, depositing soiled plates and silverware by the sink. Then, when the song was over, Julia shooed them out of the kitchen to resume their painting class.

Donna asked if they could have hot chocolate before bed, then added, "I just felt like a little kid asking mommy for a special treat," she laughed. "I think I'm regressing."

"I'm flattered dear," said Julia. "Let's say eleven, that will give everyone time to clean up after painting."

Chapter 44

Friday Night Painting and Hot Chocolate

Barbara was helping Jan set up since she had missed the earlier class. Jan, with new enthusiasm, jumped right in and was excited to get started. Donna was carrying on like an old pro while Gia and Sharon were finishing up shading. Sheila needed a little more help, but she was progressing nicely.

Barbara made a general statement to the class, "I would like to reiterate, because it is so important," she started, "keep thinking of the relationship of one subject to the next and in your mind's eye you can even start seeing the negative space as shapes."

N.C and Lynn were working next to each other and reminding each other of the things Amanda had taught them and what Barbara had said earlier.

"Ladies, I can't impress on you enough how important your drawing is to the final painting. One of the exercises you can do at home is to take a picture of a simple still life, blow it up, turn it upside down and then draw. This makes it easier to focus on the lines and shapes rather than the objects themselves."

"Um, and don't you think we've heard that one before too," whispered Lynn.

They worked on and N.C. told Lynn how this reminded her of suggesting something to her husband, say taking a certain vitamin or doing certain exercises. Then, it may be a month or a year later and some stranger at the gym, or casual acquaintance, would suggest the same thing.

"It's like he never heard it before, he'll even tell me this 'new' information and have absolutely no recollection of our previous conversations. If he wasn't so wonderful, in so many ways, I probably would have strangled him a long time ago."

Lynn laughed and said, "I know, Chuck does that to me all the time—I think I'm like white noise at home. I guess it serves me right for being a 'know it all,' but I can't help it if I know it all," she chuckled.

Barbara passed around a chart that demonstrated a scale of shade variations from white to black. She wanted to impress on them how subtle light changes could improve the appearance of their painting.

Barbara was diligent with her students and seemed able to catch their little mishaps, almost as they were happening, and therefore prevent a chain reaction of error. They were all pleased with their own progress. Even Sheila, who started out in a tentative manner, now seemed determined to acquire more skill.

The time went by quickly and Barbara's watch timer went off at ten-forty five. She announced it was time to clean up. They all needed to wash the charcoal or paint off their hands so most went to their bathrooms to clean up except Sheila and Barbara, who went to the kitchen sink.

"I'm so excited about this, I never thought I would ever draw, much less paint," said Sheila.

"A great deal of talent is lost to the world for the want of a little courage," said Julia, as she stirred the hot chocolate.

"I agree with you," said Sheila

"Oh not me, my dear, Sydney Smith," said Julia.

"You are doing so well, Sheila. This is a wonderful creative outlet and it's a shame that more people don't try. Once people reach adulthood the majority avoid challenges. They stick to the same pastimes and lack the patience to attempt new skills. They miss so much joy life can bring. That's why the brain starts to stagnate, when we lose interest in learning new things," Barbara insisted.

The others had returned to the kitchen and Gia noticed the soft singing in the background, "Vivian, who is that singing? I really like it."

"Billie Holiday, I'm surprised you haven't heard of her," Vivian responded. "She was just one of the best blues singers ever. Her interpretation of lyrics makes you really feel the all the emotion she's trying to get across."

Mamie and Jan admitted they hadn't known of her either but they all agreed they liked her and wanted to hear more, so Vivian started the CD from the beginning as they all found places at the table. Julia and Rose had been filling mugs with steaming hot chocolate as they started discussing different parallels in music and art.

Julia raised her voice a bit so they could all hear, "Did you know that, in the thirteenth and fourteenth centuries, artists were so competitive for commissions that a few even plotted to kill their rivals? Here, my dears," she said to Barbara and Maddy, "will you help me put the mugs on the table?" Then she took out the remaining cookies and placed them on the table.

"That's sure taking ambition to the extreme," laughed Sheila.

Sipping from their mugs, they were still excited about the evening's class and the chit chat going back and forth at the table was mostly about interest in continuing classes when they got home. NC. and Lynn were reconsidering lessons by Amanda, if she would have them back.

Mamie said, "Isn't it a shame that so many great artists never made any money or even recognition when they were alive?"

"Oh yes," said Maddy, "that is true dedication; to continue without financial reward, and many faced ridicule and humiliation, that is quite amazing."

"I don't think you see much of that today," said N.C.

"Look at poor Van Gogh, few people knew or appreciated his work when he was alive," said Barbara. Then, changing the subject, "Now, we should make a plan for tomorrow. If the rain doesn't let up, you can have an early yoga class then breakfast about nine-fifteen."

"If I get up early, can I get a cup of coffee? My eyelids don't respond well without sufficient amounts of caffeine," said Lynn.

"Certainly, no problem, I will have coffee and juice ready first thing in the morning," Julia assured her. "But I would suggest you don't have anything too close to yoga or you may have a problem with some of your postures."

Rose called out to Mamie and N. C., "Can I see you both, first thing in the morning before you eat or drink anything?"

"Sure," they both said in unison.

Chapter 45

Saturday Morning Yoga, Breakfast and Jacuzzi Time

They were scurrying around getting themselves ready for yoga. At seven-thirty Lynn, Jan and Gia were the first vying for the coffee pot. N.C. and Mamie had already been to see Rose in the back office. The rest of the group weren't as caffeine-needy and were gradually assembling in the kitchen.

Donna warned that if they didn't go easy on the liquid, they would taste it all over again in class. That sent cups retreating to their saucers.

It hadn't taken long for N.C. and Mamie to drink down Rose's concoctions and rejoin the group. They had finished their cocktail before seven-thirty and, with everyone ready, they started class a few minutes early.

Julia, Maddy, Vivian, and Barbara were all preparing breakfast. Julia was stirring the oatmeal while Maddy took the spinach and sausage quiches out of the oven and placed them in the warming oven underneath. Barbara set out the plates, silverware, glasses and more cups while Vivian gathered sugar, honey, salt, pepper, butter, jelly and almond butter for the table. The toaster and various types of bread were on the side table near the coffee pot and electric tea pot. Barbara returned the cream to the side table along with a second jar of jelly, then Julia and Maddy put the juices back out.

Rose had been in the back office mixing up another batch of herbs for N.C. and Mamie. She now joined the others and they all selected a beverage and sat down to wait for their guests. Julia sighed as Sammy rubbed against the leg of her chair. They sat talking about the current events and the changes that had occurred in the history of the United States.

"I think it very unfortunate that people tend to whitewash history rather than embrace all its nuances," said Julia. "There was certainly a dichotomy of thinking going all the way back to the founding fathers."

"George Washington had three hundred slaves yet he was ideologically against slavery," said Julia. "And the same with Thomas Jefferson. Jefferson even fathered children with his slave, Sally Hemming, but did not have the moral fortitude to fight against slavery. Yet both were great men who were dedicated to their country and made great contributions and sacrifices, no one can deny that; they were both human and made terrible mistakes too."

"I find it particularly poignant that after Washington had his famous victory against the Hessians, who were fighting for England, he wrote a declaration to them," said Maddy. "He said he knew they were forced into fighting as mercenaries, against the colonies, by an agreement between the English King and a German Prince. Then he made them an offer: any Hessian soldier who would like to stay and settle in America was welcome to do so. I have never seen anything like that. Who, in history, has ever made an offer like that to an invading army? About fifteen percent took him up on that offer."

"Americans should be embracing the truth, even in its ugliest forms." Julia added. "Overcoming the dark side of their past is the greatest of victories."

"But not all have 'overcome'," said Barbara, "prejudice is still alive and well."

"Yes, but I believe the collective conscious understands the immorality of it," she agreed. "There are those individuals, and some groups, who have anger issues. They may feel inadequate for reasons they don't understand and it serves them to hate someone of a different race or religion, rather than the father who beat them or the mother who neglected them."

"If I had to live in the old days here, I think I would have been a Madame," said Rose, looking like she had been thinking seriously about it.

"Why Rose, you little tart," laughed Maddy.

"I was thinking of the early west. Women had so few choices and so many died in childbirth. Then there were the widows who had children and were left with no resources. At least a Madame had some influence, and a lot of them were helpful in the Wild West. In the gold rush camps they acted as nurses when an epidemic went around. They helped establish and support the local schools."

They were smiling and then Vivian burst out laughing and Rose looked indignant.

"Ok, ok," Vivian said, "we hear your cry for the long lost ladies of the night, but I had a mental image of you in a saloon, with a sassy dress and boa, and it just tickled me Madame Rose."

The group was on their way back to the dining room and Mamie said, "What's up with Rose?"

"Oh nothing, we just think Rose was a Madame in a former life," laughed Barbara.

"You laugh but you know I'm right," Rose countered.

Julia and Maddy took the spinach quiches and oatmeal out of the warming drawer and eight hungry women buzzed around with clinking dishes, glasses and cups until they found places at the table. The quiches were cut and passed around and the large bowl of oatmeal glided on towel from one end of the table to the other.

"Julia, are these pork or turkey sausages in the quiche?" asked Sharon.

179

"Turkey, but not all brands are created equal, you have to try a few to get the taste you prefer," she answered.

"Hmmm," crooned Donna.

"This oatmeal is delicious. What kind is it?" Gia asked.

"I only use steel cut oats," she said emphatically. "It takes about a half hour to cook but the nutritional value is so much greater than the fast-cooking oats. And it helps lower cholesterol."

"I don't think I've ever had steel cut before, I like the texture," said Gia.

"And how was yoga?" Barbara inquired.

"Great," said Gia quickly. They all made comments. Donna felt the whole class was improving. Jan complained that she really was enjoying yoga but didn't know if she could keep it up, with her busy schedule, when she got home. Mamie was saying she thought it took about six weeks to establish a habit, if Jan could just figure some kind of time slot in her work week.

Donna turned to Jan saying, "I had a client who could only come one day a week. After about a month she was doing as well as the people coming three days a week. I asked her if she was going to another class, besides mine, but she said she could barely make mine. Her secret was that she would do postures when ever and where ever she could. First thing in the morning she would do head rolls, hip rotations, standing wheel, twist and cat pose A modified tree poise, if she had to stand any length of time at the deli counter, the car wash or a check-out line. On her breaks, at work, she would find an unoccupied room or office and do the warrior pose, downward facing dog, you get my point. Some of her days weren't over until nine or ten o'clock at night and she would do a class, at home, with my DVD. The fact that she was feeling better gave her the reinforcement she needed to continue. That was years ago, right Sheila?"

Sheila was blushing, "It sure was, about ten years. I was a full-time nurse and taking advanced classes at night. My son was still at home and the days seemed to melt away. I think the yoga helped maintain my sanity."

"I have to admit," said Donna, "I've used your story, more than once, to make my point," and she turned back to Jan. "Now that you are familiar with the postures, you can even find yoga programs on T.V. You just have to know yourself, the best way for you. Some people can self discipline and others prefer the dynamic of being in a group. Figure out if it is important enough to you to make the effort and it really will help, in so many ways."

They were all impressed and let Sheila know it, then they started moving around, picking up seconds or trying whatever had previously not made its way to their plate. Some had second cups of coffee or tea. They all just wanted to sit and relax a while after their hearty breakfast. Julia overheard N.C. and Lynn debating which meal was most important. She interjected that there were several schools of thought about when the majority of calories should be consumed. She still considered breakfast and lunch should have the bulk and a light dinner, with as many raw fruits and veggies as possible. Processed foods and sweeteners should be eliminated altogether, along with carbonated beverages that just leach the calcium from the bones.

Vivian nudged Julia, as it was one of their signals for being too preachy, and said as a distraction, "Do you want to play a game, ladies?"

This was met with the inquiry as to what kind of game and she answered. "If you could be anyone in history, say for a day or two, who would you be?"

"We know Rose would be a Madame, in the Wild West," she teased, "but let's find out who you all would be."

Gia was the first to respond, "I would go back to the beginning and see what it was like being a cave woman. I want to know if they had any power or if they were at the mercy of the men."

Julia said, "The thing women need to learn is that no one gives you power, you just take it."

Sharon said, "I like the sound of that. Another of Julia's profound statements."

"No dear, that was Roseanne Barr. Excuse me ladies." The rain had stopped and Sammy seemed agitated, "I need to do something in the office, carry on." She rose from the table as she informed the group, "Well you wouldn't find Maddy in a cave with ripe smelling animals and people. She has what we call 'olfactory aversion.'"

"Very funny dear," said Maddy. Raising her voice as Julia walked away, "and the only way we would catch you in a cave would be if it had air conditioning and a flat-screen T.V."

The group thought it funny, listening to two old friends good-naturedly quibbling back and forth.

"I love history" said Lynn, "and I would have loved to have been Josephine Bonaparte for a day. It was such a crazy time in France and I wish I knew what that Napoleon was really like."

"Did you know her name was really Rose?" said Rose. "Well it was Josephine too. Her full name was Marie Josèphe Rose Tascher de La Pagerie but she was known as Rose until she was in her thirties and met Napoleon, who preferred Josephine."

"So much for feminism in the eighteenth century," said N.C., "I think I would like to have been Mata Hari for a day. I did a paper on her once and she was quite a character. I would love to know if she really was a spy, responsible for the death of thousands of French soldiers, or just a colorful scapegoat. You know October 15, 2017, one hundred years after her execution by a firing squad, her court file is going to be reopened. Doesn't do her much good but it could be interesting. What about you Vivian?"

"I think I would like to be William Shakespeare for a day," she replied right away. "I would quickly write my autobiography so that everyone would know what a fun loving, charismatic fellow I was, or I think he was. Donna, how about you?"

"I would love to have been, no, just to have seen, Joan of Arc, at the height of her popularity," said Donna. "I can't imagine how a teenage girl could have convinced solders to make her their leader, especially back then when women were basically chattel."

"Would you like to continue outside in the Jacuzzi, ladies?" said Maddy. "This may be your only opportunity since I heard there may be another storm front coming in an hour or so."

"How did you hear that?" asked Sharon.

"We have a computer dear. You are the guests but we are the worker bees," she explained.

The group agreed it would be fun and they finally extracted themselves from their chairs and started moving to go change.

Rose, Maddy, Barbara and Vivian joined Julia in the office. Julia suggested that lunch should be a little later today, say one-thirty, and that Barbara could start the painting class as soon as the ladies were finished cleaning up after their Jacuzzi.

"Rose dear, you and Barbara go turn the heaters on and then announce, on the intercom, the time change for lunch while Barbara sets up for class. Vivian and Maddy will finish up in the kitchen and help me prepare for lunch, I'll be just a few minutes, unfortunately we require another storm."

"Why", asked Rose.

"We can't use the force field in case any of the walk-a-thon people want to put up signs. I'm sensing a possible problem and a heavy rain my deter, or at least slow down, any intruders."

Rose and Barbara went out to set up the four heaters near, but not too near, the Jacuzzi. Rose was tilting and rolling the last one in place and said, "I think that should do it." She could see Mamie, Jan and Gia walking through the Great Room and out the front door to the patio.

"Aren't you ladies forgetting something?" asked Rose.

They had been discussing historical characters and Rose heard Gia say, "Oh please, Madame Curie would be boring, you can do better than that. Oh, we forgot the towels."

Maddy hurried off and Rose told them not to worry, she would have one of the other ladies bring them out. It was chilly and damp outside and they delicately placed feet in the tub to adjust themselves to the hot water temperature.

Rose was on her way back to the bedroom hallway when she spotted Sharon and N.C. and asked them to bring the other three towels. Lynn, Donna and Sheila were not far behind.

Ten minutes later they were all finally ensconced in the hot water and still carrying on as if someone could really snap their finger and give them a day in someone else's skin; but it was fun to think about. Sharon said she didn't even care about being someone else, she would just want to be invisible and 'observe' a day in the life of someone like Jesus and see what he was really like.

"Wow, now that's a good one, why didn't I think of that?" said Sheila.

"Well I don't have a monopoly on fantasy; you're welcome to it if you happen to come across a time machine," said Sharon.

"Wouldn't a time machine be great to have in your backyard?" N.C. mused. "Then we could go take a look at Moses and see if there was, just maybe, something out there in the desert he really didn't want to leave."

"I know this will sound strange, but I would love to see what Hitler was like as a kid. What were his parents like and what could have made him such a crazy son of a bitch," said Jan.

"Well, I don't care if his mother didn't give him his binky or his father beat him. I wouldn't waste my time with that monster," said Lynn.

"On a lighter side, if you could be him for a day you could commit suicide and change the course of history," said Mamie, "or how about Jack the Ripper."

"Now you're just getting freaky morbid," laughed Donna.

"Of course I wouldn't want to be him, but I love mysteries and it's curious to me how he got away with it," said Mamie. "You know there is a theory that he was an artist. One of the mystery writers did an investigation and wrote a book about it."

"You know Hitler wanted to be an artist," said N.C. "but he was rejected by the Vienna Academy of Art. God, when you think about it, if he had been a better artist history might have been very different. I'll have to ask Barbara if there is any connection between artists and nutcases."

"Could be," said Donna. "Look at Van Gogh. Hey my fingers are puckering up. I think it's time to get out," and the others agreed and started moving about and grabbing towels from a chair they had placed near the Jacuzzi. There were loud squeals when they climbed out and hit the cold air. The water on the slate patio was slippery and Jan somehow managed to get one leg over the side of the Jacuzzi and slip when she brought her other leg over. She fell and hit her shoulder and the side of her head. Sheila and Mamie were right there and Sheila said firmly, "Don't move." She checked to see if anything was broken and asked Jan if she was ok. Jan had been stunned but said "yes" and after the precaution of asking her name and the date, they got her up. The adrenalin rush had worn off and they were all shivering as they escorted her into the house.

Vivian and Rose saw them coming in, helping Jan. they followed Mamie and Sheila and told the others they would handle this; the others dispersed to shower off the chlorinated water. Rose went to the office to mix up some calming, healing herbs and make some chamomile tea. Julia joined Vivian, Mamie and Sheila and took a good look at Jan. Julia put her hands on either side of Jan's head and added a little pressure. She held Jan's head for another moment and asked Jan to look this way, than that way.

"You'll be fine dear," said Julia, "but after two accidents, I would like you to take it easy today. Do you have a good book to read?" Jan said she was reading a wonderful book, the first book in the Outlander Series by Diana Gabaldon.

"Wonderful, then how about you rest and read. We'll call you for lunch and dinner and you can join the group for the evening activity, if that is agreeable to you, dear."

Jan said she didn't often allow herself the luxury of reading for fun, and she had this great book, so it was almost a treat. Mamie made a joke about Jan falling on purpose to get a little alone time and that she better just excuse herself, next time, before she does any real, permanent damage.

Jan was embarrassed about her clumsy second fall and said, "Oh I'll do anything for attention."

Julia and Vivian, Mamie and Sheila left Jan, as Rose was on her way in with tea and an herbal tonic; they were out in the hall. Mamie went to take a shower but Sheila turned to Julia concerned that, after two falls, Jan should have an MRI.

Julia put her hands on Sheila's shoulders, stared deep into her eyes and said, "Jan is fine, and everything is going to be fine. All you need to do now is go shower."

Sheila looked back at Julia and said in a rather robotic tone, "Yes, everything is fine and I'm going to go shower."

They walked down the hall and Lynn poked her head out the bedroom door, "Can I get a message, Vivian?

"Sure, follow me."

CHAPTER 46

Saturday Painting Class and Lunch

Lynn was having her massage, Jan was resting and the others were all refreshed and ready to get back to work. Sheila was admiring Sharon's painting. Then Sharon turned around, and looked at Sheila's painting.

"You're doing great. Remember, I illustrate my ideas all the time, I should know what I'm doing. I can't believe how well you've picked this up." a few moments later she asked, "Hey, is it true that Jan's boyfriend is your ex-husband?" Then quickly added, "Oh, I'm sorry. Is that too personal a question?"

"Oh that's ok, Tony is a great guy and we've been divorced for years," said Sheila. "We were still teenagers when I had my son, Chris, that's really the only reason we got married. I've been very close with Tony's parents. He and I are like brother and sister now, and trust me, if I didn't like Jan he would know it. Not that it would matter, but he could tell. I'm just glad that's not an issue, I think she's great too."

"What was it like when you first met?" said Sharon. "Oh, there I go again, boy am I the noisy one. I guess I'm curious because I'll be

187

meeting my boyfriend's family soon and there may be some awkward moments ahead."

"Awkward might be a good way to describe our first meeting, but I'll leave it up to Jan to tell you about that; it's what made her immediately beloved by the whole family," Sheila revealed. "My son thinks she's good for his dad and I kind of think of Jan as my future sister-in-law."

"That's really generous of you," said Sharon.

"Not at all, when you get to know Jan better you'll realize she may be a bit of a tough cookie at times, but she's got a big heart and would do anything for you. More important, she loves Tony and she's good to my son."

Barbara was moving around the room advising and encouraging. Gia, N.C. and Donna were looking at each other's work then back to their own canvas. N.C. remembered their earlier conversation and said, "Barbara, were many of the great artists a little crazy?"

"I guess that depends on your frame of reference," said Barbara. "Who and what are you referring to?"

N.C. explained their conversation about Jack the Ripper, Hitler and Van Gogh.

"First of all, the Ripper and Hitler may have considered themselves artists but the world certainly did not. It's far too much of a generalization to say most great artists were a little crazy. How about we have a group discussion before the next session," Barbara suggested. And they went back to work.

It was eleven-thirty when Lynn came in and said, "Sheila you're next up for massage with Vivian, and Rose said she can take you now, Sharon."

One-thirty seemed to come around quickly. Barbara had stopped the class ten minutes earlier to wash up for lunch and they all arrived in the dining room about the same time. It was a little chilly so Maddy adjusted the thermostat and assured everyone it would be comfortably warm in a few minutes.

There was a huge pot of tomato-basil soup and Julia, Maddy and Rose were behind the island ready to prepare some specialty sandwiches. Rose gave out small pieces of paper for the ladies to write down their choice of: lox, cream cheese and capers on a toasted English muffin drizzled with olive oil, tuna melt with cheese on rye or whole grain bread, or turkey layered with coleslaw, tomato and avocado on a Kaiser roll. Several were made up already and they made their choices while Barbara ladled out the soup. There were crispy pickles, potato salad and condiments on the table and, once the soup was distributed, Barbara was asking how many wanted hot coffee or tea. No one wanted coffee so only the electric tea pot was on and there was always green ice tea ready and waiting. There was a large fruit torte, stuffed dates, custard pudding and a variety of nuts on the side board for dessert.

"I've never had lox on an English muffin before," said Lynn, "I'm liking this; the capers give it a little kick."

Sheila said, "Jan, Sharon asked about our first meeting. I couldn't help laughing, but my lips were sealed."

"Well telling this story they'll know that I am ridiculously clumsy and it will explain my latest, ah, mishaps," said Jan. So Jan went through the story of her Thanksgiving introduction to the family. They were all hysterical, especially at the part when she went sailing across the floor revealing her winking Mickey Mouse tushy tattoo.

"You had to be there to get the truly full picture of complete humiliation," said Jan, "I think Mary wanted to cry over her beautiful rug, but they were all so kind and sweet to me, I fell in love with the whole family."

"And they fell in love with you," said Sheila, "but don't be surprised if they back away when they see you with a hot pot or knife in your hand," said Sheila, and they laughed again.

Then the other women started telling stories about awkward moments. Mamie described the evening her parents were meeting her future in-laws. Her father was a practicing alcoholic at the time, and before dessert arrived he excused himself from the table. The others thought he was going to use the restroom but Mamie and her mother knew better. He just decided to go home, and she was mortified.

"You mean he didn't say anything about leaving?" asked Gia, incredulous.

"No, and it wasn't the first time," Mamie laughed, "but luckily it was the last. He got really sick that night and it scared him. He quit drinking and never went back. So there was a happy ending."

There was finally a lull in the conversation and Julia addressed the group, "Ladies, it's already two forty-five. How about resuming class at three and we'll have a snack in the great room about five-thirty, meditation if you like, at six, and dinner at seven?" They all agreed

"Geez, how can you think about dinner, I'm stuffed," said Donna.

The rain had started back up and it was really pounding now.

Sharon said, "It doesn't look like we'll be back in the Jacuzzi any time soon."

Sammy jumped up on the table and did what looked like a little dance, then sat as if waiting for a reward.

"Now you know better than that Sammy," said Julia, "no jumping on the table, get down." Sammy slowly picked up his paws and slithered down using N.C.'s knee as a step to push himself away from the table. He meekly meowed and circled Julia, who couldn't resist giving him a piece of tuna fish.

Vivian reminded N.C. that she should take advantage of another acupuncture session and N.C. agreed, asking if she could come in about four, she wanted to listen to Barbara's discussion first. They finished up dessert and went off to use the bathrooms before class. Jan was happy to go to her room, she was really enjoying her book.

They gathered in the great room for class, each taking a chair and forming a circle. Barbara posed the question, "What do you ladies think of our topic: sanity or the lack of it in artists."

Lynn started with, "You always hear stories about certain 'mad artists' like Van Gogh or Silvia Plath. I wrote poetry when I was young and it seemed like I wrote best when I was depressed."

"Did you write very much at other times?" asked Barbara.

"Now that I think of it, only when I had to for a class, the other times were usually when there was a boyfriend breakup."

"I think that is more the youthful expression," said Barbara, "Young people have very acute feelings when dealing with a budding romance, or an extended one for that matter. Their bodies have changed so quickly and they haven't developed the emotional sophistication to understand the signals the other person may be giving. They may be attracted to someone physically and assume that person has all the wonderful character traits they want in a mate. Therein lies the disappointment and drama that young people go through."

"I'm still not over that stage," said Gia, and they laughed.

"The difference would be, I hope," said Barbara as she smiled at Gia, "your discovery and recovery time would be much shorter. You might get angry, hurt or upset, but unless we are talking about a long term relationship, you wouldn't feel like you were in the middle of a tragedy of epic proportion. My point is there is a difference using an art form as an outlet and being truly committed to a lifelong pursuit of that art form. My other point would be that just because someone is an artist, and a bit crazy, does not mean their work is good."

"I was in a poetry class once," said Sharon, "And one of the craziest girls I knew was really into writing. She would write pages of poetry and make copies for the whole class. The problem was we couldn't understand any of it. It was embarrassingly disjointed and incomprehensible. We all wanted to be kind but most of us were speechless and could only say 'well that's you alright' or some other inane comment. I think she took the attitude that we were just not on her intellectual level."

"In college it seemed like a lot of the art students relished taking on a persona of being different, kooky and eccentric," said Mamie.

"You know the theory of the artist insanity goes back to the Greeks," Barbara offered, "Aristotle was the first to connect creativity with depression. Plato, in Phaedrus, said that artists were bestowed with Divine Madness. Socrates dismissed poets who were 'not touched by the madness of the muses.' He thought sane poets were 'eclipsed by the inspired madmen.' And yet recent studies suggest that people are most creative when they are in a positive mood. And, generally speaking, the artists who we consider to be certifiable did not create their great works while they were having an um, let's call it 'a crazy episode.'"

"I did a rotation in Nursing School, in a psych ward," said Sheila, "and I didn't see anything impressive about their art work. Maybe knowing the anticipated reaction of say Aristotle, Plato or Socrates— artists may have behaved in quirky, flamboyant ways to satisfy that expectation."

"Good point," commented Barbara.

"And who today really knows what they considered to be madness?" responded Barbara. "Throughout history the usage of words and the perception of the definitions can change too. If someone had a seizure they might have thought that was temporary madness, or that person was touched by the gods. I think someone like Bernie Madoff was crazy, but not in the sense the ancients would perceive. Madness has to do with the expectations of society too."

"I wonder if the ratio of crazy people in business, politics, blue collar workers, secretaries, etc. would be all that different," mused Sharon.

"I have always thought that there is an element of creativity in all walks of life," said Barbara. "A business deal can be very creative. A salesperson can be very creative in the approach taken to deal with a client. The so-called experts seem to only apply the 'creative insanity' to the arts. The cavemen ancestors had to be creative too. But ladies, if you want to finish your paintings, I suggest we get to work."

They went back to their canvases. A while later Sammy was meowing at the door. Barbara excused herself and said she would be back in a few minutes and N.C. went to the massage room for her acupuncture treatment.

Vivian went through her ritual of washing hands and dampening the cotton swab with alcohol. She wiped the areas to be punctured and proceeded administering the needles. She put some soothing music on and N.C., once again, proclaimed she would probably be asleep in a few minutes.

"That's good, it works best if you are relaxed," advised Vivian. "One of us will come back to turn the needles in about ten minutes."

Vivian went to find Rose, who was now inspecting what needed to be cleaned, straightened or replenished. They went to the other office, what they were calling the herb office, to consult about a fertility treatment. They decided that a good detox of yellow dock, burdock and dandelion should be the first step. Then a tonic of nettles, red clover, red raspberry, oat Straw, lemon balm, skullcap and rose hips; and finally a hormonal balancing compound of vitex, kong quai, maca, false unicorn, wild yam and squaw vine.

"Hopefully, that will do the trick," said Vivian.

"Why can't we just cause her to be fertile? It would be so much more reliable," said Rose, as she used the mortar and pestle to grind down the first three herbs. Vivian was removing the different, and clearly labeled, canisters of herbs from the shelves and arranging them in sequence of use.

"Hasn't Maddy drilled it into you that we make every possible effort to use only the things of the earth?" Vivian emphasized. "We only want to make a ripple in the ocean of humans, not a title wave. We try not to interfere with the natural course of things or events. We just want to give them a little nudge. Besides, in the interest of full disclosure, we did that centuries ago in China and see what happened."

"How about the Force Field, wasn't that interfering?" Rose stated flatly.

"We do what is needed at the time, I didn't say never. But the Force Field only senses beings and sends them a mental command to go elsewhere. They recipient isn't aware of how they get that information, they just move to a different location. By the way, making the beds with your mind power is just not acceptable, those things don't go unnoticed. We need to understand the human condition and there is no cheating, understand? Oops, I better go tweak N.C.'s needles."

CHAPTER 47

The Neighbors

The road, leading to the ranch, was about a quarter mile and then it forked. The long ranch driveway was on the right and a poorly maintained, weedy driveway was on the left. That driveway winded around and up about an eighth mile and dead-ended at an abandoned and sadly, dilapidated old farm house, probably built around the turn of the century and neglected since the fifties. The family who originally owned the property had grown over the years and the now twenty-two descendent owners never seemed to be able to agree on when to sell. So the old property stood as testimony to an earlier time.

One of the descendents was a nineteen year-old student dropout, Devin Connolly. He and his parents lived in Encino, California until he enrolled in the University of California at Santa Barbara. He started out well enough; then he found a girlfriend. He was shy and never popular in high school, so in an effort to impress his new found love, he started experimenting with drugs. This escalated from dabbling on the weekend to scoring cocaine as often as possible. He ran through his allowance money and attending classes started to interfered with his lifestyle. By the time his parents caught on, he and his girlfriend, Lisa Brunell, had a committed relationship with crack.

They had both sold everything of value they owned and had very little left of a small trust fund left by Devin's grandmother. There was a second trust fund, from his grandfather, with a substantial amount of money, but Devin could not touch that until he was thirty. In his case, that was a wise decision.

Lisa and her sister, Lauren, had also been at UCSB. They joked that they were Irish twins, born ten months apart. Lauren delayed college, at first, and then took classes at Santa Monica City College before transferring to UCSB with her sister. Their dysfunctional family left them with few tools to deal with the temptations before them. They had been good students in high school but, in the College atmosphere, the lure of drugs overcame them and now they did little else. They were both disowned by family and friends as a result of their lifestyle. The once sweet, young girls had evolved into seedy characters who took a contemptuous attitude toward the rest of the world.

Lauren had recently hooked up with Donny Davis. He was a little older, twenty three, and took over the role of alpha male in the group. On Devin's suggestion, they had retreated to the old farm house to party and figure out their next move. They recently added a string of burglaries and shoplifting to their resume. They were smart enough to wear gloves and only went into homes when there appeared to be no one home; but they were becoming desperate and bolder. It was too difficult to unload goods, so they focused on finding cash.

Lisa was the taller of the sisters at five foot six to Lauren's five foot five. They both had sandy brown hair with the remnants of lighter blond streaks almost grown out. Thin and gaunt, the once, not so long ago, pretty faces had blotches of red and a few scabs that testified to their habits.

Devin and Donny were a contrast in looks and temperament. Devin was about five-nine with a thin frame and a wispy beard that did nothing to improve his appearance. Once, twenty pounds heavier, he had shiny brown hair and a clear complexion. Now he was wiry and sallow looking.

Donny, until a couple of months ago, had been taking better care of himself. He had been fired from the family manufacturing business and then obtained employment at a local hardware store. He was able to work and party on the weekend; then it was every night—until it all caught up with him. He was six foot, with black hair, hazel eyes and balanced features, but his good looks were fading fast.

The farm house was a wood frame with three bedrooms, one bath, a kitchen with adjacent eating area, and a living room with a fireplace. The few outbuildings, dilapidated as they were, consisted of a chicken coop, storage shed and the remaining traces of a burned down barn. A decaying stove, toilet, and sink littered the front yard. The house had wood planks and large punched out holes in the walls. Cobwebs draped the corners and only a few windows remained intact, most of them stuffed with rags or old newspapers. There was dirt and debris strewn on the floors and one old carpet. A dusty mid-century couch lay flush to the floor, it's stubby legs long gone. Three old crates performed double-duty as tables or chairs, depending on the need. The kitchen was devoid of appliances, and pieces of wall where cabinets once hung.

They were able to clean up the fire place, it was their only source of heat, eating beans and hot dogs, held on sticks over the flames. They had been trying to figure out what to do next when Lisa spoke up, "There are people at that Serendipity Ranch, up the fork in the road, and four or five cars. Maybe we could steal one and sell it."

"Brilliant, should we put an ad in the L.A. times or the Ventura County Star?" Donny said sarcastically.

"She's only trying to help," Lauren said giving him an evil eye. "Maybe Lisa and I could go down and look around, see who is there."

"Now that's better, but it's pouring out," Donny reminded them.

"Even better, no one will be out and it's dark. We can even peek in the windows. There's a box of plastic garbage bags in the car that we can wear. If we get caught, we're just a couple of poor homeless girls looking for a handout," said Lauren.

"Well that's not a stretch, you are," said Donny laughing and slapping Devin on the back. Lauren cringed at that uncomfortable revelation. She hadn't had that image of herself, but now, especially looking at her sister, she realized how far they had spiraled out of control. She put those thoughts out of her mind.

The rain was pouring down as Lisa and Lauren carefully maneuvered themselves through the wooded area in between the two properties.

"I think we should have taken the road," Lisa yelled over the storm at Lauren.

"I doubt it, that road is like a stream right now and I don't want to get caught in anybody's headlights while we're walking around," Lauren shouted back.

They huddled together, each in a raincoat fashioned out of black garbage bags and holding a large piece of cardboard over their heads. By the time they reached the ranch house they were reasonably dry in the midriff but their hands, heads, arms and legs, from the kneecap down, were soaking. Shivering, they approached the window of the back door, but all they could see was a small mudroom entrance and a long hallway. They struggled in the puddles around the left side of the house, the mud sucking at their thin tennis shoes. They could see a few empty bedrooms, but no people, and they back-tracked to the other side. They saw a woman sleeping on a massage table with needles protruding from various parts of her body.

"What is this, some kind of treatment center?" said Lisa.

"Who knows, but I haven't seen any men yet, and that's a good thing," said Lauren.

"Ok Martha Stewart, so now what? Do we just go in and steal whatever we can and make a run for it?" asked Lisa.

"Come on, Lisa. The plan is to look the place over and get back to the guys," chided Lauren.

They went a little further but a couple of the windows had the shades drawn. They continued and came to a large window with the drapes open. Lisa was the closest so she squatted for a moment and peeked over the ledge. She reported back to Lauren that there were a bunch of women painting in there and she still didn't see any men. They didn't think it could rain any harder, but it did. The wind picked up and caused water to rush sideways, so now the rain was dripping down their necks like a cold shower.

"If there are no men it shouldn't be too hard," said Lisa.

"Difficult," Lauren corrected as they continued their struggle back the way they came. They were almost to the parking lot area, by the back door, when Lisa fell in the mud dragging Lauren down with her. Suddenly, two older women appeared before them, with umbrellas, helping to pull them to their feet. Lisa thought they were incredibly strong for old ladies; the shorter one had a grip like a vice.

"Oh dear, are you alright, no broken bones I hope? You girls had better get in the house, you'll catch your death out here," warned Julia.

They moved in tandem to the back door and were greeted by a smiling Rose. She had towels on the floor and in her arms. The three fussed over the girls, removing the plastic bags and wrapping their wet heads. They ushered the girls to the public bathroom where there was a small table piled with clean sweat suits and more towels. Maddy was running the hot water as Barbara came down the hall with two cups of tea. Julia had locked the back door and, after introductions were finished, she explained to the girls that Rose would be helping them with whatever they needed while they cleaned up. Excusing herself to go start dinner, Julia heard Rose encouraging them to drink their tea while she, Maddy, and Barbara walked down the hall planning what to do next. Vivian found Julia, Maddy and Barbara in the business office waiting her arrival.

"Another thing we didn't have to contend with in the old days; drug addicts," complained Maddy.

"Oh, we did too. There have been drug addicts for centuries, in different and varying degrees," said Julia.

"Oh you didn't come when we were here in the sixties and early seventies, Maddy. We had to help with a very gruesome scene, one of the worst. You know it all started out so beautifully, flower power and love. Then it gave way to hard drugs and that idiot Tim with his LSD. I asked him once if everyone dropped out who could afford all the parties he loved so much, and all he could do was laugh," Barbara told them.

"I heard all about it. There was that other nasty little piece of work, Charley, who turned father-hungry teenagers into killing machines," said Maddy.

"And he didn't even have the cojones to be there himself," added Vivian.

"That's why we needed that little inspirational chat with that nice attorney. Thinking outside the box is what they call it now," said Julia. "But let's get back to our present dilemma, shall we. This is going to be a difficult business if we don't go about it carefully."

"How do you want us to proceed?" asked Barbara.

"We too need to think outside the box," Julia started, "Let's invite the girls to dinner. Barbara has already put a mild sedative in their tea, just enough to take the edge off without making them groggy. If they get along with the group, we might get them to stay the night. Let's see how things pan out. We'll have to change the evening activities depending what the girls do. We need to be flexible and we may need a diversion. I'll leave that up to you Barbara."

"Sure, should I tell the others about our new arrivals now?" Barbara asked.

"You might as well, but try to keep them in the Great Room while we sort a few things out. Serve them some wine and cheese," Julia said.

"Maddy will you go ahead and help Barbara with a couple of trays for the ladies?"

"Sure, do you think the men will show up?"

"Probably, but who knows when," said Julia.

Vivian went back to the massage room to tweak the acupuncture needles, for the second time, and found N.C. still fast asleep on the table. She did what she needed to do and tip-toed out of the room.

CHAPTER 48

Rose, the Girls and Dinner

Sharon loved being in the kitchen with Julia and had excused herself from the class to see how she could help with dinner. Julia had Sharon combine pine nuts and garlic in the food processor for fifteen seconds and then add the basil leaves, kosher salt and black pepper, and while the processor was running she added olive oil until the pesto was pureed. Then spinach and lemon juice was added and pureed, and finally the parmesan cheese. Sharon placed the pesto in the refrigerator. Meanwhile, Julia had cooked the fusilli pasta. She told Sharon that once the pasta was room temperature, she would add the pesto and cooked peas along with more parmesan cheese.

Julia had Sharon pounding chicken breasts, sprinkling salt and pepper, dipping the breasts in egg whites, the bread crumbs while she was slicing mozzarella cheese and finishing up the tomato sauce. Once the chicken was prepared, with cheese slices on top and tomato sauce generously poured to drench all, it was put in the oven. They then rinsed the asparagus and snapped off the ends. Julia salt and peppered the stalks and then Sharon drizzled the extra virgin olive oil back and forth. That was set aside to be placed under the broiler a short time before dinner. All the while they chatted amicably as Julia retrieved a huge bowl of strawberries from the refrigerator. They cut up the berries and placed them in a large pot with orange juice and Triple Sec Liqueur.

"We'll bring that up to a boil," she explained, "let it simmer a minute, and then cool down. It's simple and delicious poured over my angel food cake with a dollop of whipped cream."

Julia chose this time to tell Sharon about the two young ladies, who are probably drug users and homeless, explaining the hosts felt the need to feed and shelter them tonight. She was concerned about the reaction of the other guests.

"I do hope the other ladies will understand and not object to the intrusion," confessed Julia.

"As long as I have my bed, you can invite an army, I don't care," said Sharon

"My only concern Julia, and please forgive me, but I hope you are not being too naïve about the ways of the world. We should really keep a close eye on them, just to be on the safe side," Sharon concluded.

"Oh you are so right dear," said Julia inwardly amused, "but if you don't risk anything, you risk even more. Well that's what Erica Jong said once." Julia excused herself to go check on the girls.

Rose was no-nonsense when it came to getting the job done. She had the shower water at the right temperature and helped Lisa out of her jeans, which were soaked and caked with mud. She had set out the soap and shampoo so as Lisa stepped in she was helping Lauren with her jeans and sweatshirt. She piled the dirty things on top of a towel and rolled it up like a giant snow ball.

Not wanting to leave them alone, she went about cleaning up the mud splattered floor and sink until they were both scrubbed spotless. When they were ready to get out she handed them towels.

"I can help you detox your bodies if you like," Rose said, in a very matter of fact tone. "I know those sores on your faces, and skin discoloration, are fairly recent from crack. I have an ointment that can help, as long as you stop using. Your teeth aren't too bad yet but I'd say within a year, if you're not dead, then you'll be toothless and look like you're in your forties," as she was talking, Rose pulled a photo from her pocket and showed them the picture of a woman. "See this girl, she's twenty-four" and the girls gasped.

"No way, are you kidding?" they chimed.

"Shit, I don't believe it, she looks like my alcoholic mother," said Lauren.

"You want to be a real chip off the old block?" Rose said rhetorically with an almost challenging smile as she handed them sweats and underwear. They had heard this all before, but for some reason, it seemed to hit home with more impact. Maybe it was the cool, laissez-faire attitude that Rose projected with no coddling, pleading or sympathizing; just the facts.

"So who is that?" Lisa asked as Julia knocked on the door.

Rose grabbed the bundle of wet things and, as she turned to exit she said, "Oh that's you in three years."

Julia walked in as the girls stood, in various stages of dress, with their mouths open.

"Oh dear, have you two been the recipients of Rose's two minute analysis? That young woman is uncanny. I don't know what she said to you but trust me, she regurgitates the truth. How did you enjoy your tea?"

They still looked befuddled but came around saying "Thank you, it was good." Julia thought that somewhere, along the way, someone took the time to teach them a few manners.

"My pleasure, you are welcome. Now come along, I want you to meet our other guests." Julia handed them each a pair of flip flops. "Oh, you might want to dry your hair first." She disappeared for a few moments and was back with another hair dryer and clean combs and brushes saying, "You may keep these." She then closed the door but waited outside until the hairdryers went silent. She escorted them to the Great Room and on the way stopped by the kitchen, made introductions and told Sharon to join the group in the Great Room too.

Barbara and Maddy had brought two large trays containing wine, glasses, cheese, crackers and fruit. They opted for small plastic dessert plates to make the transporting easier. Maddy had a white table cloth over her arm and, in a matter of moments, set up a lovely display of refreshments on a card table.

Barbara went around to each easel to admire and assist shading with paint. She then announced that they should take their break and perhaps finish up for the day so they could do a half hour meditation before dinner. Once the ladies were sipping their wine she explained the current situation with the two young girls and said, "We are hoping that you ladies do not object to our decision to help two young girls who appear to be in distress. There was chatter and claims 'of course not' or 'as long as they're not serial killers' and laughter. Only Sheila, the nurse, thought a little deeper, having seen so many homeless in the ER and knowing many were drug users. She, like Sharon, feared the older ladies were too naïve to realize these girls could be trouble.

N.C. had been poked and tweaked enough and she returned to the Great Room to find the ladies cleaning up and preparing to do a guided meditation; Maddy doing the guiding. She advised Gia that Vivian was waiting for her and Gia walked out as Julia and Sharon were escorting Lisa and Lauren in. Introductions were made and more chairs were added. Julia, Barbara and Rose returned to the kitchen to finish dinner, set the table and collect their thoughts.

Meanwhile, Donny and Devin sat around the fireplace with a six-pack and a joint. They had no hard drugs left and, had they not been exhausted from their antics the night before, would have been much antsier. They both had been from affluent families but Donny was newer to this vagabond existence than Devin; he didn't like it. They had pounded an old couch, with a couple of pieces of wood, to get the dust and loose dirt off when Donny turned to Devin saying,

"Holy shit, those bitches have been gone more than an hour. They probably did something stupid."

"What do you think we should do, get over there?" Devin asked. "Or wait a few hours, I don't want anyone messin' around here."

"Let's go into town and get some more beer. I think we should take a look around in a couple of hours, if they don't get back before that," said Donny. "If the cops come by here when we're gone we'll be able to see their tracks in the mud when we come back. But I don't think the girls are stupid enough to say anything about us."

"Maybe not Lauren, but I don't know about Lisa. I think she may be a few rungs short of a ladder," added Devin and they both cracked up.

The kitchen was a busy scene with Julia and Barbara carrying dishes to the table as Rose got out the silverware and napkins. Sammy was meandering around, trying to find a comfortable spot to nap.

"What shall we do about the rain?" Barbara asked Julia.

"I think it is to our advantage to leave things as they are, I don't want to make it any easier for them. And the Cancer Society will get an even more generous check than I planned," Julia added.

Rose looked at Julia with a questioning expression, "Do you think they are salvageable?"

"Always one who gets to the crux of things, you are Rose, but I don't know, free will is at hand. It is perplexing and not at all logical why one chooses a path of destruction. Some will claw their way back to society while many feel they have gone too far and no longer have a connection to decency. The ego can become enmeshed in a subculture, with its own mores and vernacular, to the point of losing oneself; their old life having no relevance any more. How strong the pullback to the dominant society is, for them, what will make all the difference. We just have to let things play out and hope for the best."

"They were both attractive girls. It's sad to see them deteriorating physically like that," said Barbara, then caught herself. "But I guess it would be sad, no matter what they looked like."

Rose got the glasses and wine out. Barbara mixed up a salad, adding almond slivers, pumpkin seeds and raisins. Everything was about ready when Jan came in the kitchen, looking rested and relaxed she said, "Hey, did I miss anything?"

Then she proceeded to the side table and poured herself a glass of wine. Julia filled her in on the new guests. Jan was feeling a lot better; her only comment being "the more the merrier, as they say."

The group in the Great Room had sat on chairs with their feet on the floor as Maddy repeated the same instructions given the night before. She led them in some visual imaging exercises and they were now trying to quiet the mind and clear their thoughts.

It wasn't easy, especially for Lisa and Lauren. They were actually relaxing and both were kind of enjoying themselves. That is, until thoughts of Donny and Devin crept in. They had talked about the boys before and came to the same conclusion; things were getting really bad. Devin had been a nice guy at first and Lisa actually felt she was the one who coerced him into doing crack. One minute she would feel badly about that and the next she would tell herself that he was a big boy, she wasn't responsible for him. He had changed though, a lot, especially since meeting up with Donny. The kindness seemed to have leeched out of his body and now he was attempting to sound like a rapper on the loose. She knew he was trying to impress Donny, but in doing so he seemed to have lost any real feelings for her. She admitted to herself that she really hadn't cared for him and had used him to get what she needed. But they had spent a lot of time together and, until recently, she developed a sort of brotherly love for him.

Lauren had joined her sister before Donny came along. They all met at a party and Lauren was attracted to the big, manly looking guy; that didn't last long. He had a way of using people up and dismissing them from his attention when they served his purpose. Everything had to be his way, a true alpha male with a mean streak that screamed to be unleashed. The girls were starting to fear his moods. Lauren could see the vacancy in his eyes, like her father, that could sometimes chill her to the bone.

Lisa was thinking how funny it was that the old ladies had taken them by surprise. They were so dirty, wet and cold; they decided to just play along.

They were kind of like twins in that they could give each other a silent look and know that they had the same idea, they were checking the place out for what they could steal, but they hadn't had a chance to verbally communicate. They had someone with them every minute and Lauren was suspicious about why these people were being so nice; but it was good to feel clean and warm. The tea really relaxed them and she wasn't looking forward to being back out in the rain.

CHAPTER 49

Devin, Donny and Dinner

D evin and Donny had gone into town for beer but after, on Donny's suggestion, they were planning to go to the home of Two Tone Jenkins. His real name was Henry and no one seemed to know where the 'Two Tone' moniker came from, but no one dared call him Henry. He was a notorious local dealer in everything from grass to heroin. Donny planned on ripping him off and Devin was there to help.

The house was outside of town and looked like any three bedroom ranch house in any lower middle class section of California, with one exception, it was immaculate. The rest of the block might have parts of old cars or toys lounging about lawns and crying for attention, but not Two Tone's. He was compulsive about order and cleanliness and on a night like this, with the potential of mud being tracked into his living room, he was cautious about allowing anyone in the house. They rang the bell. There were a number of locks that had to be undone before the door opened to the spectacle of this character. Two Tone was about five foot eight and the his fast food choices made him look as wide as he was tall—a heart attack waiting to happen.

"Hey assholes," was his typical greeting. "What are you looking for tonight?"

Donny and Devin had based their plan on being in the house, so not gaining entry left them dumbfounded. Finally Donny spoke up, "Can you let us in double T? We're soaking." Donny asked.

"Exactly, so I see, and that's why you're not messing up my crib, dog," Two Tone answered. "Go around to the back door."

"Now what?" asked Devin as they negotiated across puddles and stepping stones around the house to reach the back.

They got to the door and could hear another series of locks clicking off, and then the door opened. They were told they could enter but only stand by the doorway on the sheet of plastic strategically placed and taped down securely. Once inside the kitchen, to the right of the door, was another man seated at a pristine nineteen fifties Formica table with a shotgun facing the newcomers.

"So you're in, what do you want?" Two Tone asked impatiently. He loved that his profession of choice allowed him the luxury of calling people assholes and basically being rude anytime he wanted.

"Just a couple of joints for now. Can you roll them? My papers got all wet," he explained.

"You fucking jack offs, you're bothering me for a couple of joints? Are you crazy," said Two Tone.

"No we'll be back later," Donny insisted, "we're gonna hookup with the bitches we live with and hit that ranch on the top of the hill. A bunch of old women are up there, it should be an easy score. The girls are up there now checking everything out. I was in the area and wanted to know if we could pick up two ounces of coke later. I dropped my phone in a puddle and I don't have your number now."

Devin was thankful that Donny came up with a halfway plausible story, but Two Tone looked suspicious and glanced over at his buddy. He told Devin and Donny to put their hands up and he frisked them. He only came up with a pocket knife in Devin's jacket and laughed. Then he asked his friend," Cap, have you got a couple of joints for these losers?"

Cap stood up holding the shotgun by his side. He reached in his pocket and took out an old Prince Albert tin, he flipped open the top revealing his stash of joints. He walked over and handed two of them to Two Tone, who in turn gave them to Donny. Two Tone didn't take drugs, other than an occasional joint or a beer, and looked down on his clients as lowlife losers. Donny came up with the last of his money and they left.

They got back in the car and Devin said, "What were we thinking? This guy wouldn't be in business as long as he has without being ready for trouble."

Donny was an amateur boxer and thought he could surprise double T with his fisticuffs using Devin as back up. They never saw anyone else at Two Tone's and were unaware that there was always back up. Double T liked to keep his body guard in the next room, viewing through a two-way mirror. He figured he was better able to size-up whether a customer was trouble, or not.

"Fuck, well that's just great," said Donny. "We've got a half tank of gas and we're broke. Those bitches better have come up with something," and they drove off.

Meditation time was over and the group was getting up and stretching. Sharon went out first to see if she could do anything for Julia. Rose was keeping a close eye on her charges while everyone washed hands before dinner. Julia had just placed the last dish, asparagus, on the counter top. It didn't take long for a queue to circle the kitchen as dinner was set up buffet style. Lisa was the first to chow down and said, louder than she meant, "Oh my god, this is really delicious."

She couldn't remember the last time she actually sat at a normal dinner table, relaxed and enjoyed a healthy, homemade meal; she was relishing every bite. Lauren didn't stop to comment but anyone could see they were in culinary heaven.

Everyone was hungry since dinner had been somewhat delayed, but once they had put a dent in their caloric intake, the chatter began again. None of them wanted to put Lisa and Lauren on the spot, but they were all curious about their backgrounds. Lauren was sitting next to N.C. who could have had a doctorate in extracting information from people, if there was such a thing. N.C. was gentle in her tone and had a way of making you feel you were talking to your long, lost best friend; people just trusted her.

Lauren put their lives in a nutshell, explaining that both their parents and paternal grand-parents had been alcoholics. The family had been financially comfortable, their father being a well known successful attorney. They were functioning members of the community until the girls reached high school when the cumulative effects of their lifestyle could no longer be hidden from the outside world.

Their father's drinking resulted in a bitter and abusive temperament, while their mother seemed to retire behind a curtain of depression. The girls found themselves basically on their own. They were embarrassed to have company at the house and found their shame caused a riff in other relationships.

They were both able to attend UCSB, but when their grades reflected non attendance and failures, their parents cut them off, their father spitting curses at every fiber of their being. They were both book smart and without guidance in the terrain of society's underbelly, they ended up clueless and dependent.

Lauren was tired of it all and disgusted with herself. N.C. had asked if they had any relatives that might help them and was told their maternal grandparents were kind and loving people but lived in Northern California, and were not close. There had been a falling out between the grandparents and their mother and there had been no communication, other than birthday and Christmas cards, for a number of years. All this had been said in hushed tones while the others were talking back and forth at the table, entertaining each other with show business gossip.

Julia got up and whispered to Maddy, Rose and then Vivian to come in the kitchen and help her with desert. Barbara was talking with Lisa, so she was left undisturbed. They went in the kitchen and were breaking up the angel food cake in a large bowl. Julia got another large bowl out of the refrigerator containing strawberries that had been cooked in orange juice and triple sec. She was pouring the mixture over the angel food cake and whispering to the others, "Those little wankers will be here within the hour and we need a plan," Julia advise., "Let's not make it easy for them."

So they decided they would coerce the girls into having whatever treatment they might like while the others had their yoga class, maybe followed by a zumba class or anything to distract. They would leave that up to Barbara. Now that the cake was covered with the strawberry mixture, they ladled it in to small desert bowls, squirting whipped cream and a strawberry on top for presentation.

The talk and laughter went on at the table while Lynn was summing up a story about Hans, from the cooking show she had been on, and his soon to be ex-wife, Emily. Hans had a long time girlfriend waiting in the wings, stage left, as his wife arrived and was waiting, stage right. The wife recognized the woman and had previously seen rather racy emails from her that Hans had printed out and left unattended on his desk.

"As soon as the director said 'cut', that's what Emily planned on doing. She ran on the set and grabbed a knife, before anyone realized what she was doing. Hans had his back to her and noticed the horrified face of a stage hand looking behind him. As he was about to turn and look, Emily stabbed him in the ass. Then the girlfriend, scared to death, ran off as the rest of us snapped out of shock and had to subdue Emily while they continued cursing and screaming at each other; talk about the 'War of Roses'."

They were laughing and then realized the older women were clearing the dishes to make way for dessert. The rest of the group followed suit and as they deposited the dishes near the sink, they picked up their dessert plates from the counter. Everyone loved Julia's 'strawberry delight' and several went back for seconds. Julia was trying to move things along but, when she suggested that they do their yoga class, the response was less than enthusiastic; they were moaning and rubbing tummies. Even Donna was saying they were probably too full to perform well. Barbara suggested they play games in the Great Room and listen to some R&B music. They could let their stomachs rest a while and then have a Latin Dance lesson; that agenda was received with a more enthusiastic response.

The coffee, tea and wine were on the side table. Vivian suggested they bring their beverages to the Great Room. They had listened to soft jazz, Anita Baker, during dinner and everyone seemed happy and mellow. Sammy was sharing the favor of his presence among all the legs under the table. Compliments went out again for the dinner as they deposited the remaining dishes on the counter and picked up the various libations to take to the Great Room.

Jan excused herself and returned to her room to read and relax.

Vivian and Maddy took Lisa and Lauren to the massage rooms for facials.

CHAPTER 50

Bad Boys

They drove back to the old house and finished their liquid courage; Donny was saving the joints for later. He had a big hunting knife that he kept in the trunk, but no other weapons.

"Hey man, you got anything better than a pocket knife?" he said to Devin.

Devin searched the place and found an old baseball bat saying, "This is all I could find," as he swung at an imaginary ball. They still were not sure who or how many people were at the ranch, and they needed to come up with a strategy.

"Do you think the cops picked them up?" asked Devin.

"Those stupid cunts, how am I supposed to know? They've been gone long enough that if anyone called the cops, they would be at the station by now. If they said anything about us I think the cops would be here by now; unless they were here and gone already, but I didn't see any tire tracks," he surmised. "We better go through the woods and stay clear of the road and driveway, just in case."

So they took their weapons and started out through the wooded area, between the two properties, commiserating about alternatives on how they would enter. Donny impressed on Devin that they had to be quiet, and the best scenario would be if they could sneak in and out without any confrontation. They were almost ankle deep in mud, with the rain still coming down. Devin suggested, when they find a way in, they should take off their shoes. They could now see the parking lot, but things looked very dark from where they stood. They decided to split up and each take a different side to check things out. Devin went to the right and passed several windows, but the shades were all drawn and he couldn't see or hear anything. He moved along cautiously in the deep mud toward a faint light. This was the kind of house that was reversed he thought. The front faced the view while the back faced the parking lot.

The windows were much larger, with only a very faint crack in the drapes, not wide enough to see anything. He could only hear music and a few muffled voices. He thought it was an old Marvin Gaye song. Then the music changed to something Latin. The view window in the front, might have afforded a better opportunity, but he didn't want to risk his shadow alerting them to his presence. He started working his way back to find Donny.

Donny had gone to the left and passed by several windows. He could only make out, in the crack between the shade and window, one dark bedroom. He could see lights as he moved forward and gradually heard music. The only window he thought he might see into was too risky to approach. He moved backwards and bumped into Devin behind him. "Shit," was his automatic response as Devin went down on one knee. Donny quickly turned and helped to keep Devin from a full fall into the mud whispering "Asshole." The bat served to balance him too but the thick end was now about five inches in the mud. Donny, looking like he had done this before, took off his jacket and wrapped it around his hand and forearm. He had dropped his knife during the collision and decided it wasn't worth the trouble to retrieve it. They moved further back towards the parking lot and the vacant bedroom. Thinking most of the occupants were in the front of the house, he tapped the pane of glass with his wrapped fist once, twice and on the third time he cracked and broke it. He then tried to find the latch but had no luck and decided to break a second pane. When the second was done he hoisted Devin up so he could put his hand in and locate the latch. Having unlocked the window, Devin was able to push it up and, once open, Donny pushed him through, followed by his shoes.

To his surprise, Devin landed on a carpet of sticky mouse traps saying, "Oh fuck." They were the kind that would trap a rodent in the sticky glue of an eight by five inch pad, rendering the animal unable to move. The animal would then either die of starvation, be killed by the trapper or be eaten by something higher on the food chain. Now Devin was wrestling with about five of the pads to no avail. The one on his head was the most disconcerting; Devin had a sneaking suspicion he would have to cut a good chunk of hair off to remove it. One of his socks had fallen off on the way into the house so he was able to dislodge one foot by removing the other sock, but not so for the bare foot that was now hopelessly stuck on the gooey surface. The window ledge was too high for Donny to hoist himself up without help. He heard Devin curse and make some frustrated sounds.

"What's going on, are you ok? said Donny in a loud whisper, "I need you to open the back door."

"You'll see, I'm going to need your help too," said Devin. "Go ahead to the back door."

Devin had the look of someone in a slapstick comedy. He had fallen in the house, mostly on his right side; his head, right hand, right forearm, right foot and kneecap had each been caught. The knee cap offender he was able to dislodge from his jeans, leaving a very thick sticky residue just waiting to attach itself to something new. But when he tried removing the pad attached to his foot, without sitting down, he lost his balance and fell on the floor, sitting on another pad. He gave up and tried hopping on one leg down the hall to unlock the back door. Just before he got to the door he could hear footsteps coming down the hall and one of the doors open. He hurried, thinking they might make a getaway, but as soon as he unlocked the back door Donny pushed his way in, apparently abandoning the idea of subtlety.

Rose and Julia were coming down the hall, Julia carrying what appeared to be an old fashioned doctors' satchel; Jan was peeking out her bedroom door. Julia was passing Jan's door and turned to her saying, "Please go back to bed, dear. We have a little situation here but I don't want you to be alarmed. It will be no problem, I assure you."

Jan, as much as it was against her nature, retreated back to her room but listened by the door. Donny was dumbfounded when he got a look at Devin and then caught sight of a pudgy, elderly woman and a young thin petite woman walking toward them. Mentally, he sized up the situation and thought, 'no big deal.'

"Caught a big one didn't we?" Julia whispered to Rose.

Before the women could say anything to the men, Donny said, "We don't want any trouble, we won't hurt anyone. Where are the girls?"

Julia smiled and in her most proper, pleasant, English accent answered, "Well young man, that is certainly a relief, and we don't want to hurt you, but we will if it becomes necessary," still with a smile on her face. Rose, on the other hand, seemed to have her typical expression of untroubled observance.

Donny was confused at their response. He had expected fear, a scream or at least concern.

Julia addressed them again but this time with a confident, no nonsense and frighteningly cold voice, "I think we can sort this out quickly, we want you to leave. If you do not do exactly as I wish, you will suffer consequences you cannot even imagine."

Jan could not quite hear what was going on and couldn't stop herself from opening the door a crack. The men seemed stupefied for a moment and then Donny snapped out of it and started walking toward Julia, who said with great conviction, "I will not warn you again." He didn't stop and, when he was within two feet of her, Julia calmly kicked him in the balls with more force than he could conceive possible. The pain was excruciating and while he was writhing on the floor, Devin seemed to be immobile.

Julia was hoping to take care of the situation without the other guests being aware. The Great Room was far enough away that, with the music blasting now, no one over there could hear them. There were many other things she could have done but, remembering Jan behind the door, she was being cautious. Julia asked Rose to go check the room Devin had broken into for their shoes. Donny was cursing and moaning, still in pain. Julia looked at Devin saying, "People today just don't listen, do they young man? I gave him a fair warning, didn't I now? I hope you have a little more sense than your friend here."

Even though, on some level, Devin felt the power of this woman, he also felt the obligation to assist Donny. He started walking towards Donny, who was still on the floor, as Rose came back with the muddy shoes that somehow were clean and appeared to be dry. Julia opened the black bag she had carried down the hall, and handed Rose some plastic ties saying "secure his hands and feet please," and Rose sat on the floor to do so.

"I can't let you do that," said Devin, and as soon as the words came out of his mouth, and he leaned over to grab the ties from Rose, Julia zapped him into submission with a stun gun saying, "Oh dear, did you think I was asking permission?"

He had a severe spasm and passed out. Donny was still in pain but angry and frustrated he rolled toward Julia and attempted to grab her leg. She could see it coming and stood her ground. Rose scrambled to her feet and observed the astonished look on Donny's face as he tried to pull Julia's leg from under her, and nothing happened. It was like trying to dislodge a marble pillar. Rose looked at Donny shaking her head. He looked from Rose to Julia, who had a smile on her face as she said, "It's not nice to fool Mother Nature." She zapped Donny and, when he passed out, she turned to Rose, "I've always wanted to say that," and they laughed as they used the plastic ties to bind their intruder's hands and feet.

That being done and Julia being aware that Jan was nearby, they dragged the men into the same room where the window had been broken. They worked unnaturally fast, removing the sticky traps and glue stained clothes Devin was wearing and put him in a clean sweat suit. Julia found a pair of scissors and duct tape in her bag and they cut a piece of Devin's hair to get the trap off his head. By then both men were starting to revive and Julia cut some duct tape into strips to put over their mouths.

Donny's eyes were wide and fearful as he said, "What the fuck?"

Julia gave him that dreaded cold stare and said, "We'll take the tape off in a little while and don't worry, if you are good boys, I have a little surprise for you later. You should have played nice when you had the chance," and she slapped the tape over their mouths.

Two joints had fallen out of Donny's pocket when they dragged the boys into the room. Julia picked them up and put them in her pocket. They cleaned up the room and Rose took an empty box from the closet in the mud room and cut neat card board pieces that were placed and taped in the empty panes. Sammy wandered in the room and Julia said, "You can keep an eye on our guests Sammy." She reached in her pocket, pulled out a treat and threw it in his direction. Sammy jumped up and caught it in his mouth as Julia said, "Nice Sammy, you never miss."

Jan had been mesmerized as she peeked out the crack in the doorway. Luckily, for Julia, the angle did not afford Jan a view of the leg grabbing incident. Even so, she was amazed at the quick thinking and ability, of these two women, to subdue two men with calm, ease and even humor. She thought they were absolutely her new heroes. Things were quiet now and she stepped out into the hallway as Julia and Rose were closing the bedroom door.

"Julia, you guys are amazing. How did you get a stun gun and how could you be so calm?" Jan asked.

"That is a little trick I learned a long time ago. If you are being confronted by dangerous people you must get a little crazy, and quickly, before fear paralyzes you. I hope you remember that," Julia said. "But really dear, don't you think you have had enough excitement for one evening, please rest for a little longer and I'll call you for some hot chocolate when it's ready. I need to go call the authorities and, oh how do they put it, let's keep this on the down low, I don't want to upset our guests."

"Sure Julia, but don't forget me, I love your hot chocolate," said Jan and she returned to her room closing the door behind her.

"Those mouse traps were a nice touch," said Rose brushing off any residual dust from her pants.

"I think this is going to be a long evening and we've had enough rain," Julia said to Rose as they walked down the hall.

Vivian and Maddy were giving the girls facials in the massage rooms. Their eyes were padded and they were facing in the direction of steamers. They hadn't heard a word of the commotion from the back door area. Rose came by to resume keeping the girls under her watchful eye. She left the doors open a crack and alternated her view of each one. Vivian and Maddy had stepped out of the room to talk with Julia, who informed them "We have another problem."

They spoke for a few minutes and then Maddy and Vivian returned to the massage rooms. Rose went to the Great Room with Julia who said, "I don't think we have much time."

Rose asked, "Would this be a code 13?"

"No dear, I'll explain that later, we have other things on our plate right now."

They got to the Great Room to witness Barbara giving salsa lessons. Julia decided they would run back to the kitchen and grab a couple of bottles of Limoncello Liqueur, as a special treat, and some fruit, cheese and cookies. Rose carried a tray of glasses and one bottle while Julia had another bottle and the rest of the goodies. They made it back in record time and Julia, realizing she was needed elsewhere, gave the two joints to Barbara saying with a wink," Get the party started."

She and Rose went back to the massage room to check on the progress of the facials. Julia, with a look, told Vivian and Maddy that it would be helpful if the girls were pampered for a while longer. Oops, there was another complication.

The back door had been left open and two men, with ski masks, surprised that the door was unlocked, slowly entered. Jan heard their boots in the hall. She turned off her light and opened the door a crack. Unbeknownst to her it was Cap, from Two Tones's house, with one of his buddies, not wanting to miss out on an easy score. Jan caught a glimpse of one of the men and she was sure they could hear her heart pounding like a drum. She quickly hid under the bed.

The men went from room to room collecting whatever valuables they came across. Jan wasn't going to give up her engagement ring easily and, as she lay on the floor, she took her ring off and wedged it between the leg of the side table and the wall. Hers was the third room they entered and she could hear one of them whispering, "I guess we got here before those jack offs, we might be able to get out of here without being seen. They rummaged through her bathroom, checking her makeup case and the medicine cabinet for drugs, before going through the drawers and then the closet and suit cases.

"Nothing but crap," said Cap. Jan was glad she didn't bring any valuables, except her ring. She was still sure her pounding heart might give her away even as they left the room. Then she remembered what Julia had said and realized she had allowed fear to paralyze her. She started taking deep breaths to calm herself down and made up her mind to get crazy. Then she rolled out from under the bed and went to the bathroom to find a weapon. The only thing she could find was a can of hair spray and a bottle of perfume, she grabbed the hairspray. She heard one of them say, "This is better, we may end up with some good stuff yet."

They finished with the next room and were standing in the hall with their backs turned when Jan quietly rushed at them, kicked the back leg of one guy, right behind the knee. He went down as the other turned in her direction she sprayed his eyes. The one on the floor quickly turned as his buddy was yelling, "Fuck you, bitch," and she sprayed him too. She didn't have a plan B so she just ran down the hall.

The two men had been sufficiently surprised and were now scrambling to feel their way to a bathroom. Bumping into each other, they managed to find the public bathroom two doors down. Grabbing towels and repeatedly rinsing off their eyes, they gradually regained their sight and were ready to ring Jan's neck. Being fooled by a woman was humiliating. They put their masks back on and Pete, the bigger of the two, was mad as hell as they started down the hall.

Jan didn't go to the Great Room but opted to duck in the closet off the Dining Room. She figured they would go looking for her in the Great Room and maybe she could pull a similar trick again from behind.

Pete and Cap were walking down the hall when a woman entered the back door cautiously. She too was surprised that the door was open and slowly made her way down the hall. The men before her had gone from one room to the next on the right side of the hall until they were interrupted. The woman was opening each door, from left to right and peeking inside. The third room, on the left, held two men tied with their mouths taped shut. A big grey cat jumped up and ran out the door. She didn't know what to think. They tried to implore her with their bulging eyes and finally she untapped, the closest one, Devin.

"Please Miss, we've been like this for an hour and we think the women here may need our help. Can you find something to cut these ties?"

She was about five foot six, with olive skin and brown eyes that were staring at Devin and trying to figure out what was going on. Devin thought she was cute and under different circumstances—but right now she had a concerned expression on her face. She looked in the adjoining bathroom and found a pair of nail scissors and started working on Devin's wrists. Donny was making muffled protesting noises and she stopped to rip off the tape from his mouth.

Donny was thanking her as she resumed working on Devin's wrist bands but it was futile. Donny remembered there was a pair of what looked like hair cutting scissors in the bathroom adjoining the room across the hall. She went to retrieve the scissors and, upon seeing the tousled condition of the room, wondered if these men were victims or perpetrators. She wasn't so quick to release them without further investigation. Donny seemed agitated when she got back, insisting that she hurry up, but she wanted some answers first. Who were they and why were they there?

Donny felt her trepidation and tried a different approach. He explained that their girlfriends were there and, when they tried to visit, they were ambushed by a man with a gun. He tied them up and now they feared he might be harming their girlfriends. Donny gave a great imitation of a boyfriend's sincere effort to get help. She asked a few more questions about names and where they lived and then decided to release them. A few minutes later they were rubbing their wrists and ankles. Devin was at a loss as to how they would proceed. Donny suggested the woman stay in the room and they go and investigate; fat chance of that happening. She pretended to agree but was only giving them a few minutes head start; she wasn't going to wait around.

CHAPTER 51

Masked Men

Rose and Julia walked out of the massage room and down the hallway that was on the other side of the ranch from the long bedroom hallway. This led to the back of the kitchen which faced the dining room. The two men in black masks were now entering the dining room and were taken aback to see an older woman and a young woman walking towards them. Rose wasn't sure how Julia was going to proceed and waited for her lead. She was surprised to hear a very cheerful.

"Why Pete and Cap, it's so nice to see you both, we have been waiting for you. Now why don't you take those silly masks off, don't they get itchy?" said Julia as she and Rose kept walking towards the men.

Cap and Pete had been in a fury but, upon hearing their names, they were totally incredulous and there was a long moment of suspension in the air. Julia kept smiling and Pete said, "Damn it, did Two Tone call you?"

"No," said Julia, "but I will give you thirty seconds to turn around and get out or I'll make you wish you had."

Pete and Cap looked at each other, as if coming to their senses, relaxed their stance and smiled as if they had been talking to two children who didn't know what they were up against.

Julia turned her head to Rose and, with a smile on her face she said, "Would you like to try your hand at that one dear?

Rose made a miniscule nod, stepped forward and, within a heartbeat, punched Pete in the stomach and head. Picking her leg up, she wrapped it around the back of his kneecap and pushed him backwards to the floor where his head hit so hard he was knocked out.

Cap was in shock as Julia smiled and said to Rose, "Very nice, dear." Then she looked at Cap saying, "It probably wouldn't do any good, but I will ask, would you like to take your friend and leave now?"

He snapped to attention and his hands reached out to grab the closest one to him, Julia. She made a slight turn and elbowed him in the solar plexus.

"I thought so," said Julia, just before she head butted him into unconsciousness.

"Well done," said Rose, and Julia responded, "Thank you, dear."

"I do hate making such a display," Julia said. "But no one will believe them anyway." Then she sensed it was best to do something about Jan, in the closet.

"We need to clear up this mess quickly and I think baby animals are much easier to deal with than criminals, and pleasing to have around."

There were two kittens on the floor as Sammy walked into the dining room.

"Sammy, these are your two charges. Take them to the office, or better yet, to the bathroom next to the office with the litter box, they'll need some training." So Sammy pushed them along; sometimes picking up one in his mouth, by the back of the neck, to quicken their pace.

The closet Jan had been hiding in was to the left of the bedroom hallway, on the far side of the Dining Room. It was deep with and filled with cups, saucers, glasses, dishes, linen, trays, candlesticks, vases and various platters to accommodate any occasion. The door was thick and although Jan could hear voices, she wasn't sure who they belonged to. If she opened the door it would make a click noise and the light inside the closet would go on. She decided to stay put until it was quiet. The kittens were now out of the way and Julia walked over to the closet to retrieve Jan. She opened the door to a wide-eyed Jan holding a heavy candlestick in one hand and a bottle of hairspray in the other, ready for a challenge.

"You can put that down now dear," said Julia, "Everything is under control. What have you been up to?" said Julia, knowing Jan had a heroic tale to tell. So Jan related her story quickly and Julia praised her courage adding, "I'll explain the rest later but go ahead and join the others, only please, until the authorities come, can I trust you not to mention anything, and I mean anything, to the other ladies? They're having such fun and I don't have time to explain everything just yet." So Jan agreed and went to the Great Room.

The ladies had played backgammon, scrabble and then got a dance lesson from Barbara. They were taking a little break after Julia and Rose had arrived with more refreshments and Barbara asked if anyone would like to indulge in a little cannabis. Heads turned and different women made various comments. Sheila laughed and said, "Sure, I haven't done that since college." Sharon and Donna said basically the same. N. C., Lynn and Gia said they smoked on occasion and Mamie said she had never smoked in college but had been using it regularly since the cancer.

They pulled their chairs around and lit up, passing the joints around and telling stories about their 'first time smoking' and different escapades when they were high.

There was a lot of laughter and Lynn took center stage. She told the story of how she and a friend were having breakfast, in a diner, at two A.M., after smoking a joint in the car. The place was noisy and crowded with dance club evacuees but they managed to get a centrally located booth. They ordered and were starting to feel the giddy effects of the weed when they happened to see a man in shorts, with very bowed legs, and were trying not to laugh.

Then Lynn began explaining how she had dated a very cute medical student for a while. His upper body was well developed but, from his small waist down, he had skinny little legs and walked a little pigeon-toed. The waitress brought their drinks and she resumed. Not realizing, because the noise level was moderately high, the next few words came out of her mouth like a scream when she said to her friend, "I JUST COULD'T FORGIVE HIM FROM THE WAIST DOWN." You could hear a pin drop in the diner and then an uproar of laughter, even some clapping; The Great Room was laughing too.

Donna was saying she could never go out in public after smoking. She would get paranoid and think everyone was looking—they all knew. Gia said she had smoked a lot with her cousin but she gave it up when the marijuana munchies ended up on her hips. Donna said she couldn't imagine Gia fat.

The Carlos Santana cd was over and Sharon was saying they should put the music back on, "If we don't I'll nod off in about five minutes, weed is like a sedative for me, but I want another lesson."

"You just want to show us up, swivel hips," said N.C.

The music went back on and Barbara was demonstrating the Samba.

Jan walked in and felt she had gone to a different reality than the one on the other side of the door. N.C. gave her the remainder of a joint. Jan shrugged and took a puff. She thought she deserved to let off a little steam, so she joined the dance party.

Jan had just walked into the Great Room when Devin and Donny came into the Dining Room followed by a woman. They could hear the music playing and the woman made a B-line for the Great Room. The men, still furious, headed for Julia and Rose who were standing by the island in the kitchen. They were saying "You crazy bitches, I'm gonna kill you!" Rose just gave them a head shake as if saying "you'll never learn."

Donny wasn't going to give Julia another opportunity to kick him in the balls. He looked around, grabbed a chair and waved it in front of him like a lion tamer saying, "It's the last time you mess with me, bitch."

"I'm sure you're right about that," Julia smiled. Devin followed closely behind Donny, weary that he might be zapped again. Julia, looking amused, gave Rose a knowing glance. Donny wanted to get close enough to grab Julia by the hair, but when the chair was a few inches from Julia, she grabbed the leg. She pushed it towards him, with great force, causing Donny to fall back on Devin. Both crashed to the floor as Julia said, "Look Rose, our own domino effect."

Devin had the wind knocked out of him. Donny rolled over on his left side, the chair having fallen to the right, and when he got on his knees Julia put her foot on his back and pushed him to the ground. In one quick motion she leaned down and put her knee on his back, then twisted and pushed his arm toward his head.

"You're gonna break my arm, you crazy fucking bitch!"

"Young man I'm just so tired of you referring to me in that nasty way, apologize," Julia insisted.

His response was, "Wait 'til I get my hands on you." Julia punched him unconscious.

Rose had opened the black bag that sat on the counter and taken the stun gun out. Devin needed another moment to regain his breath, but on seeing Rose with the stun gun, he cringed and froze.

Rose looked at Julia and said, "Sammy is going to have his hands full with these two, or at least that one," pointing to Donny. "How about a couple of mice?" she asked.

"That sweet face is hiding a wicked sense of humor Rose, but no, we've made a bit of a mess and it is important that-" at this point Devin tried to make a run for it and Julia literally froze him in his tracks.

"So, what is it important that?" asked Julia.

"Ok, ok," Rose smirked, "that we leave as little a footprint here as possible."

Julia leaned toward Donny and picked up another kitten saying, "Well that's an improvement."

Rose picked up the other kitten and Julia handed Donny off to her, asking if she would please take them to Sammy and give them food and water. "Quickly, we have some other things to handle."

CHAPTER 52

Solving problems

A minute after Jan had walked in, another woman entered the Great Room. The music was loud and everyone had their backs to the door, focusing on Barbara, counting out steps and demonstrating hip and arm movements. It seemed, out of nowhere, Donna was being pulled away from the others by her arm. They were all frozen for a moment and couldn't hear what was being said, except for the words 'bitch' and 'whore', and they knew it wasn't a friendly visit. Mamie, closest to the iPod station, turned the music off as both Gia and Jan went into action; then the others gathered around.

No one needed to tell Gia to get her 'crazy on.' She and Jan reached the woman about the same time but Gia was fierce in her attack. She grabbed the woman's hair and swung her around so hard that the woman lost her balance and was on the floor. Jan, her adrenalin pumping, ran to the woman, who was face down and pulled her arms, crisscrossing her back and pinning her to the floor.

"Who are you, what do you want?" asked Jan, who was basically squatting on the intruder's back.

"Why don't you ask Donna?"

All eyes went to Donna who was now sitting in a chair, head down, her shoulders making heaving movements as she cried her heart out. N.C. was stroking her back and trying to calm her down. Donna was too upset to speak yet; the eyes turned back to the other woman.

"I'm Syd, her girlfriend. I'm here to take her home," she said.

The moment seemed suspended as the rest of the group took in this revelation and recalled the bruises Donna had displayed at the dinner table.

"I don't think Donna wants anything to do with you," said Jan as she looked over at Donna again, waiting for affirmation. But Donna seemed isolated in her own bubble of emotional, unrestrained tears— unable to meet anyone's eyes.

Julia walked in, ready for whatever. Quickly taking charge, Julia relieved Jan's position, restraining Syd, and with a commanding voice ordered everyone out, except Donna. She asked them to take a seat in the dining room. A few "but" mumbles could be heard as Rose walked in, then Julia said, "Please, ladies, this is under control." Rose and Barbara helped corral them out of the Great Room and then Rose stepped back into the Great Room, closing the door behind her.

With the others gone, Donna manager to pull herself together, but was still tearful when asking, "Syd, how did you find me, what are you doing here?"

"I tricked your aunt. I had my brother call her and say the moving company had broken something in the truck and they needed to talk with you," she answered, still struggling under Julia's restraint.

Julia addressed her captive saying, "Young woman, you are trespassing and you have a great deal of nerve being here. I have a stun gun and trust me, I'm not afraid to use it. My young friend here," Julia gave a nod to Rose, "is a black belt and she too has a bit of a temper. So I will let you up, but behave yourself and we will listen to whatever you have to say."

Syd was frustrated and when she got up she lunged again toward Donna. Rose, in a dash, put her foot out and Syd tripped and went down again. Rose calmly pulled the woman up by her armpits and, once again, crisscrossed her arms behind her back. Syd kept struggling so Rose strained her arms further.

"Ok, ok," yelled Syd, "I won't move."

"Do you have difficulty hearing or are you just obstinate, young woman," Julia sighed, "My patience is wearing thin, just what did you hope to accomplish by this intrusion?

Rose steered Syd to a chair opposite Donna, still holding her wrists behind her back.

"I'm here to take her back," she said looking at Donna.

"Syd, I'm never going back, don't you get it? I spelled everything out in the letter I left. I won't be your punching bag, or your prisoner, anymore," Donna said with conviction.

"Please, Donna, it will be different. You know I love you and you love me," Syd pleaded.

"Listen to me Syd," Donna responded, "I don't love you anymore and you don't know how to love. I care for you as a person but you need help and I can't help you."

"I'll get help, I swear, if you come back with me, I'll do it right away, I promise," she pleaded.

"No, no, you're not listening. I will never go back. I don't want to see you ever again." Donna was getting all worked up and her voice was getting louder, "You don't know how to love, you only know how to hurt. I'm sorry about your background but you are an adult and you are doing the hurting now. I DON'T LOVE YOU ANYMORE AND I DON'T WANT TO SEE YOU EVER AGAIN, DO YOU GET IT NOW?"

They were both exhausted and crying when Julia asked Rose to take Donna to the dining room. Rose released her grasp on Syd. She and Donna started walking out. Syd began to rise, looking toward the door.

"I don't think so," Julia said. Syd had anger seething from her eyes and as she tried walking around Julia saying, "Out of my way old bitch,"

Julia chided herself for taking such pleasure in stunning Syd. She walked to the door and poked her head out telling the group that all was well, they were having a chat, and she did not want to be disturbed.

Julia held the stun gun like a pistol when Syd was sufficiently recovered. She had her black bag in hand and ordered Syd to 'get a move on' as they went out the front door that faced the view. They went around the side of the house and walked to Syd's car in the parking lot. Julia reached in the black bag and took out a pair of cufflinks. She directed Syd to get in the back seat of her car and hook herself to the small bar handle over the door. She then proceeded to drive Syd's car down to the fork in the road and turned right to the old house where Devin and friends had been squatting.

"Where are we going?" and "What are we doing here?" Syd repeated several times, with fear entering her voice.

Julia would only say, "I'm not turning you in, dear. You should be thankful for that; it would cause too many undesirable complications. I have a surprise for you. Do you have a spirit of adventure?" Syd was confused and just said, "Huh."

Then Julia pulled the car around the back of the house, away from Donny's car, and returned to the ranch with another kitten. The others were sitting around the dining room table, all of them having been shaken up by Syd's untimely appearance. Barbara and Rose had made and distributed Chamomile tea to calm everyone's nerves.

Jan had kept her promise and had not said a word about the two men tied up in the bedroom or the intruders whose eyes she had hair sprayed. She didn't know what happened to them but apparently they were no longer a threat. She felt like the whole day had been surreal and she had become some kind of conspirator.

Of course all eyes were on Donna to unravel the mystery of how Syd had known where to find her. "I can't blame my Aunt; I should have explained how cunning Syd can be. She had someone call claiming to be the moving company and they needed to get a hold of me," Donna explained. She had not come out to the group when she arrived, about being gay, and now she felt embarrassed and exposed.

She cried for a while with N.C. on one side and Sheila on the other. She was being consoled and told it was not her fault, but Donna felt responsible and made the point that she had allowed the relationship to continue long after she knew it was over. She had spoiled the weekend and felt terrible about it. Donna pulled herself together to address the group saying, "I'm really sorry I didn't tell you guys that I'm gay. Syd was so jealous that, other than my yoga students, I lost contact with a lot of friends. I just wanted a quiet weekend before I started a new life. I wanted to make new friends, no strings attached. I didn't want my being gay to get in the way or put anyone off, at least not until they got to know me," Donna said with a shy, tearful smile.

"Where do you think you are, honey?" Lynn said to bolster the mood. "This is Southern California and you're moving to the San Fernando Valley, not the bible belt. Half the people I know are gay. This is Show Biz territory, and trust me, I wouldn't miss your class for anything."

The others made supportive comments and jokes that Donna appreciated, but she was still nervous.

"Do you think Julia is alright in there? It's pretty quiet?" she asked.

"No need to worry about Julia, I don't know anyone as capable," Barbara assured her.

"I've seen her in action and believe me, no one gets the better of her," said Jan, with admiration in her tone. She was itching to tell her story, but keeping her promise.

"What have you seen?" Mamie asked.

"Um, I think Julia should be the one to explain that," answered Jan.

Before Julia changed Syd, she looked deep into her eyes, telling her she was never to come after Donna again. Syd, seemingly hypnotized, answered back, "Never look for Donna again."

Julia walked in the back door and locked it before opening the black bag and saying to its contents, "Make a peep and I'll ring your little neck." She quickly breezed through the dining room waving her hand and saying,

"I'll be right back, I want to use the restroom and put my bag away."

She went to deposit the furry little ball with the others. Sammy looked up and Julia said, "I know, I know, don't worry, you will be rewarded."

Everyone was surprised by the direction she had come from, thinking she was still with Syd in the Great Room. She returned quickly saying, "Well, that's taken care of. I walked Syd out the front door to her car and I promise you, she will not bother anyone here again."

Turning to Jan she continued, "Jan has had quite an eventful evening, has she told you about it?" said Julia addressing the group. They were now looking at Jan and shaking their heads to indicate no.

"I can keep a secret," said Jan with a smile of satisfaction.

"Let me explain quickly. The girls were here to look around and as they say in old films, 'case the place,' for two men who would come back later and rob us. I have a stun gun and Rose is proficient in martial arts so we were able to subdue them. However, they had let two other men know of their plan and the other men decided to try their hand at robbing us too. Well thanks to our brave Jan here," everyone smiled and looked at Jan, "she heard them in the hall and ran up behind them, kicking one in the back of the knee before he saw her, and then spraying them in the eyes with hair spray. They came in the kitchen and we were able to subdue them. The police were notified and I asked them not to run their sirens when they came up the road. When Jan went to the Great Room the police were at the back door to collect the men. I'll have to go down and fill out some reports soon, but they allowed me some time to explain all this to you."

"Oh my god, do you mean all this was going on while we were dancing and smoking weed," said Sharon astonished, "and Jan was the only one who knew about it?"

"Exactly, Jan hasn't had what you would call a relaxing evening," Julia maintained as Jan turned a bit pinkish with all the attention and questions being asked at once.

Julia needed their attention and knocked on the table with her fist as if it were a gavel, "Ladies, I need your attention, feedback and cooperation. I do believe you all have had an impact on Lisa and Lauren. I have an idea on how I might proceed with them but I'll share that with you tomorrow. For now, I think it would be best if they know nothing about the intrusion by the four men. Talking about the incident, with Syd, is fine since it has nothing to do with them. Now what do you think about that, are we in agreement?"

"They do have a maternal grandmother who sounds very nice. Maybe she would take them in," said N.C.

"Yes, I was thinking the same," agreed Julia, "but they have been on the streets a while and should have some psychological help, that's what I will look into first."

The others agreed and were chatting back and forth on the subject. Sheila said she thought the grandmother lived in Northern California and she volunteered to escort the girls on the flight and deliver them wherever Julia wanted.

It was getting late now and Maddy, Vivian and the girls came out from the massage rooms to join them. Vivian suggested Julia make her hot chocolate and she did; within the hour everyone went to bed. Lauren was in a double room with Rose and Lisa with Vivian. The girls did not want to be separated but Julia told them she didn't want to go around changing the rooms where the others were already settled. It was N.C. and Lynn's room that had two window panes broken, but it was patched up nicely and the incident had been explained to them.

CHAPTER 53

Sunday Morning

The sun was out, the sky cloudless, and everyone was waking up early this morning. Rose had knocked on N.C.'s door and handed her an orange juice size glass with a muddy liquid in it saying, "I thought you might like a last herbal treatment this morning."

"Thanks for room service, Rose. I was just about to go looking for you," said N.C. "Do you think I could get an acupuncture treatment too?"

"Sure, later this morning," said Rose.

Julia and Maddy had the coffee pot brewing, tea pot boiling and juices on the side table. The toaster was set up there too, next to the Ezekiel, rye and whole grain breads so anyone could make toast at their leisure. The jelly and jams were on the table and the steel cut oats were just ready. Julia had a huge frying pan and was scrambling eggs, adding caramelized onions, avocado, tomato and a little goat cheese; there were muffins and sweet rolls on the counter too.

Jan was the first one to the coffee pot saying, "I guess all the excitement really knocked me out. I slept like a baby."

"Oh that's lovely dear, and how are you feeling this morning?" inquired Julia.

"Perfect, but hungry," replied Jan as she leaned over the pan Julia was working on. "I'd love some of that," she said just as Julia was adding a little salt and pepper.

"It's just about ready," and after a moment Julia picked up a plate and scooped the eggs on to it, adding a few grapes, slices of melon and orange for presentation.

Vivian, Lisa, Lauren and Maddy were the next to enter the kitchen, quickly followed by the rest of the group, who also seemed to be drawn by the delicious aroma of coffee.

A couple of extra chairs were taken from the Great Room to accommodate the swollen numbers. The hustle and bustle went on as everyone made their breakfast and beverage selections. Rose looked at Sharon's choices: a plate with a few pieces of fruit, a sweet roll and a cup of coffee.

"Where's the protein?" Rose asked in her usual frank manner. Sharon looked at her in surprise and Rose went on, "You really need to add protein, especially when you're eating refined sugar."

"Julia moved over very quickly with a small bowl of almonds saying, "Rose is a real purest. You see, we do not eat refined sugar and we only eat Ezekiel bread, very little dairy, mostly fish and a little chicken. I've been giving you some choices that are not normally in our diet but, unlike some people," and she looked at Rose, "I don't believe in proselytizing diet beliefs without some indication that the listener is curious or interested in the information. She is right though, would you like some nuts if you don't care for eggs?"

"Sure," said Sharon, amused by Julia's reprimand.

They were all starting to appease their hunger pangs and the critique of the weekend began.

"I had a wonderful time this weekend, and I'll never forget it," was Jan's declaration.

"And how could you?" was Maddy's response chuckling and sipping her tea.

"You mean a fall, a near death experience and tangling with criminals complete you, honey," laughed Vivian as she got up to refresh her cup and the others chimed in with comments.

N.C. was whispering to Lauren, and Sheila to Lisa, explaining Jan's falls.

"Ok, ok so maybe I'll be more careful already, but something happened to me here, and I don't know, I guess I feel sort of at peace with myself." She picked up her orange juice glass, stood up and made a toast.

"To Julia, Maddy, Vivian, Barbara and Rose, thank you for your kindness and understanding. I'm sure I speak for all of us when I say we will never forget you and hope we can do this again."

They all agreed and clinked glasses and cups.

"So, when can we come back?" asked Lynn.

"We have your contact information ladies, but we are booked for the next two years. We will be on our way to Europe tomorrow," said Julia. There were moans and groans of disappointment going around the table.

"On a happier note," interjected Maddy, "Sammy apparently is a Samantha and has five kittens. You can go in and take a look but I wouldn't advise any touching. She is a very protective mother. I think I know someone in town who might be willing to take them all."

"I could take a couple of kittens," said Lynn.

"Thank you dear, but they need to stay with their mother for a number of weeks before they are weaned," added Julia.

"Who is up for a morning hike?" Barbara proposed. They all seemed anxious to get out on such a beautiful day. "I think up here there is so much gravel on the trails that they drain pretty quickly, so as long as we don't go off the beaten path, it shouldn't be too muddy. But I'd leave my slippers by the back door, just in case."

They were all commenting on different aspects of the weekend when Julia leaned over to Jan saying, "Jan dear, would you agree to see Vivian after breakfast? She believes that you may have an inner ear problem that is affecting your balance."

"Sure, that would be great, I'd rather put the blame on my inner ear than my clumsy self," she answered, "but can I be greedy and get a massage too?"

"Sure can," said Vivian.

"Can I get a massage too," asked Gia.

"I can take you after breakfast," offered Rose, "I think Vivian is pretty busy today."

Gia and Donna were unusually quiet this morning and, to the observant eye, they were avoiding each other.

Barbara suggested, "After your walk a yoga class would be nice, and then you can do a last touch up on your paintings before lunch, or anyone having a treatment can finish up after lunch."

Maddy said, "If you would like, I will run a guided meditation this afternoon and I encourage you all to continue this practice at home, there are numerous mental and physical benefits."

"Ok, Maddy," teased Vivian, "I think you're preaching to the choir here."

Donna had been waiting for a lull in the conversation, feeling the need to make an apology. "Everybody, I have something to say," Donna started feeling self conscious, "Last night was the best and worst night I have had in a very long time. I really appreciate this whole group, and I want you all to know how really sorry I am for the horrible interruption."

Lisa and Lauren seemed clueless but the others understood the heartfelt sincerity of Donna's words.

"Hey, no problem," Lynn said loud and clear, "you gave us the gift of yoga, and a good story too. You have to get used to the idea that nothing is sacred in this group, and we'll all have a good laugh about this, probably at dinner next week. How about it?" There were nods of agreement and smiles all around.

Donna was getting overwhelmed by the spirit of generosity in the room and said, "That would be great."

Sheila was bemoaning the loss of Donna from Northern California, "I just hope your replacement is half as good or I may just have to move."

N.C. started to ask about what happened to the men last night but caught herself, "What happened to, ah, to the music Vivian, are you slacking off on the last day?

Vivian went to her iPod station on the side table and chose, "I Will Survive, from our late, great Donna Summer," she announced.

They were finished eating and they started moving to the rhythm of music, and singing, while they cleared the table and placed the dirty dishes by the sink. Lisa and Lauren shrugged at each other and got up to do the same. Barbara told the group she would meet them by the back door in ten minutes. Then they all went off to get ready for the rest of the day. Sheila had an extra pair of walking shoes she gave to Lisa and Rose had a pair for Lauren.

Rose was passing through the kitchen, on her way to give Gia her massage, when Julia stopped her for a moment and said, "Don't be too hard on her, a little tact might be helpful."

Rose gave Julia her wicked impish smile saying, "Aren't you the one who told me I didn't have any tact? So how am I supposed to do that?"

"It didn't take you long, now did it. You're getting as bad as Maddy," said Julia, pretending annoyance.

Just then Gia, Jan and Vivian came out of the hallway and they all proceeded to the massage rooms

CHAPTER 54

Vivian and Jan

"Sit up here, honey," Vivian said to Jan as she patted the massage table. She had the same type of scope used by ENT doctors and she peered into Jan's ear.

"I think you need to lie down, there's something in there," said Vivian, "I think I may need some help." She left the office and came back a few minutes later with Maddy.

"Now hold her head very still," she addressed Maddy, and to Jan she said, "Don't move your head, I am sorry honey, but this may hurt for a minute," she told Jan. Using something like very thin tweezers, Vivian carefully yanked something off the back of Jan's ear drum.

"OW" Jan screamed, "That really hurt."

But rather than soothing words or apology, Jan heard Vivian say to Maddy, laughing, "This is one for the record, first time I've seen that."

"What?" said Jan?

"When was the last time you had acrylic nails?" Vivian asked.

"I guess it was sometime before Thanksgiving, I decided to get them taken off and go natural, why?" said Jan.

"I think you may have removed one yourself, in the middle of the night," and with that Vivian showed Jan a perfect pinky nail, polish and all.

"Oh my god," said Jan, "I don't believe it. It must have been when my manicurist put a fake nail under the acrylic. I guess I must have scratched my ear but I sure don't remember."

The three of them laughed and Vivian said, "Yes, you must have scratched your ear in your sleep and it came off and lodged down in there. I'm going to rinse out your ear with a little peroxide. I think you should be fine, but if you have any irritation in the next few days, go see your ENT doctor. Here, a little souvenir," and she handed the astonished Jan her pinky nail.

"Now hurry along, catch up with the hikers, you could probably use a good dose of vitamin D sunshine, but be careful," Maddy gave a last warning.

"Oh, I will be. Thanks so much," Jan was saying as she hurried out the door.

Vivian and Maddy were shaking their head and laughing. They straightened up the room and walked out the door, stopping by the bathroom in the hall to check on the kittens. They were very cute, in this incarnation, but appeared somewhat feral as they swatted each other and rolled around the floor. Sammy was keeping them from doing any real damage, like a diligent mom.

They decided to give Sammy a break so he, now being called she, could run around a little. Maddy told Vivian, "It's a bit of poetic justice that now all these bullies are the same size."

CHAPTER 55

Rose and Gia

Rose was in the other massage room playing soothing music and massaging Gia's head. Rose noticed something on the back of Gia's neck, right under her hair line, and she asked, "How did you get the scar back here?"

"My cousin and I were playing pirates with sticks. The one he was using had a jagged edge that got me pretty bad. I think he did it on purpose and then felt really bad when he saw all the blood," Gia related.

"Why was he mad at you?" Rose asked?

"When we were kids, I was a tomboy and always pushing him into rough-housing games he didn't want to play. He was a gentle soul," she concluded.

"What do you mean was, did he die?" Rose said, knowing full well the answer to her question.

"Yes, he committed suicide, recently," Gia said. "It was heartbreaking, we were very close growing up."

Rose was working on her arm now and said, "He must have been very unhappy, why do you think he did it?"

"His dad was a homophobic," Gia explained, "My cousin was gay, and I think because his father never accepted him that way, he really didn't accept himself."

"That's very difficult, isn't it Gia?" Rose said in a quiet tone that puzzled Gia, "I mean accepting yourself."

"I guess it is for a lot of people," Gia responded.

"What about for you," asked Rose?

"What about for me?" answered Gia, annoyance in her voice. "What are you getting at Rose?"

Now at her other arm Rose said, "Relax Gia, why are you tensing up? Just relax, we don't have to talk," and Rose continued the massage knowing she had touched not just an arm, but a nerve.

So Rose was quiet but, about five minutes later, Gia asked, "Rose, what did you mean, really?"

"I observe people and I've seen the way you and Donna relate to each other, look at each other, it's special. Now that she has admitted to being gay you've been avoiding her, and you look very sullen. I think you too got the message, from your uncle, that it was wrong to be gay. You can't help who you love, you didn't choose this. When you think about it, the people that say it's a choice are probably gay and religiously intolerant or they would understand that no one chooses to be heterosexual or homosexual. You just are what you are. The choice I see is whether you want to be happy or keep living a lie for the rest of your life."

"Sharon told me you were very insightful and direct, I sure didn't see this coming. I did feel an attraction to Donna but I never really admitted it to myself—until now. I guess I was scared when she said she was gay. I've never been with a woman, even though I never felt the way I thought I should, about a man. I thought some were handsome but the erotic passages in books or movies never did much for me. I guess on some level I knew, I just don't know how my friends are going to react."

"Well guess what; I bet on some level they know too," Rose insisted in her common sense tone, "They're not stupid, and you heard Lynn last night, I don't think any of them really care. Ok, roll over again, you have some knots in your back, but they'll loosen up."

The realization of the conversation was starting to hit Gia like a sledge hammer and she was starting to panic, "Rose, I don't know what to do."

"You don't need to do anything, just be," Rose said casually, "You know, one step at a time. I find it helpful to think about what you want to say and store it in your head, at the appropriate time it will come out, no pun intended," she smiled and continued working on those knots. "Actually, if I was you, I would start by giving Donna a smile, I think she feels she's upset you."

"You make it sound so easy," Gia complained.

"Just do it and it will get easier every time. Think of it this way; a lie or a secret makes other people more important than you; it means you care more about what other people think than your own happiness. Ok, you can sit up now, you're done," said Rose.

"Thanks Rose, you're good, really good," said Gia, "and surprising."

"Never underestimate a person based on appearance, at least that's what Julia says," Rose admitted, "Enjoy the rest of your day and stop worrying so much, just be you."

And with that, Rose left Gia to get dressed and went to the kitchen.

Chapter 56

Plans for the Future

Sammy's break was over and Vivian and Maddy went to the kitchen to do some cleaning up; a few minutes later Julia came in.

"I've been on the phone with the rehab center in San Francisco and I've already transferred the money for a six month program. I'm going to ask Sheila if she wouldn't mind dropping Lisa and Lauren off at the center, before she goes home, that is, if they agree to go. They are booked on the same flight, which took a little doing, believe me," and Julia rolled her eyes.

"What are we going to do with the, ah, the kittens,?" asked Vivian with eyes wide.

"I will have them change back at one hour intervals tomorrow," explained Julia, "first Syd, her rented car is parked by the old house; then Devin and Donny, and an hour after that Pet and Cap. I moved their car from the bottom of our driveway to the old house last night. Sammy knows what to do. They will be naked, tired, hungry and confused, so they'll want to get away from here as quickly as possible. I left clean sweats in their cars, along with their keys."

Rose asked, "So we leave them at the old house across the way?"

"Exactly," answered Julia.

Barbara asked, "What if they come over here?"

"I think they have had a harrowing experience and I doubt they will want to be anywhere near here, besides I gave them a little mind suggestion. And as a precaution, I have contacted a security company and employed them for two days, they start tomorrow. I don't want any nonsense going on here when we leave, in case Cap and Pete have any other friends wanting to snoop around. Wednesday a group of body builders are scheduled to take over the place for ten days, I don't anticipate any problems," Julia said emphatically, then added, "I just love the internet."

"I've been toying with the idea of eliminating the old farm house and out buildings; it has been a location of trouble for a long time. Sammy will stay with our changelings until they are all gone, then he can take care of it."

"So much for that footprint," Maddy reminded Julia of her words.

"A little tweaking is fine," Julia answered, "You didn't mind when you showed Sir Fleming that corn steep liquor could increase the production of penicillin 12 to 20 times, now did you"

"Touché," answered Maddy as the group came trickling in the door.

"Touché?" said Lynn. "Are you two bickering again?" she laughed.

"We're fine," said Julia.

They were all in the kitchen now and Donna, after consulting with Barbara for a moment, announced that yoga would be in twenty minutes to give everyone time to clean up and change. Jan was going to get a massage with Vivian and Mamie was having a therapeutic touch session with Maddy. They all went off to prepare for yoga while Jan and Mamie went to take quick showers before their appointments. Rose and Barbara were keeping an eye on Lisa and Lauren but also observed that N.C. and Sheila had taken them under their wings and suggested that the girls join the yoga class.

Rose was joining the class too, just to be on the safe side.

The yoga class was about to begin when Gia walked in and gave Donna a shy smile. She might as well have poured fairy dust on

Donna, who had been walking around sullen and distracted. Donna perked up and seemed immediately energized. N.C. and Sharon noticed the change too.

Lisa and Lauren had never taken yoga before and Donna made sure she observed their movements and gently guided them when they needed help with the more difficult postures; always reminding them to go at their own pace and not to be in competition with anyone.

The class proceeded and after the last Namaste, the group clapped and thanked Donna for her fabulous instruction. N.C., Sharon, Lynn, and Gia all said they would exchange emails and phone numbers at lunch, and declared they would spread the word about her classes. Lisa and Lauren agreed they would like to continue with yoga.

Gia held back until the others drifted towards their rooms and walked beside Donna, who said, "I thought you were avoiding me and didn't want anything to do with me," she began.

"I'm sorry, I wanted to work out some things, I mean I needed to get used to the idea," and they both understood what she meant.

Jan and Mamie were finished with their sessions. N.C. was on her way to the massage room for her last acupuncture treatment with Vivian and Sheila was having a massage with Maddy. The others were taking a few minutes before returning to the Great Room to finish up their paintings.

Rose was off to town on an errand for Julia.

Julia had asked Lisa and Lauren to help with lunch preparation. There was a barbeque off the side door, near the kitchen, and Julia decided to make use of it. The meal would be a simple one: salad, salmon, brown rice, grilled asparagus, with a kiwi lime pie and other fruits for dessert.

Julia had Lisa washing and snapping off the ends of the asparagus. Lauren was washing and arranging some of the other fruit.

"Ladies, have you given any thought as to your future?" Julia addressed the girls.

Lisa and Lauren looked at each other, surprised at the question. They had both been feeling vulnerable, wondering if Donny and

Devin were going to show up and cause trouble. Lauren spoke first, "We need to tell you something." She proceeded to tell Julia about the boys and how sorry they were for possibly putting everyone in a dangerous situation. They had no plans but thought they should call the police, everyone had been so kind.

Julia assured them that presently Donny and Devin would be no problem, explaining they had been here last night while the girls were having a treatment. She and Rose were able to trick them and used the stun gun on them until the police arrived. Julia said she didn't want to upset the girls since they seemed to be enjoying themselves.

Lisa and Lauren were relieved at first, then fearful that the police might want to come back for them. Julia assured them that was not the case but said in a day or two the men would probably be out of jail and the best thing for the girls would be to get out of town, that is, if they wanted to get a fresh start. She asked how they would feel about going to a rehab and confessed that their tea and hot chocolate had been laced with some calming herbs but the effects would wear off in a day.

"I have made contact with a treatment facility in Northern California and perhaps we can contact your maternal grandparents," said Julia who then went on to tell them she had sent Rose to purchase some clothing, saying they couldn't very well travel in sweats.

This was quite a lot for the girls to take in. They were both surprised and confused and couldn't understand why these women had been so generous. They could hardly speak.

"We had better get back to our food preparations, we can talk about this after lunch, if you like, but we will all be leaving in a few hours, so you will have to make a decision soon," Julia informed them.

Preparations continued in silence as Julia sprinkled salt, pepper and dill on the salmon, then drizzling lemon juice and extra virgin olive oil on top. Except for the dill, she did the same with the asparagus, hoping the girls were paying attention for future reference. Then she heard, "Yes," from Lauren and, "Me too," from Lisa.

CHAPTER 57

Treatments

Maddy was massaging Sheila's neck and Sheila was saying, "That feels so good."

"Have you enjoyed the weekend?" asked Maddy.

"Oh yes, we were all talking and wishing your schedule wasn't so full," bemoaned Sheila, "this has been such fun and we were wishing we could do a weekend like this every six months."

"We have enjoyed all of you, such a lovely group," said Maddy. "Now tell me, did I hear you may be getting engaged?"

"Yes, rumor has it that maybe it will be on my birthday next month," Sheila confessed, "I am so excited, but at the same time, I was glad this weekend took my mind off other things."

"You don't have any doubts, do you?" asked Maddy.

"Oh, not about Jim," Sheila said emphatically. "It's my parents. I really don't know if I want to invite them. I haven't talked to them in months and there have been times when I would go for two or three years without any communication. When we would talk, it didn't take long before another fight and another few years had gone by."

"What in the world did you people fight about?" asked Maddy

"What didn't we fight about? They are very critical and opinionated. The only one in the family I ever got along with was

249

my Aunt Tootsie, her real name was Loretta but Tootsie was my nickname for her. She was wonderful. She died last year. She tried to keep the peace between my mother and me. She always said that it was my father's influence that turned my mother into such an ice queen, but I suspected mother was a hardcore narcissist. Tootsie was my anchor. She was the one who taught me about love and kindness. I always thought it was a mean trick of fate that my mother had children and Tootsie didn't."

"Fortunate for you, that she didn't though, or quite possibly she wouldn't have had the time for you."

"Hmmm, I never thought about it like that," Sheila considered.

"But let's get back to your parents," said Maddy as she left one arm to work on the other, "and do you have any siblings?"

"Yes, my brother Thomas, he's five years older than me. We don't have much of a relationship. He's an attorney on the east coast. Thomas gets along with my parents a little better than I do, he would just 'yes' them to death and do what he wanted. Of course he moved as far away as he could. In my parent's eyes, Thomas chose an honorable profession, one they could be proud of in front of their friends. Nursing was for middle class girls. I have this weird irony going on about Jim. The angry little girl inside of me would like to tell them I was marrying a guy who flips burgers rather than a doctor."

Maddy asked, "Is that why you married Tony?"

There was a silence and then Sheila said, "Honestly, until you just said that, I never thought about it that way."

"You have so much anger towards them," said Maddy, "why are you even thinking about inviting them?"

"I guess I'm always hoping it will get better, that they would be happy for me like normal parents," said Sheila. "I love Tony like a brother, and Mary like a mother and I don't want my parents making any snide remarks or nasty innuendo."

Maddy asked, "What does Tony do for a living?"

"He's an attorney now, but when I got pregnant and we married, we were just graduating from high school," said Sheila.

May I make a suggestion dear?" Maddy asked and then added, "You can roll over now."

"Sure, what are you thinking?" said Sheila, grateful for any help she could get.

"Why not write them a very respectful letter and express your feelings and your fears. You could tell them you would love for them to be there, but under your conditions. If they don't want to abide by that, well it's their decision," Maddy concluded. She then went on, with concern in her voice and said, "I'm worried about you and your anger issues. Being a nurse you know how anger can affect a person's physical well being. I would like you to consider forgiving them. That doesn't mean you have to invite them to your wedding, or even see them again if you choose. But let it go, the best revenge is living well. You can't change them but you can change you, or rather the way you think of them. Are they happy people?"

"Not my kind of happy," said Sheila. "They have moments of triumph, like winning a gulf game or being honored at a charity event, but it's all superficial, there's no real joy."

"That's where you start, dear," Maddy pointed out. "Shouldn't you feel pity rather than anger? Think of the joy you feel just looking in the eyes of your son or holding Jim's hand. Don't you feel sorry that they are not capable of that kind of loving? Why, you have had the love of Tony's parents, that's an accomplishment in itself. You have an extended family that admire and respect you. You don't need negativity of any kind in your life, let them know it and let the anger go," Maddy almost demanded. "You can sit up now; I'll just work on that shoulder a bit more."

"I know Maddy." Sheila admitted. "Thanks so much, I never even thought about forgiving my parents, and I do feel sorry for them, but I'm feeling better. You are right, I do need to forgive and let go."

"You're done dear," said Maddy as she patted Sheila's shoulder. "Remember, we can't become what we need to be by remaining what we are."

"You are so profound," admired Sheila.

"Thank you dear, but I learned that from Julia—it's a quote from Oprah," admitted Maddy.

Vivian was finishing up with N.C.'s acupuncture and advising her to seek someone good in her area.

"Better yet, if you like, I can look online for someone for you. I may be able to tell, a little easier, the good ones, based on their education and recommendations. Of course, some schools are better than others."

"That would be great; do you really think that all this will work?" N.C. asked.

"Oh, honey," Vivian said in a sympathetic tone, "I don't want to get your hopes up that this is a sure thing. We are doing our best, but you know, what will be will be. From what I can gather, you have a wonderful husband who loves you, and a very comfortable life. You need to focus on the positive and take care of that man of yours."

"I know what you're saying, I've been blessed," she said.

"I never understood what people mean by that," Vivian confessed. "No offense, but I don't think anyone picked you over someone else to bless. I think you were lucky to be born into a comfortable family, you were well educated, worked hard and applied yourself. But there I go rambling about one of my pet peeves, sorry honey; let's get back to the baby situation. You can still have a plan B if this doesn't work. If you are too old to adopt a baby, you might try a child a little older or a minority child. You know you don't need to go to Africa to find a black baby, if you're so inclined. And there are orphans all over the country."

A noisy growl emitted from N.C.'s stomach and Vivian said, "I think lunch should be ready, let's go.

Chapter 58

New Clothes

Rose came back loaded with packages and Julia commented, "That was fast." She turned to Lisa and Lauren saying, "We have a few surprises for you, ladies."

"I found a store Savvy, on State St. and Erica, the owner, helped me," said Rose. I gave her the sizes and in twenty five minutes she had it all done."

That's lovely dear," replied Julia. "Will you take the girls and bags to their rooms? You can change for lunch, if you like, but don't be long, it's almost ready,"

Rose marched the girls, with bags in tow, to the room Lauren occupied. Their eyes were like saucers. Rose gave them seven tops, seven pants, seven pairs of underwear and socks, three bras, two pairs of Toms' shoes and two jackets. Fortunately, there was a Marshalls nearby on State St. and Rose was able to pick up two large suitcases. She left the girls and went to the car to retrieve the luggage. When she came back, Lauren had her arm around Lisa and the two were crying. Rose, not sure what to do with this emotional display, tried to make light of things. She picked up some of the clothes and said, "What, you don't like my selections?" And they laughed.

Lauren wiped her eyes with the back of her right hand, still holding on to Lisa with her left, "It's just so much, how can we possible take all this? We have nothing to give," she said.

"First of all," Rose started, "you can take it in these suit cases, and second of all, no one is asking you for anything, although I know what Julia would tell you. Did you ever see the movie Pay it Forward?"

"No, I heard about it though," said Lisa.

"The whole idea is that someone gives to you and, when you are able, you give to someone else. What goes around comes around. You were lucky enough to be part of this group and you have an opportunity to change your life. If you don't have the courage to do it for yourself, do it for each other, that's what sisters should do. We better wash up for lunch, you can try this stuff on later."

Chapter 59

Sunday Lunch

Most of the group were assembled and all were ready. They picked up plates, made a queue and walked by the kitchen counter as Barbara spooned the veggies on the plates. Maddy was scooping up the brown rice and Julia slid a generous piece of salmon on each plate. There were salads and extra cut lemons all ready and set on the table.

Vivian had Bill Withers, from the 1980's, playing in the background. Sharon said, "Oh, great choice, Vivian, I love Bill Withers. My Dad used to say he had too much integrity for the music business. He made enough money and just decided to walk away, rather than be pushed into doing music he didn't love."

"That's right baby, and aren't we the ones who suffer when the music business screws with people," said Vivian.

Rose walked in with Lisa and Lauren. Julia thanked the girls for helping her earlier. It was obvious that the girls had been crying and Julia said, "Oh no, has Rose been practicing her karate chops on you two?"

She was able to coax smiles from the girls as she filled their plates. Lisa and Lauren wanted to express their gratitude to the whole group. They looked over at Rose, for a bit of confidence, and Rose gave them a nod. So, they stood, with plates in hand, and Lauren started, "We wanted to thank you all for being so kind to us, especially since we didn't deserve it." At that point she was getting all choked up and Lisa took over saying, "and we are going to put it forward, I mean, pay it forward, too," and as they sat down everyone had smiles on their faces.

It was a beautiful southern California day and they all seemed happy and energized. The salmon was delicious and Sharon asked what Julia had done with it.

"Only a little salt, pepper, lemon and dill. There are no secret ingredients," Julia replied emphatically as Maddy mimicked behind her back, 'sure' and rolled her eyes.

"The trick is making sure you don't cook it too long and dry it out."

Mamie said that after her treatment this morning she stopped by the bathroom, where Sammy and the kittens resided, and was shocked. "Those kittens are cute, but what nasty little buggers they are," said Mamie. "I went to pick one up, very carefully so as not to upset Sammy, and it swatted me so hard it drew blood. Funny thing, Sammy swatted the kitten and it backed away. She sure has her paws full with them, poor thing looks exhausted."

Julia asked, "Has everyone finished their painting?"

"I think everyone except Jan; she has a few minutes work to do. We will have our gallery open after lunch for your viewing pleasure," Barbara said. "I think you will be pleasantly surprised."

They started expressing sadness at not being able to get together with their hosts when Maddy changed the subject to avoid further inquires.

"Ladies, I think we should all be packed and ready to go by four. There are planes to catch and we, the hosts, need to leave everything in order. I was thinking that, after lunch, you can finish packing and Jan can finish up her painting. We will all meet in the Great Room to look at the finished masterpieces in an hour, and then perhaps do a twenty minute meditation before you all leave."

They continued chatting and all had finished eating, but it was as if they were psychologically stalled, as no one seemed to want to move. Vivian switched the music to Ray Charles and turned the sound up a little. 'Hit the Road Jack,' was just what they needed to snap out of it. They sang and moved along with the rhythm as they deposited the dishes by the sink and cleared the rest of the table.

Julia had told Sheila that 'the girls' had agreed to go to the treatment center. Sheila was very happy about that and said it would be her pleasure to take them to the airport, drop them off at rehab and get in touch with their grandparents. Julia advised her the last part was not necessary, she had already tracked down the grandparents and they were delighted to renew a relationship with the girls. Their efforts to do so, in the past, had been thwarted by their son-in-law. That was good news, but Sheila also volunteered to be a contact person and stay in touch.

CHAPTER 60

The Great Room

J an had packed up earlier and was in the Great Room finishing her painting. Little by little the rest of the group were assembled and admiring the results of their efforts. The paintings were lined up, on easels, with a couple of feet in between each. Even though they had all painted the same still life, they had been viewing at different angles and each painting stood as a testament to the personality of the painter. Julia, Maddy and Vivian walked by and viewed each one, then Julia was the first to speak, "I think you ladies should be very proud of yourselves, each and every one is lovely."

Lynn was the first to speak up saying, "We all want to thank Barbara for her patient instruction and enthusiastic inspiration," and the ladies applauded Barbara.

Lisa and Lauren walked in with Rose and everyone stopped and stared. Rose had helped them pack and pick a suitable outfit for the plane. She then took them in the bathroom to cut and style their hair. Both of them had been using a salve that rose and Maddy had concocted to help heal the lesions and blotchy patches on their faces and, with a little makeup borrowed from N.C., they looked transformed.

"Wow, who are these two?" said Sharon. "You ladies look amazing! A little fashion twirl please," and Sharon motioned for them to turn around. The girls were blushing but anyone could see how pleased they were to have so much positive attention. They gave a mocking model turn and then bowed to their audience with a giggle.

Julia hated to break up the moment but needed to move things along, so she addressed the group, "Ladies, time is marching on, we better transport the paintings to the cars. What are you doing with yours Sheila? It's still wet."

"Jan is taking mine," said Sheila. "Once it's dry they'll bring it to me in San Francisco."

Everyone began to help moving the paintings to the cars and stacking the easels to the side of the room. Rose, Lisa and Lauren took their luggage out to Sheila's rented car. There was a roll of butcher paper they used to line the trunks to prevent the paint from escaping the canvas onto the carpet. While that was going on, the hosts had taken the stacked chairs and made a circle.

Finally, when everyone was finished, they came in for their last meditation and sat silent for twenty minutes. Barbara was the first to speak. "We know this was a short meditation, but we have a schedule to keep and thought it would be a nice way to end our time together."

"We hope you remember some of the things we talked about," said Vivian.

"It has been our pleasure to be your hosts for the weekend," said Maddy.

"Remember what Julia says, if anyone bothers you, get your crazy on," smiled Rose and they laughed.

"What lies behind us, and what lies before us, are small matters compared to what lies within us," said Julia.

Lynn chuckled and asked, "Ok, Julia, who said that?"

"Why that was Ralph Waldo Emerson, dear," Julia smiled.

They all got up, folded and stacked the chairs and walked to the back door. Julia picked up some papers she had left on the side table, in the dining room, and said to Sharon, "Here dear, your promised recipes."

Then she gave N.C. a paper with a phone number and the name Bing Lin on it. "I believe Vivian promised you a good acupuncture referral."

There were hugs and kisses, their departure being bitter sweet; then waves to the cars as they pulled away.

Vivian said, "Now that sure was a nice group of women, I hope they'll be ok."

"Now can I ask," said Rose, "what's a code 13?"

"I don't know why we decided to call it that, I really like the number 13," said Maddy.

"That dear is why we are here," said Julia. "We don't want them destroying themselves. And if they keep cutting down trees, not protecting the bees or making wars—that could very well happen. Let's go, we have other fish to fry, as they say."

"One more question?" asked Rose.

"And what would that be?" said Julia.

"Why didn't you just turn those men into kittens right away?" Rose asked.

"I thought being overtaken by women was a little lesson in humility, and sometimes we need to have a little fun too," she said with a twinkle in her eyes.

They went inside and scooped up the kittens into a box that Rose carried. Barbara grabbed the cat food and a large rectangular cake tin. Vivian carried a jug of water and Sammy followed them outside. They walked it all over to the old farm house, put the food out and filled the tin with water.

"You know what to do Sammy," said Vivian.

Barbara then addressed the kittens, "Now you better listen closely. You will be turned back, but not all at once. When you do turn you will stay away from the other kitties and get off this property immediately. If you do not do that you will die, understand? I suggest you tell no one about this, they will not believe you and may entertain the idea of having you committed. Now behave or Julia will be back to get you." And with that warning, they left Sammy and his charges.

Julia had written a note for the security company and left it, and the key, in an envelope. Maddy taped it to the back door just as the rest of the group joined them in the driveway.

"You know we will be found out, Rose," said Julia, "you didn't do a full enough sweep of the ranch, that was your assignment."

Rose looked forlorn and said, "I thought I was doing well."

"Not to worry dear, for your first trip, you did very well, but you must remember to cover all details," said Julia. "Believe me, it's not as bad as Maddy's Babylon debacle," and she laughed.

"Oh, not that again," said Maddy. "I think it's time to let that one go."

"What did you do Maddy?" Rose asked in a whisper.

"It's time to leave," said Julia.

Maddy was saying, "Some other time Rose," as they all disappeared.

CHAPTER 61

Jan and Mamie-
The Ride Home

They had been talking over events of the weekend for ten minutes when Jan went to scratch her left hand and said, "Oh my god, where's my ring?"

"When do you remember having it on last?" asked Mamie.

"I think at dinner," she started saying, "oh no, I remember, I was afraid the men might steel it. I stuck it behind the leg of the side table in the bedroom. With all the excitement, I forgot about it."

She turned the car around and, in another ten minutes, they were back at the ranch house. When they pulled into the driveway, it was clear that there was no one else around. It seemed all the energy had been sucked out of the place. They found the note and key for the security company and hurried inside.

Jan ran into her room and, sure enough, found the ring exactly where she left it. They were about to leave but Jan said, "I want to look around a minute." She went into the kitchen and opened the refrigerator to find it pristine. Not a thing to be seen in all the cabinets, the place was immaculate.

Mamie had gone to take a last look at the view from the Great Room and came back to tell Jan that there were no easels or paints around. They checked the offices but could find no herb jars or any sign of the tinctures, salves or poultices used over the weekend. They were confused and wanted to get out of there, it felt so strange and antiseptic. They were silent for a while, not knowing what to make of it.

"There is no way they could have cleaned and gotten rid of everything in twenty minutes," said Mamie.

"Who were these women? I don't understand," said Jan, and she never really would.

The End

Epilogue

Syd

Syd was the first to transform. It didn't take her long to get in the car and drive to the airport. She didn't understand what exactly happened but she wanted to get away from that place as soon as possible. She had a lot to think about and, not long after, she did seek help.

Donny and Devin

The experience sobered Donny and Devin up very quickly. They didn't even know what to say or how all this had happened. Devin asked Donny for a ride home, to Encino. This was not the life he wanted anymore and he was willing to do whatever to get back in his families good graces.

Donny went back to his family to make amends. He was very humbled and asked them to forgive him. They took him back but he would be on a very short leash for quite a while.

Pete and Cap

Pete and Cap were the last to change. "This is wacked," was all Pete could say at first. They had left their car near the fork in the road but someone had moved it closer to the old farm house.

Cap said, "What the hell happened?"

"I think we had some kind of cosmic intervention," said Pete. "I'm going back to Kentucky; I'm tired of this shit."

"Can I hitch a ride as far as Oklahoma," asked Cap "I want to go home?"

N.C.

A week after the retreat N.C. received the call she had wanted for so long. Her friend, Andrea Jackson, did a lot of pro bono work in the Crenshaw Area and knew the community well. A young, pregnant woman had been shot in the head by a stray bullet and was lying, still alive but brain dead, in a hospital bed while doctors were preparing to deliver her baby.

The young woman's only relative, her grandfather, was desperate to find a home for the baby. He was seventy-six and his wife had died two years earlier of cancer. The father of the baby was killed three months before in Afghanistan and he had no relatives able to care for the child. There were several families who expressed interest but were put off by the grandfather's stipulation; he wanted to be able to see the baby, at least once a month. This child was the only thing that kept him interested in living and he wanted to make sure the child had knowledge of his roots and was treated well.

N.C. and Kevin had no problem with that and said that if he were to allow them this precious gift, they would be more than happy to accommodate his request and would be happy to put that in writing.

They were in the delivery room to see the baby being taken away from his unaware mother. It was a touching moment for N.C.; to see the lovely face of her child's mother, seemingly asleep. A moment later the cry of a healthy baby boy filled the room and N.C. was given the baby right after he was cleaned and swaddled.

N.C. asked to be alone, for a few moments, with the baby and his mother. They complied with her request and, as she stood holding her child with tears streaming down her cheeks, she promised to be the best mother she could be and thanked the woman she would never be able to meet.

That's how Andrew Clayton Allen came into this world. His grandfather, Andrew, was delighted to have a namesake and the baby's father's last name was Clayton.

Two months later, N.C. found she was pregnant with a little girl. They decided to name her Tisha after little Andrew's mother, Latisha.

One year later they decided to set up a trust fund for the education of underprivileged children and a camp, in the nearby mountains, for inner city kids.

Lynn

Things were good in the Kahn home. Lynn's new show started two months after the retreat and was a big hit. Lynn even got some writing credits for all the input she was giving. More important, she came home with a new appreciation for her husband. She realized, with a little help, that her husband had been an afterthought in her life for quite a while. She didn't know how it evolved to be that way, but she was determined to do something about it, and she did.

The Goodwill store was the beneficiary of lots of flannel night gowns and pajamas. She initiated date night and, when Amanda was out with her friends, there were romantic dinners prepared. Chuck, thrived under this new love light and experienced a renewed interest and passion for his wife.

Amanda had decided to go to Cal Arts in Valencia, Ca., which was only about a half hour away. She still wanted the experience of living in the dorms but, to Lynn, this was the best of both worlds; having her daughter in college less than an hour away.

Later that year Lynn organized a telethon for abused and neglected children.

Gia and Donna

The relationship between Gia and Donna progressed beautifully. Donna thrived on being in love with someone who reciprocated without injury. It did take her a while. She was very cautious, even talking about her students, fearing jealousy would rear its ugly head again. Finally, Gia assured her she could have other friends too. Gia was not a jealous person and, for weeks, did everything she could to make Donna feel comfortable. It seemed to be working. Six months after the retreat, Donna and Gia found a lovely Spanish Revival house in Studio City.

They saw the other ladies frequently in class or out for ladies night dinners. Neither family nor friends were terribly shocked by the relationship; those who were got over it. Donna's family was particularly happy that she was no longer in danger and her aunt was a frequent visitor.

Gia and Donna organized an after school yoga program for 'at-risk' kids and spent lots of their spare time mentoring young people.

Sharon

Sharon and David were married seven months later. It would have been sooner but David's divorce needed to be settled. They purchased a beautiful new home and, between the two of them, it had become a showplace of interesting objects, color and design. Sharon was able to charm Gloria, the housekeeper, as soon as Gloria was assured that her situation would continue, and perhaps become easier, with another woman in the house.

Then came the announcement that Sharon would be having a baby. David and Sharon were cautious about telling Lexi, not knowing how she would accept the news. Their concern was unwarranted; Lexi was delighted. Most of Lexi's friends had siblings and she looked forward to being a big sister.

Sharon, even with all that was going on in her life, decided to get the training to council young rape victims.

Sheila

Sheila had a beautiful wedding. Her parents chose not to attend, having been insulted by the ultimatum about their behavior. Sheila was relieved at not having to worry about them on her special day. She didn't need them, she had a wonderful family. Her brother came, even after their parents threatened to take him out of their will. That was the last straw for him; he had his own money and wasn't buying into their control issues anymore.

Sheila and her new husband decided life would be even more rewarding if they signed up for 'Doctors without borders'.

Mamie

There was nothing as sweet as the words "cancer free," to Mamie's ears. She and her family invited Jan and Tony over for the good news. The real relief would come in about five years, but this was exciting. She was so proud of her family and the way they had handled themselves during their crisis. She had heard of men who just couldn't deal with this kind of illness, but Bill was really there for her. He told her she was beautiful, and nothing would change except their love would be even stronger.

The girls made special cards for her, picked flowers and followed the lead of their big sister, Jules, who tried to keep sisterly bickering to a minimal.

Mamie had done so much research about her illness that she decided to put her knowledge to work. She started a mentoring program for cancer patients.

Jan

Jan had felt a renewed spirit of life. She and Tony were married, surrounded by family and close friends. She vowed not to be a slave to her job, remembering that Rose had once said to her, "You know

I don't think anyone dies thinking they wished they spent more time at work."

It wasn't easy, but it got easier to delegate responsibility to her assistants. Eventually she found that trusting her employees was rewarding to all concerned.

She and Tony were even entertaining the idea of adopting a child. There was no pressure. Tony said he hadn't been around for a lot of his son's growing up and he would be happy to support whatever decision she made.

Jan, skilled at computers, ran into an old teacher friend of hers and ended up volunteering to help teach computer science, two hours a week, in one of the poor neighborhood schools. She loved it so much she recruited friends and acquaintances and started a whole new after school program.

Dakini Teachings I

Of all living creatures, not a single one has not been your father or mother. So as a way of repaying the kindness of those creatures, set out to work for their welfare.

CPSIA information can be obtained at www.ICGtesting.com
Printed in the USA
LVOW01s0132040114

368035LV00026B/981/P